SEEK AND YOU SHALL FIND

# the Magnum Opus

A NOVEL BY

Christopher & Christine Kezelos

# The Magnum Opus

ISBN-10: 0-9984628-0-2
ISBN-13: 978-0-9984628-0-6


Cover art by Christopher Kezelos
Copy edited by Ellen Michelle Koehler
Interior design by Christopher Kezelos

CREATIVE

zealouscreative.com

Give feedback on the book at:
themagnumopus@zealouscreative.com

Twitter: @ZealousCreative
Facebook @ZealousCrtv


First Edition

Printed in the U.S.A

Dedicated to all the Makers in our world.

*"You are a Maker, you must create,
make haste for time should never waste."*

# Overture in A

# CHAPTER 1
## *The Workshop*

In a time and a world long ago forgotten, there was a workshop. If a stranger ever found themselves within its walls, they wouldn't know where to marvel first. Perhaps they would start front and center, where there was a solid wood workbench with towering shelves on either side neatly lined with an uncountable number of mismatched boxes and jars of various sizes, all meticulously labelled and begging to be snooped. The bench drawers brimmed and burgeoned with every tool or material one could possibly know or never imagine, poised ready to create anything and everything conceivable. In the middle of the bench was a magnificently curvaceous hourglass with grains of sand that dazzled like jewels, held heroically in the arms of two bronzed figures.

On either side of the workbench, a multitude of musical instruments, strange and unusual in design, hung from ornate golden hooks spanning from the floor to the tall, tall ceiling. A French horn with three different sized bells and tubing that endlessly looped and coiled, a cello that had a neck resembling a bassoon, and a smallish harp that perhaps once thought it was an umbrella, just to name a few. What rapture and delight would greet anyone fortunate enough to hear and see a tune or two played from such instruments.

1

Farther down the wall, an oversized potbelly kiln burned fiery hot, heating the room to a cozy never-want-to-leave feeling. Throughout the workshop stood grand bookcases filled with volumes of leather bound books, which were finished in an assortment of regal colors and majestic gold leaf flourishes. Against the back wall, hundreds of tiny supply drawers were stacked, each contained powders and potions both potent and pure.

Upon closer inspection of the room, it would become evident that everything within the workshop had been crafted by skilled hands. From the perfect plane and stain of the mahogany wooden floorboards, which ran to meet the delicately hand-painted floral papered walls, to the hand blown light bulbs cradled in spiraling wrought iron light fixtures. Even the large wooden beams that ran across the ceiling were not to be outdone, with detailed carvings of constellations from within the celestial sphere. Everything had been considered, and everything had been surveyed and studied with the keen eye of finesse. Yes, any stranger that found themselves within these walls would have come to the conclusion that this was the workshop of a master craftsman. They would also come to the startling realization that there were no windows or doors in the workshop. The question would then be raised, "Where in the name of all things great and gargantuan am I?"

Which is the exact same question a solitary creature that stood in the midst of the workshop asked himself at that particular moment. His large hazel eyes darted around the workshop, uneasy and unsure as he observed his surroundings. He was unlike any beast or being from the known world, for he wasn't made of flesh and bones. Instead, his entire body was sewn from finely crafted linen, printed with subtle navy blue stripes. He stood about the height of an adolescent and tapered thin in all proportions. He could be compared to a rag doll, but that wouldn't be quite right, for he was very much alive just as sure as any other critter lives and breathes. How could such a fantastical individual be possible? The power of the ages and the energy of the world—that indescribable force that creates trees and birds and stars had been harnessed to breathe life into the creature, and my, what a creation he was to behold. Why, there was magic in that room.

His face was sculpted from clay, yet was fluid enough to convey every emotion one could possibly feel through the journey of life. His ears were like those of a rabbit, tall and long, which rose and fell in unison with those same emotions. Right in the center of his forehead was a large indented black treble clef, which starkly contrasted against his smooth porcelain-like white 'skin'. He wore a thick, black, lightly pinstriped waistcoat and matching suit pants with a crisp white cotton shirt—all crafted with professional-grade stitching and tailored to perfection. In fact, he looked quite dapper. His hands consisted of a long linen thumb that joined two linen fingers, and in those hands he grasped a deep tan leather bound book, thick and heavy with bulging pages that looked as old as time itself.

He traced one of his long, linen fingers over the intricate leather design on the front of the book. His confusion was paralleled by waves of calmness and peace that seemed to soothe him. A most peculiar and somewhat unsettling place to be. For he could not remember anything before that moment, yet he seemed to know so much. For instance he knew that the leather of the book was definitely the hide of a wild Ochaa Beast, roasted in the sun for at least twelve moon cycles and then stained with the berries of a Crimson Cleric. The complex leather imprint had been carved with a standard swivel knife. A fine selection for sure, though he would have perhaps also used a decorative stamp, but that, of course, was merely a personal choice.

He also knew that his name was Allegro, but he most certainly didn't have any memories of birthdays or family dinners. As he stared at the front of the grand old book, engraved with a rare and antiquated language, he knew instantly that the words read *The Making*. Interestingly though, he couldn't recall where or how he had actually learned to read. He didn't have much time to truly consider his conundrum for as he opened the book to the first page and read the first words…

*You are a Maker, you must create,*
*make haste for time should never waste.*

…he was distracted by a deep wooden creak. The hourglass atop the workbench had turned upside down and as the sparkling sand started to fall, Allegro was seized by a great sense of urgency and rushed to the bench. In perfect synch, the most magnificent music burst from large tubular horns, affixed to every corner of the room. The Maker's ears perked upright and his back was rigid straight as the music infused his entire body and made him feel more alive than he could believe possible. It was the music of maestros. The cadence, the expression, the brilliance of the tone and the dynamics. He heard the mastery in each and every note, which blended into the perfection of the entire orchestration. He had to resist every desire to grab an instrument and play along, for a far deeper urge beckoned him back to the book. He had something important to make.

# CHAPTER 2
## *The Making*

In life, we can feel compelled by a force far greater than our own will. Humans call this power all sorts of names and have honored it in endless scrolls and upon countless pages of revered tomes. This same force surges throughout universes and worlds, unknown and unexplored. It races through each and every living vein and in its purest, most channeled version, it pushes us onwards and upwards. It inspires us to evolve and causes us to create beauty that mirrors life itself.

It was this same force, this need, this raging urgency that was in control of Allegro as he raced to the work bench. He stood over the book, gently, yet quickly, turning the pages and reading as fast as he could. *Why, yes of course,* he smiled and thought to himself. *Of course this is what I have to make.* Allegro took a deep breath, scanned the array of materials at arm's length, and then began his task working both furiously and systematically.

As per the book's instructions, springs, cogs, and rods were assembled and soldered with clean precision. Clay was kneaded and rolled, then fashioned into the desired shape. A long handled branding tool forged with twisted wrought iron was softly pushed into a precise location of his clay creation. Allegro then walked to the kiln and placed his handiwork deep inside the searing hot kiln.

Rolls of pink paisley linen were then laid neatly across the bench and chalk patterns were created. With great flair, Allegro wielded scissors and meticulously cut piece after piece. All the while, his eyes darted to the falling sand in the hourglass, aware that he was racing against time. The crescendo of the music blared through the horns across the workshop floor, which carried him faster and faster forward.

With thread and needle, Allegro painstakingly stitched and cross-stitched the fabric pieces together. From within one of the drawers, he found candy-colored wadding and began stuffing his creation.

Allegro was not aware of how much time had passed, only that the sand was now far heavier at the bottom of the hourglass than the top. It could have been hours, or it could have been days. He was so consumed with his making that time felt irrelevant—the only thing that mattered was finishing. He allowed himself a precious moment to survey his current progress, and was quite pleased with his craftsmanship; however, the music swelled in urgency and compelled him on once more.

What was this curious little creature so intensely constructing? This Maker was no different than any of nature's other creatures—one always brings forth the next. Slowly but surely by the skill of his own hand, he was creating a body. A female body, to be precise. Slightly more delicate in design, but still in his own likeness with distinct long limbed features and characteristics.

The book was Allegro's constant companion and he followed it step-by-step. He used a pair of long forceps to remove the piece of clay now baked to perfection in the kiln, then plunged it into a barrel of water. It hissed and gurgled, and when the steam and bubbles subsided, he drew out a smooth, exquisite porcelain mask that he carefully carried back to the bench. He pulled open a drawer containing rows of neatly displayed glass eyeballs that shimmered with colors of the earth and sky. Allegro was taken by the greenest of emerald irises and affixed them gently to the mask. Finally, he attached the mask to the body, which melded fittingly.

Allegro stepped back to admire his handiwork; he gasped in awe at the vision that lay across the workbench in front of him. *Truly magnificent,* he thought to himself, *yes, a masterpiece if I do say so myself.* For a few deep breaths he basked in the joy of his creation, but his ears twitched nervously when he looked at the depleting hourglass. He flicked through the pages of *The Making* book and knew there was still more to do.

He stood poised with needle and thread staring at the lifeless maiden. "What to call you?" he wondered aloud, then he smiled as the ideal name came to him. With great care, he embroidered 'Sonata' on the lapel of her linen blouse. He stepped back once more as his eyes gleamed with joy, for she was now complete.

Allegro returned to the book, and as he read, a wide grin spread across his face, "Ahh wonderful, wonderful," he said as he skipped over to the instruments hanging on the wall. He selected a viola with three fingerboards and far too many strings. He then hurried back to his creation, dragging a music stand behind him and propped up *The Making* book. There, upon the pages, were musical notes to *The Making* song. As he began to play, his fingers had a natural affinity as if they had always known what to do. His soul knew the nuances needed to bring the notes on the page alive. Allegro played with vigor, passion, and, most of all, relief. For ever since hearing his first note of music, he desired nothing more than to truly be a part of it.

The music filled the air. It flowed with such richness and depth that it could almost be held and felt. As he played, a low rumble passed through the workshop; bottles and jars began to shake and tinkle slightly. As if beckoned, his sleeping progeny gently levitated above the bench, then floated towards him as though she were being carried by unseen hands. He was unafraid, for he trusted in that moment. He was electrified with awe and gratefulness that he could live to experience this time. Sonata hovered upright before him, as the notes danced off the page, driving him towards a great crescendo. Then, her eyelids snapped open. Allegro gazed into a world that was so vital and full of the same precious life that was flowing through him.

As Allegro's performance drew to an end, Sonata's feet touched the ground. He carefully rested the instrument against the music stand then stood face-to-face with his progeny as they blissfully smiled at each other. He reached out and held her hands, a birth had taken place, he had brought this life into the world and he glowed with pride. Allegro was a Maker and Sonata was his greatest creation. He glanced over at the hourglass and saw that only a few grains of sand remained, an overwhelming feeling of sadness permeated his joy.

He reached for *The Making* book on the music stand and handed it to Sonata, like his Maker had done with him. Now, he truly understood what life was as tears that brimmed with beginnings and endings stung his eyes. He gave Sonata the warmest of smiles, and she stood unaware of what was about to happen. He did not speak a word, for he knew she had everything she needed to find her own way. As the last grain dropped through the hourglass, Allegro burst into a shower of sparkles and light that engulfed the workshop. Tools and instruments swooped back to their places while materials magically replenished, returning to their original burgeoning neatness.

Sonata stood alone in the quiet workshop completely shocked, but still calm. "Oh boy, oh joy, what manner of boggle do we have here?" she said softly. The wooden creak of the hourglass interrupted her thoughts as it turned. The exhilarating music once again surged through the horns, and as she began to read the pages of that wondrous book, she too was overcome by that same fervent desire to make.

The Making cycle continued in this fashion for countless moons, each Maker begat the next and so on and so forth. That was, until the day a young female Maker named Melody was creating her progeny. Dainty but strong, her crisp linen body was patterned with petite pink roses. She wore a fine laced linen dress that draped just to her knees and a light fur jacket completed the outfit. Her piercing blue eyes burned with flecks of amber that perfectly matched the fiery sparks of her nature.

She had followed the steps precisely and was thoroughly enjoying the process. Melody had taken great pride in all his folds and seams and believed she had created a fine gentleman, whom she named Ario. However, when it came to branding him with his musical symbol, try as she may, it would not stamp. It was most perplexing and she frowned with concern. She poured over *The Making* book as her ears twitched furiously, but it offered no solution whatsoever. Conscious of the falling sands, she gently placed the face in the kiln and moved on.

Being a resourceful young lady, when Melody took the baked face out of the kiln, she used pots of black and white paint to replicate a perfect bass clef on Ario's forehead. Such were her painting skills that with her subtle shading, the flat surface looked like it was indeed indented and had been branded all along. The sands in the hourglass stopped for nothing and she pressed on, soon young Ario had taken his solitary place in the workshop.

Ario was eager and earnest in heart, and was simply thrilled by the prospect of creating a new Maker. The music that blared through the tubular horns gave him chills and thrills all over his body as he worked steadily and exactly. Cutting, sewing, wedging, and rolling the clay, he was as skilled as any Maker who had come before him, and what a fine specimen he had created.

He stood over the latent body, so proud of his craftsmanship and artistry. He searched his heart for a name. *What was fitting? What was apt?* he pondered. As the music crescendoed around him, he felt a grandness of emotion and held a sweeping vision for the future. Makers danced and sang, and this sleeping beauty's voice rose above them all. She could be like a new day; she could show a new way, for isn't that what every new being comes into the world for? They were indeed lofty ideals, but even as a fledgling Maker, Ario saw the world with a largeness—he was unable to think small. Though he could get down to the detail, it slowed him and tripped him up as he ran towards his big ideas.

He smiled down at her and delicately touched her forehead, "You shall be Renaissance," he said. "I don't know what the world holds beyond this room, but, my word, it will be stupendous."

With that, he picked up his instrument and stood ready to wake Renaissance. This was the moment he had longed for. He had all the desire to play, he felt the same flood of passion that every Maker before him had felt, as they waited poised and ready. He drew the bow to stroke his elongated violin-fused-guitar, but his fingers felt awkward and he had no idea what to do. As the bow moved across the strings, the most discordant sound reverberated through the workshop. His hands slightly trembled, for he knew this could not be a good sign. He tried again and again with no luck. In distress, he grabbed other instruments from the wall: a mandolin with two faces, a pan flute with strings to pluck, and a glockenspiel that you wore as a vest. With each attempt he failed to execute a perfect note or tune. He wanted nothing more than to create music and wake his sleeping progeny, but over and over the sound he made was unkind and cruel to his finely tuned ears.

As the sand in the hourglass continued to fall, he desperately flipped through the pages of *The Making* book, looking for help, a possible solution, anything. It would seem that this scenario had never been considered by the author. As Ario wrestled with the book for an answer, he accidentally pressed a button hidden in the carvings on the spine. A small compartment sprung open and within it was a silver compass. It was etched with fine flourishes and swirls, in the center the needle spun endlessly out of control. He turned the compass over to discover an ornate inscription engraved on the back, it read:

*Only together is life complete - Magnum Opus.*

Ario scratched his head, extremely disappointed for this was of no help whatsoever. He caught sight of the all but empty hourglass and his heart sank under a gigantic wave of failure and defeat. He looked at Renaissance lying so peacefully on the bench, as the last few grains of sand fell. The music stopped abruptly and the silence was shattering. *Hazy mazes, what's wrong with me?* he thought to himself. He didn't know where he was going, but he knew he was in all sorts of trouble. With the compass in hand, Ario disappeared in a shower of psychedelic sparkling light.

The workshop lay still, the progeny remained lifeless and the bottom of the hourglass was full of glistening sand. A faint draft whistled through the pipes in the wall. The age-old Making cycle had been broken.

# Passage in A Minor

# CHAPTER 3
## *The Processing Station*

In a daze, all that Ario could see was a blinding white light, but it was the cold that seized his senses. A deep chill pervaded his toes and crept quickly up his body through his bones to the tips of his ears. As he looked down at his feet, his vision started to clear and he saw that he stood upon a dark marble disk, engraved with golden Maker words:

*Step forth and make.*

He still grasped the compass in his hand, and he noticed the spinning had stopped and the needle now pointed north. He flipped it closed and looked around. The workshop was replaced by a long, thin room. To his intrigue, the walls were fashioned with large hand carved blocks of thick ice, interspersed with solid steel framework frozen within. The gray chalky colored walls filtered dim light from beyond as it stretched to dark double wooden doors far on the other side. He was surrounded by cogs, pulleys, wiring, and rigs that were Maker in design.

Ario looked eagerly around, waiting to be greeted, to be welcomed, to talk to someone about what had just happened in the workshop. He was ready to explain himself, ready to go back and try again, for he felt instinctively that it was his most imperative priority.

He was slightly disappointed to not see anyone, and was just about to step off the disc when he heard a loud buzz crackle from an overhead speaker. All the cogs and pulleys sprang into action. *Wonderful,* he thought, until a large metal claw picked him roughly off his feet and dropped him onto a conveyor belt that ran the distance of the room.

"Muddle me!" he cried as the belt jolted into action. He regained his balance and composure as he whizzed along at a swift speed until an abrupt stop sent him hurtling towards the wooden doors. He covered his face with his hands, but at the very last moment, the doors swung open and Ario landed rather ungracefully at the foot of a large solid wooden desk.

Ario picked himself up from the ice-covered stone floor in an otherwise sparse stone room. He was just tall enough to curiously peek over the desk, past the multiple levers and buttons, where he met small oil-black eyes that glared at him. Ario gasped and stumbled backwards. The eyes were set deep within a swollen and puffy face, with rolls of pale blue sallowed skin framed by unruly furrowed white brows. His scowling lips hung over multiple chins, which draped over an almost indistinguishable neck. Ario wondered who this sullen man was.

In an attempt to melt the chill in the room, Ario gave him a beaming smile, but the creature simply grunted then looked away. The man lifted a blue, chubby, pale hand that squeezed out of a coarse, navy blue coat, trimmed with dense gray and white speckled fur. He held a stamp and slammed it on a pile of paper. "My name is Officer Festus," he said with complete bureaucratic boredom. With a sigh, Officer Festus continued stamping page after page. He really didn't like his job, having to deal with these Makers on a daily basis, but he reminded himself of the importance of his role. He did a great service each and every day and he stamped his paperwork with a little more gusto and pride.

Unsure of the proceedings, Ario commenced with some pleasantries, "Good day, fine Sir. My name is —" No sooner had the first syllable left his lips than Officer Festus yanked at a nearby lever. A mechanical arm sprung from a trap door in the desk before him, and with great force, thumped Ario on his chest. Ario cried out in a combination of shock and pain as the wind was almost knocked out of him. The corner of Officer Festus' mouth rose ever so slightly, for that was definitely his favorite part of the proceedings. "Your designation is 367890," he said blankly. Ario looked down and saw his delicate hand embroidered name was now covered in thick black ink that did indeed read '367890'.

Ario tried to speak again, but the Officer cut him off and spoke with dry coldness, "You have arrived in the Maker Processing Station in Winter City."

Ario was becoming more confused with each moment. He wasn't too sure about this Winter City place; so far, it was a bit too cool and mean for his liking. All he wanted was to return to the workshop.

He forced a smile once more, "It's so nice to meet you Mr. Officer Festus, and I thank you for your um... processing, but are you able to direct me back to the—"

"Everyday, everyday," Festus mumbled, then drew a long wheezy exasperated breath. He stopped his stamping and fixed his eyes upon the repugnant little rag creature who was wasting his time. *I really need a promotion,* he thought to himself, *or at least a vacation, maybe out to the seaside, it's particularly frosty this time of year.* He basked in his delicious daydream for a moment until he remembered that this rather persistent pest was still in front of him and unprocessed. "No one knows it's location, it's a one way ticket out. You'll have no need for workshops where you're going," he said.

Ario shifted on his feet uneasily. There was something deeply menacing about those eyes, but he persisted nonetheless—surely there had to be a way to get back there. "Well, you see, Mr. Officer Festus, there's something I really need to attend to..." he began.

Officer Festus sharply raised his hand to silence him and Ario obeyed. The Officer rose tall in his seat and, when he spoke, his voice rumbled with authority, "You are now the property of Winter and will serve our every command."

The gravity of those words gripped Ario in a chill as he gulped for air, "Pr... pr... property?"

Festus continued calmly, but with undisguised cruelty, "Music, singing, and instruments of any kind are strictly forbidden." He pulled at another lever and a different mechanical arm shot out from the desk and snatched the compass from Ario's hand then dumped it in a nearby trash can. "Personal possessions are also not allowed," the Officer said with a sneer.

Ario thought that surely this was all some huge mistake, some sort of joke, or perhaps a test? No music, no singing, no instruments... no possessions? Even though his common sense screamed at him to be silent, he felt some growing indignation, a desire to truly get to the bottom of this whole Winter City craziness. He didn't know what he had expected to happen after the workshop, but it definitely smelled and felt way better in his imagination than in this reality.

Ario frowned as he watched Festus reach for a pencil and begin filling in some more forms. "Breaking the law will result in severe punishment," Officer Festus offhandedly warned without taking his eye off the page.

Ario raised a quizzical eyebrow and decided to change his tact. "On a scale of one to ten, with one being a stern talking to and ten being the most horrid of horrids, how severe is severe?"

The banter was lost on a stoic Festus, and without a pause in his writing he reached beside him on the desk and raised a staff about two feet long. The lower half was dark polished wood, while the top half was silver and engraved with intricate snowflake patterns. On the end, a silver claw held a small glowing ball of blue crystal. He pointed it to a mug sitting on his desk and gave the staff a tight squeeze. A light tinkle could be heard as if eggshells were cracking. Suddenly, a sharp, blistering blast of frost shot from the ball and encased the cup in a small tomb of ice. Festus turned to Ario, and with a menacing snarl, used the tip of the staff to push the mug off the desk. The cup splintered into hundreds of icy shards at Ario's feet.

Ario's whole body convulsed in a deep cold shiver, as a scream of terror swelled in the pits of his belly begging to cry out, but he now knew it was truly hopeless. This was it. There was to be no grand welcoming parade, or fancy party to celebrate his arrival. Nothing. This world was not stupendous at all. He sadly thought about Renaissance lying lifeless waiting for him back in the workshop, he also knew now was not the time to mention her.

This Officer Festus was in no mood to listen to anything he had to say. All he could manage was a slow head nod as his ears slumped with sadness.

Officer Festus rapidly stamped a number of documents and looked at Ario with pursed lips then declared with great disdain, "Maker 367890, you've been assigned work in the factory."

Ario's head whirred with confusion, "What factory?" he cried. Festus rolled his eyes and ignored him as he pulled yet another lever. This time, a mechanical arm dropped from above, picked Ario up with no level of gentleness, and dumped him on another conveyor belt. Ario hurtled towards a new set of double wooden doors.

Officer Festus sat back in his plush, soft, leather seat and shook his head as he watched Maker 367890 leave. He cranked a lever on his desk. A long-armed broom with attached dustpan shot out of the floor and quickly swept the smashed icy mug away. Festus pulled open a long drawer in his desk filled with identical mugs and purposefully placed one on the same well worn coffee ring stain. With his morning task complete, Officer Festus heaved and rolled to a rise from his chair. *Time for second breakfast, double-frosted sneezleberry muffins.* His mouth salivated with the thought as he shuffled off to the employee's exit.

# CHAPTER 4
*The Factory*

Ario found himself once again landing rather unceremoniously, this time in a sturdy wrought iron cage. As he frantically looked around, he saw the cage was sitting atop a vehicle that appeared to have all the hallmarks of Maker handiwork. Part horse carriage, part tractor, it had large spoked wheels with spiked treading and an exposed engine that burgeoned with cogs, springs, and pulleys. A tall, lean Winter officer sat on the driver's bench behind a small steering wheel, dressed in a thick navy blue coat, minus the fancy fur trimming of Festus' clothing. The driver didn't bother to look around. He just cranked the start lever, which caused the engine to sputter and pop. He clunked it into gear and off they went down the alley way.

Ario looked forlornly through the iron bars as they made their way through rows upon rows of townhouses and shop facades of every shade of ash, stacked as high and as far as the eye could see. All the buildings were constructed with ice and steel, and, for the most part, were lacking in design and originality. Stalactites of gray ice tried to sparkle in the morning light as they dripped from somber street lamps and awnings along the sludgy snow-lined cobbled streets.

Despite his overwhelming glumness, Ario was still intrigued by his surrounds and took it all in as he huddled in the corner of his cage. His breath exhaled great plumes of frost as he snuggled deeper into his coat. They passed Winter citizens going about their business on that brisk morning. While they came in all different shapes and sizes, it was evident that Officer Festus' demeanor was not an anomaly. These people all seemed to have faces frozen into frowns on their pale blue faces. The fashion of the day complemented the dour mood: drab-colored felt winter coats of blue and gray trimmed with fur over large knee-high, animal-skinned boots.

Ario was struck by the endless amount of Maker contraptions used throughout the city. In between all the harsh, bleak lines of the Winter architecture, countless cogs, levers, wheels, springs, and pulleys crowded every corner. The applications were many; from a barberless barber shop operated by a scissor-cutting rig to a multi-armed vendor-less food cart serving tea and cakes to hungry citizens. The Makers had created everything possible to ensure their great masters would want for nothing, or need to do anything.

The vehicle climbed a small hill on the outskirts of town and drove by a large park lined with barren trees. The park was covered in a blanket of snow that stretched under a group of Winter children who took delight in snowball fights and building snow monsters. It was from here that Ario viewed the panorama of Winter City, which sprawled to meet a towering ice wall that surrounded the city limits. The wall circled to join on either side of a sheer, rocky cliff face that was dotted with tiny holes in neat rows from top to bottom. The cliff face then rose into a snow-peaked mountain that cradled Winter City at its feet.

From his vantage, Ario also noticed that in the center of the city stood a palace both bold and bleak, encased by plainly squared turrets and towers bearing blue flags that flapped in the brisk morning winds. The palace's soaring walls of dull ice were also constructed around thick metal frames that dominated the landscape with an air of austerity. Ario wondered who lived there, but was instantly distracted by a volcano beyond the city walls. Nestled in the nearby mountains, its peak burned furious red hot amber as it billowed threatening smoke. Ario did not know much about geology, but that volcano looked even less friendly than his new Winter masters.

Farther along, as they descended once again into the Winter streets, Ario was struck with awe when they passed a group of large beasts standing on two feet, taller than any Winter person. Each beast was chained to the other by thick metal collars as two Winter officers watched them warily, ice staffs at the ready. They had been put to work. Their clawed hands and bulging arms grasped large logs like they were sticks and threw them into big piles. These magnificent creatures were covered from head to toe with gray and white speckled fur, which was matted and unkempt. Their heads were disproportionately small compared to their muscular bodies, with small tusks protruding from their mouths and large brown eyes that blinked with clear rage.

Ario flipped his coat collar and tried to keep warm. They stopped for a moment at an intersection and Ario tried chatting to the driver, "It sure is freezing back here."

The Winter officer didn't bother turning, "You're kidding, right?" he replied, annoyed he would have to talk to the new arrival. He thrust the throttle and the vehicle lurched forward, then pointed to a small group of Makers of various sizes, all armed with shovels clearing a path through the streets of sludge snow. "The ice has been melting, it's hotter than ever."

"Hotter than ever?" Ario echoed, but the driver just ignored him so Ario remained silent. He looked up at the gloomy sky where the sun hid behind thick clouds. He was unsure where the heat was coming from, but wished there was more.

They continued on the journey and passed another group of Makers working by the side of the road. An officer stood over an older Maker and bellowed, "Speed it up!" To Ario's horror, the officer thrust his ice-staff at the old Maker and zapped him with a blast of ice. The old Maker fell to the ground as he cried out in pain. The other Makers ignored the fallen one, hung their heads, and continued with their shoveling at a much faster pace. How could we have come to this? Ario wondered with frustration and despair as he hunched deeper into the corner of the cage, so sad for the world in which he had entered.

Ario didn't bother to look up again until he felt the vehicle slowing down. He saw they were approaching a large ice-walled building that stood many stories high and spewed smoke from a multitude of chimneys on its roof. *This must be the factory,* he thought, and then a dark worry gripped him, *Whatever will become of me?* He wasn't more than one morning old, but the wisps of a dream he had for life outside the workshop lay frozen and shattered. The only thing left was the desire to return to the workshop. He had to find someone to talk to, to explain what had happened, and then somehow get back there so he could finish what he had started.

The caged vehicle parked in front of a concrete loading dock that backed up to a two-storey high warehouse paneled door. A Maker wearing a dinged metallic hard hat with two holes for her ears bounded out from a side entrance with clipboard in hand to unlatch the cage. Ario was overjoyed to finally be greeted by a fellow Maker and was about to unleash an avalanche of questions and observations when something in the Maker's eyes warned him to remain silent.

"Welcome, Maker 367890," she said with an official nod and gestured for him to join her. Ario obediently stepped out of the cage and the Maker waved to the driver, "I've got it from here." The driver didn't even turn his head as he throttled off down the street.

The Maker waited until the vehicle was out of sight then turned to Ario and introduced herself, "Great greetings, I'm Carol. The factory supervisor." She stopped and cautiously looked up and down the street, "Winter leaves us to our work, but conducts surprise inspections." She then turned and checked the embroidering on Ario's coat. "Well, welcome Ario. We only use numbers as a Winter formality," she said with a wry smile. She pulled a pencil from her beige worker's vest and jotted something down on her clipboard. She seemed rather distracted, as if she had a lot on her mind and continued on in a furious pace. "It's great to have you on board. We're really busy at the moment."

Ario cleared his throat, "Look there's something I need to tell you..."

"Come, come, there's work to be done," she said as she grabbed Ario by the arm.

She ushered him through a side door into a small dimly lit office where a solitary Maker sat behind a small wooden desk. Armed with a telescope, he peered out a narrow window down the street. "This is Tenor," she introduced, "He lets us know if we have any visitors," she explained with a wink. Tenor waved politely while keeping his eye glued to the eyepiece. They approached a door on the other side of the office, "Tick-tock let's hop!" The supervisor swung it open and led him onto the factory floor.

Ario's eyes widened with wonder, He was greeted with a such a hubbub of Maker activity that his heart truly danced for the first time since arriving in Winter City. The building teemed and crawled with Makers of every shape, size, age, and design, all busy, busy, and even more busy. They bustled and hustled up and down a number of ladders that passed through a mish mash of platforms and landings that rose from floor to ceiling. Ario's ears perked at the pleasant clamor of tools from various trades in a flurry of activity. Hundreds of Makers tinkered and toiled on a large machine far bigger than any Maker contraption Ario could ever imagine. It stretched up to half the size of the factory ceiling, which was at least three stories high and was decorated with the signature Maker cogs, pulleys, and dials. In addition, there was a number of thick, wide, translucent pipes that seemed to bore deep into the factory floor.

Ario was intrigued and ready to unleash a whirlwind of questions, when a tremor under his feet stopped him. His ears darted to attention. The floor lurched violently. Unsure if the big machine was about to explode or if the building was about to collapse, Ario hit the floor and covered his head with his arms. The factory walls groaned and shuddered. Some Makers grabbed for railings while others dove for cover under nearby tables. Tools rolled and clattered off trolleys and benches. Scaffolding and platforms buckled and swayed.

Ario peeked through his arms. "What's happening?" he shrieked up at Carol, but he was barely audible above the panicked voices of the other Makers.

She responded by seizing Ario's leg and roughly dragged him to safety as a falling ladder crashed to the floor, missing him by inches. "You must keep your eyes open," she said sternly as she pulled him to his feet.

Seized by panic, Ario held onto her arm for dear life and pleaded, "What's going on?"

Carol stood unfazed. "It's an earthquake," she explained, "it's been happening for years." To Ario's greatest relief, the shaking ended just as suddenly as it had started.

The supervisor calmly surveyed the factory floor for damage as she continued, "It's the volcano. You would've seen her on the way over to the factory. We calculate she's going to erupt in six days and kill us all."

"We have to get out of here," Ario said as a ball of fear rose in his throat. He held her arm even tighter.

Carol smiled and shook her head, then pointed to the machine in the middle of the floor, "This here is the Great Freeze Machine. Pure Maker genius. It'll put that angry mountain on ice." She pried herself from Ario's grasp and hurried to the center of the factory floor. "It's all OK... let's get back to it," she called out reassuringly. The Makers swiftly rebounded from the scare and returned to their tasks.

Carol hurried back to Ario, keen to continue her induction, but Ario was in shock and aghast at the faith placed in this one machine that was not yet ready.

"Will this machine actually work?" he asked as she led Ario across the floor.

"Of course it'll work, we're Makers aren't we?" she smiled as she motioned for him to follow her up a flight of stairs.

Ario still wasn't comfortable with the situation, "What if we don't finish in time?"

The supervisor paused her ascent for a moment to think, "You're a curious fellow aren't you? I suppose that would be rather unfortunate, but with a new Maker coming every day, our kind will always be."

Ario inhaled sharply midstep, the gravity of his workshop predicament sent him into such a mental tailspin that he stumbled over a clearly visible tool box. She looked on with concern that this young Maker may be a bit clumsy.

Ario quickly picked himself up, stood tall, and took a deep breath, "Look, about the new Makers, there's something I need to..."

But the supervisor was already focused on her next duty and had no time for further chitchat. "Later, later," she mumbled as she walked up to a large metal pipe. Ario's face clouded with disappointment and he wondered if anyone was ever going to listen.

He was about to insist on being heard when Carol picked up a nearby spanner and began to bang the pipe and called out to the factory floor. "Makers," the ambience of work and chatter continued. "MAKERS!" she hollered in a voice that bounced off the walls and floors. The factory fell silent. "This is Ario," she called. Ario looked around at the hundreds of Makers who peeped over railings, down from ladders and smiled and waved from the floor below.

All the Makers replied in chorus, "Hello Ario!" which left Ario slightly embarrassed and incredibly overwhelmed. All he could manage was a timid little wave as they all turned back to their business.

Now that the introductions were over, Carol whisked Ario around the factory, intent on ensuring that he understood the protocols and safety procedures and was ready to commence work. With increasing frustration, Ario tried to interrupt a few times to talk to her about his workshop issue, but she was not interested in anything other than the many tasks at hand.

As she led Ario around, she explained exactly how the Great Freeze Machine worked. She pointed at the various tubes and pipes that channeled deep into the ground. By controlling the machine's many levers, a humongous blast of ice would freeze the core of the earth and cool the volcano, thus preventing a major catastrophe.

As Ario followed the supervisor across the factory floor, he gradually became aware of a deep pulse that he felt beat along with his heart. His ears vibrated as the sound ebbed and flowed over his body. Ario soon realized that it was the Makers. While they were intently focused on their tasks, their tools had became their instruments that worked in a unified rhythm. *Whirr, whizz, tap, bang. Buzz, clank, swipe, clang. Shuffle, jingle, rat-tat-tat, scrunch, tick, hiss, kachink, knock,* and *whack.*

A baritone, velvety hum began to gently caress the open factory space and reverberate pleasingly off the cement flooring. "I thought we weren't allowed to sing?" he said to Carol.

"As long as we don't get caught," she winked as she handed Ario a big box of knotted cables before she hurried off. Ario sat on the floor sorting the cables as he allowed the acoustics to wash over him. To his delight, a melodic chant entwined with the hum as the alto and soprano voices joined the rich bass notes. The rhythm and harmonies spurred the Makers on as they worked.

> *Make, Maker make, we must create.*
> *Hurry, Maker make, no time to waste.*
> *A Maker's task is never done*
> *Since making time has begun.*
> *Make, Maker make, we must create.*
> *Hurry, Maker make, this is our fate.*

Ario was overcome by the same desire that gripped him in the workshop, the desire to sing, to partake, to make music. He stood up, lifted his face and sang along with abandoned enthusiasm.

> *Make, Maker make, we must create.*

To his horror, what was suppose to be a deliciously harmonic B sharp melody, was at least five and a half tones out of pitch and way too dynamic for the gentle harmonies of the others.

The surrounding Makers stopped their chores and singing and looked at Ario with astonishment, "What was that?" someone muttered as they stared disapprovingly.

"Shhh, you'll get us in trouble!" said another Maker with worried eyes.

Ario self consciously slunk to the floor and returned to his pile of cables. The desire and the passion was there, but the delivery was left wanting. A group of Makers nearby were perplexed by Ario's outburst and whispered amongst themselves, wondering if he was joking, for they had never heard such discordance leave a Maker's mouth. Meanwhile the Makers continued their working song...

*Make, Maker make, we must create.*
*Hurry, Maker make, no time to waste.*

Despite his recent embarrassment, the music inspired Ario and he could not contain himself any longer. From his seated position, he attempted to once again join the chorus.

*Make, Maker make, we must create.*

He thought that all in all the melody was much better this time, but his fear and anxiety seemed to ride his exuberance. His voice soared far higher than it should have and banged about the walls quite abrasively.

This time, he drew the attention of most of the other workers as the supervisor ran over to him "Shhh, shhh," she waved.

"You sound terrible!" someone called from the rafters.

"What sort of Maker are you?" another harshly whispered next to him.

"What's wrong with your voice?" Carol queried as she frowned down at him.

Ario merely shrugged as he sat awkwardly not knowing where to look as the surrounding Makers gawked at him and Carol studied him for an eternal few seconds.

"You'd best be quiet, Ario and get back to it," she ordered as she walked away shaking her head. The other Makers also returned to their work and their chanting.

Ario hung his head in bottomless shame, unable to fathom how such a will to create bubbled inside of him, yet could not be matched with any physical ability. He gravely intended to sing no more and to merely enjoy the Makers' beautiful voices that once again drove the factory onwards.

*A Maker's task is never done*
*Since making time has begun.*
*This Winter land is our home,*
*But we hold one thread of hope.*
*Maybe we can be free.*

*Free like he, Maybe.*
*The Magnum Opus, he knows, he knows all.*
*Magnum Opus, he lives free beyond the city walls.*
*Magnum Opus, he is the greatest Maker of all.*

Recognizing the name from the compass and forgetting his previous resolve, Ario jumped to his feet and sang with what he believed was a contained B sharp minor scale.

*The Magnum Opus? I have heard of he. Who could he beeeeeeeeeeeee?*

Regrettably, his contribution was much of the same and so much of a disaster that as Ario ended his inglorious high note, all the Makers stopped dead in their song and their work. Ario stood awkwardly under the weight of that eternal pause and was almost glad when a multitude of Makers began to bleat and admonish him.

So loud was this ruckus that no one heard the cries of Tenor at the front entrance, who was trying to warn them that Winter officers were on approach. The officers burst through the doors and a wave of panic swept across the factory floor, followed by a deathly silence. The ranking officer marched directly to the supervisor, and without any questions, slowly removed her hard hat. Carol's face dropped in terror as she held her arms up and cried in futile defense.

"No, no. Wait!"

Without hesitation, he blasted his ice staff and froze her solid. The shock and horror amongst the Makers was palpable, as they dared not say a word. The officer scanned the floor of Makers and taunted, "Let this be a reminder of what happens when you are musical." A flicker of joy darted across his eyes and he pushed over Carol, who shattered into hundreds of pieces across the floor.

With eyes blazing, the Winter officer slapped the supervisor's helmet on the head of the nearest Maker. The new supervisor understood implicitly and sprang into action. He dashed to the center of the factory floor and with as much authority as he could muster shouted, "This volcano isn't going to freeze itself. Back to work everyone!"

The Makers got busy, knowing the ramifications if they did not. Each returned to their post and resumed their work as if nothing had happened. The buzz of activity settled over the factory and the Winter officers were happy that order had been restored. "Finish this damn machine," the ranking officer barked at the new supervisor, and with that, they turned on their big furry booted heels and left.

The Makers stopped their work and muttered to each other angrily, as Maker after Maker fired an endless volley of outrage at Ario.

"This is all your fault Ario!"

"Learn how to sing!"

"What are you, defective?"

On and on they cursed and spat.

Ario stood rigidly still with piles of perfectly rolled cables at his feet, weighted in the most abysmal sadness. He knew it was his fault that Carol lay in tiny pieces on the floor. *She was such a good supervisor,* he thought. Ario understood the Makers' anger and couldn't understand what was wrong with him either, he really felt like a worthless Maker.

"I... I'm sorry," he called out to the other Makers, but they glared at him even more, as one-by-one they returned to their work.

"I hope the next Maker is better than you!" another Maker lashed at him, and Ario hid his head as low as it could hang.

Ario was seized by a chill far greater than any Winter officer could inflict on him. He knew that he could not share his workshop folly with anyone now, but also knew that in no time at all his secret would be revealed.

The new supervisor strode up to Ario and growled, "I want you out of my factory. Go with Clef and clean out the troll cages."

A scrawny Maker whose own Maker clearly economized with his materials and perhaps got a bit lazy with his general workmanship, peeked out from behind the supervisor, and shook his head in disapproval at Ario.

With a deflated heart, Ario silently followed Clef out of the factory. They walked through a number of desolate cobbled back streets until they emerged onto a wider street. On one side, Ario observed Winter officers coming and going from a large block of buildings, "ith the Winter offither's Barrackth and the prothething plant," Clef pointed out with a heavy lisp on account of his mouth being slightly over baked in the making process. Ario stood for a moment looking, it had only been this morning that this had all begun. He shuddered with dread, knowing all he could do was focus on the task at hand.

Ario followed Clef across the road to the troll cages. It was a long building with a rectangular slab ice-roof and stone-slab floor. Wrought iron bars surrounded the building and separated each of the cages. Clef turned to Ario and pointed at a shovel, then to the cages, "thtart cleaning," he instructed with a haughty tone.

Ario walked up to the cages and peeked through the bars—they were filled with piles of straw and dung. He sighed, but was glad to be occupied. He slipped through the cage bars, which were wide enough to contain trolls but not much else.

As Ario started to shovel and clean, Clef leaned against a bar inside the cage, keeping a watchful eye on his charge. He chewed on a piece of straw while thinking about his fortunate turn of events. Clef had up until the last hour been the most unpopular Maker, he thought it was because the other Makers were jealous of his superior making skills, he wasn't self aware enough to know it was actually because of his misplaced air of importance and general laziness. Clef was glad this dud Maker came along when he did, now he was beginning his climb of the Maker hierarchy and he was going to enjoy it. "Tho, thith ith what if feelth like to be thecond motht dithliked Maker. Feelth good!" he said to no one in particular. Ario tried to ignore him as he focused his attention only on his shoveling.

Clef tried to offer some condolences, "Look at the bright thide, you can't get any lower than thith," which really wasn't very helpful at all.

Ario rolled his eyes, but he needed to get some answers so turned to Clef, "Tell me, who's this Magnum Opus?" Clef let out a dismissive nasal chortle, he thoroughly delighted in knowing more than this new Maker. "You don't know?" he said smugly. "He'th only the motht awethome Maker ever made."

"Why?" asked Ario, as he had decided to skip over the condescending nature of Clef's voice.

Clef gasped with surprise at the ignorance of this fresh Maker, forgetting that he too once knew very little. He stepped forward waving his hands in excitement, clearly delighted in his superior knowledge. "He'th capable of playing dothens of inthrumenths in unithon."

"What kind of uniform? Ario asked confused.

"Nooooo Unithon! TO-GETH-ERRRR," he admonished, rather annoyed that this stupid Maker was breaking his flow.

"Right," Ario nodded not wanting him to stop telling the story.

"He can thing with a thouthand voitheth and…" Clef began again. BArio, not being able to help himself, interrupted, "Wow. Where is he? What does he look like?"

Clef glared at him "Juth let me finith will you!" Ario nodded apologetically and complied. "They thay, he liveth free in the foretht and appears unlike the retht of uth Makerth."

Ario's ears sprang up with excitement, "Beyond the walls? What's out there?"

Clef puffed out his chest with importance, "Why, no one knowth, we never leave the City, ith far too daaaangerouth."

Clef was about to continue, but was once again interrupted, this time by Officer Festus who was returning a troll to its cage. The troll was in an agitated state as he thrashed and growled with ferocity. Clef stood rigid with fear and Ario backed against the corner of the cage, both trying to remain invisible.

Festus slammed down a lever outside the cage, which slid open the cage's metal gate. Festus' eyes flared with a matching level of rage as he pushed the troll inside and zapped the beast repeatedly with his ice staff. Each time, the troll roared with pain as his body spasmed under the searing freeze. "Quiet filthy beast!" shouted Officer Festus as he gave him one last shot.

The exhausted creature gave up and shrank to the floor in submission. Festus cruelly pushed the troll's head onto the stone floor and shackled his collar to the ground with a short chain and lock. The troll could only muster a groan, for all the fight was gone. Festus laughed mockingly as he shuffled out of the cages and across to the barracks, without even acknowledging the Makers in his presence.

Ario was completely distraught by what he'd witnessed; no creature should ever be treated that way. He wanted to make sure the troll was okay, so he scanned the cage and saw a bunch of keys hanging on a hook. He surmised these would unlock the shackles, so he ran over to retrieve them.

"If you're doing what I think you're doing... thtop doing that thing!" Clef ordered, his eyes darting fearfully to see if any officers were watching.

Ario ignored him and cautiously approached the troll. Ario's heart was beating through his chest. The troll lay still, but let out a low growl.

Clef was bewildered by the foolishness of this Maker, "Don't go near him. Angry trollth are exthtremely dangerouth," he warned!

Ario looked over the body of the troll, "But he's in pain."

Clef could not believe the audacity and general idiotic tendencies of this Maker Ario. He mentally wiped his hands of any association with him, "Good luck, loother," then waved as he made a quick exit and disappeared.

Thankful that Clef and his unhelpful commentary were gone, Ario turned his full attention to the troll. He slowly bent down near the troll's face, but kept a safe distance. "H... hey big guy. Y... you ok?" he nervously croaked.

The troll wearily opened one eye and growled, then closed it again. Ario, slightly terrified but determined, took a deep breath. "I'm going to help you," he said tenderly as he shuffled closer to the creature. The troll opened both eyes, but remained motionless. Ario hesitantly used the key to unlock the troll's shackles, which were clamped way too tightly. "Free!" Ario proclaimed, to which the troll only whined and curled up his body.

Ario looked down at the despondent creature; he wished there was more he could do. His heart ached knowing this poor thing had spent his life being treated worse than a Maker. He had most likely been shown no affection or care in his entire days. A nearby rake gave him an idea. The troll was soon overcome by purring delight as Ario used the rake to give the troll a gentle scratch on his coarse, hairy back. In no time at all, the beast began to rumble like a swarm of baritone bees, gossiping in their hive. Ario stopped in confusion, then realized the troll had fallen asleep. He felt a sense of accomplishment as he tiptoed away and returned to his task. And what a grubby and stenchful task it was. He shoveled, scraped, washed, and mopped, glad to be by himself. Being elbow deep in dung was preferred to the judging and hateful eyes of the other Makers.

Ario was so engrossed with his work that when he finally took a break, he realized it was sunset. His first horridly eventful day as a Maker was drawing to an end. An even icier chill had settled upon Winter City and he shivered as he drew his coat in around himself. Ario smiled proudly as he surveyed the rows of cages now neat and tidy. For it was ingrained in a Maker's mind that no matter how big or small the task, much satisfaction is gained from a job well done.

His internal pats on the back were interrupted by a succession of chained trolls being returned to the cages by two Winter officers. "Maker, what are you doing here? Go to your sleeping burrows at once," an officer barked at Ario.

He was way to scared to ask what a burrow was or where one could be found, so he nodded and hurried off trying to look as if he knew exactly what he was doing.

When he stepped out of the cages, he saw a small group of Makers headed down the street. Ario followed a short distance behind, hoping they would lead him to these burrows.

He found himself on the outskirts of Winter City. Before him, a large icy clearing stretched to the foot of the giant cliff face Ario had seen that morning. He tilted his head back in awe. What he had earlier thought were dots on the surface were, in fact, hundreds upon hundreds of perfectly round, Maker-sized holes carved into the solid stone cliff. Each dwelling had a circular door much like a ship's porthole window that promised shelter from the harsh winter night. The burrows were arranged in orderly rows, from the bottom all the way to the top of the sheer drop.

Dangling down the cliff face were a multitude of rickety wooden ladders that Maker upon Maker climbed, looking to find a burrow for their nighttime sleep. There was much pushing and shoving to get the best spots and Ario hurried to join the throng. As Ario began his ascent, it became apparent that word had spread about the defective Maker. He heard murmurings of disdain and revulsion regarding his deplorable voice and his role in the death of the much loved factory supervisor Carol. Time after time, he was shooed away from the burrow he tried to rest in. No one wanted to be the neighbor of such a clearly troublesome Maker. Slowly and dejectedly, Ario continued to scale his ladder as the sun set deep into the horizon. An icy wind moaned and blew all around him, flapping his jacket and leaving his ears rigidly cold. He reached the very top of the cliff with empty burrows all around and crawled into the narrow sleeping space. With relief, Ario closed the small circular door on the outside world and was surprised how cozy and comforting his little burrow felt.

He used his sleeve to rub the dirty glass and peered out beyond the City, wondering if the Magnum Opus was out there somewhere. He saw the volcano sputter hot red in the distance and almost instantly the burrow windows rattled, as a minor tremor shook the earth. Ario sighed, world-ending volcanoes and incomplete Freeze Machines were the least of his worries. *What kind of Maker am I?* he thought to himself. Words formed in his head and danced upon a little melancholy melody. This made him sadder still, for he possessed the same musical devotion as any other Maker, yet he was nothing like the other Makers.

*Can I somehow stop tomorrow and forget there was today?*

Alone, he dared to sing aloud. No one could hear, yes it was still off-key, but it was authentic, it was born from a desire to sing his glumness away. He sweetly yet discordantly continued...

*Maybe I can build some Maker wings and simply fly away.*
*Fly anywhere, anywhere at all. Fly far away, beyond these city walls*
*Fly anywhere, where I land who cares. Who cares anyway, if I fly away?*
*Can I somehow stop tomorrow and forget there was today?*

A burning tear rolled down his face. He sadly pulled a ratty old blanket over himself and fell into a restless sleep, as a snowy winter wind whipped and wailed at the starless night.

# CHAPTER 5
## *The Winter Palace*

On a leafless tree on a leafless, tree-lined street, a small bird no bigger than a swallow sat upon a branch heavily dusted with last night's snowfall. The bird's thick plume of white speckled with silver spots and glistened in the morning light. As is any bird's nature, she greeted the day with a chirpy tune. Unfortunately for this happy little lark, she caught the attention of Officer Festus, who passed by on his slow morning shuffle to work. With a blast of his ice staff, the song bird fell as an ice brick to the ground.

"Rules are rules. No singing," he tut-tutted to himself as he continued on his way.

Festus lumbered to the front door of the Processing Station and made his way to his desk. He squeezed into his barely forgiving chair and, with great care, unpacked his briefcase: lunch, stationary, paperwork, second lunch, and a snack. Now that he was fully prepared for his day, he pulled on a nearby lever to check the time. An hourglass sprung out of a small door on top of his desk and showed the sand almost emptied.

He popped the end of a pencil into his mouth and chewed as he became lost in thought about his sea side vacation. He had finally made the arrangements last night; as soon as this whole volcano business was over, he would be off to bask in the oh so pleasant arctic waters of the seaside.

The final grains of sand dropped, Festus sighed and furrowed his brow deeper and meaner, ready to start the Maker induction. But... nothing happened.

Curiously, he looked over to the double wooden doors that the new Maker should be bursting through. No starting buzzer, no cogs or pulley movement. Nothing. He shifted uncomfortably in his seat. *This process usually ran to precision timing.* He gave the hourglass a little tap, then waited another moment. Still, no Maker appeared.

Festus grunted with frustration as he unwedged himself from his chair and waddled over to the wooden doors. He kicked them open with surprising agility. He glared up and down the long room with growing confusion. Nothing. Never before in his working life had such an event occurred. He felt a sense of panic. Partly because of the dire ramifications for Winter City, but mostly because if this mess wasn't sorted out quickly, he would miss out on his seaside vacation. He muttered angrily to himself as he reached for a nearby lever and yanked hard. The emergency alarm bell rang.

Ario was discreetly and purposely tucked away in a corner of the factory under one of the many scaffold stairs. He was trying to engross himself in the menial task of sorting a bucketful of screws by shape and size. As he diligently surveyed each screw, he felt grateful for the task that kept him busy and out of the harsh glare of his fellow Makers.

His reception when he reported to duty that morning had been cooler than a frozen sneezleberry pie. He had learned all about the sour berry at breakfast from the less than forthcoming Maker cook. This versatile dark blue berry was really the only vegetation that grew in the harsh cold winter environment and was a staple of every meal. Winter food was served cold and all ingredients left a great deal for the palette to desire. Ario tried to comfort himself with thoughts of sneezleberry muffins for lunch, but could not shake the awful ominous feeling that crawled and scrawled in the pits of his stomach.

"Winter officers afoot," cried Tenor the Maker lookout as he burst through the factory doors. Ario sighed, he knew the time had come. He slowly stood up in his shadowy corner as the Winter officers stormed onto the factory floor.

Officer Festus' voice boomed, "There was no new Maker today."

A horrified silence gripped the Makers, then a dense swarm of panicked whispers began to rise as the gravitas of the situation hit home. Ario caught snippets:

"Ends the great lineage," a Maker close to Ario cried.

"Workforce diminished," another sobbed.

"We're doomed," Ario heard that one shouted from across the room.

His mouth was so dry and his whole body felt as heavy as lead. *If only,* he thought, *if only I could play a stupid instrument, if only I had woken Renaissance, if only Winter didn't exist, if only... if only...* But he knew that every single one of these 'if onlys,' were worthless right here and right now.

Festus' voice once again raged like fire across the factory, "Maker 367890, step forward."

The Makers in Ario's vicinity turned to him with eyes full of fury and disgust. Ario was overcome by a growing terror as he was grabbed and thrust through the crowd toward the center of the factory floor.

Even though he had known this moment would arrive, nothing could have prepared him for how it would feel. He struggled in vain and cried, "Wait. I'm only a day old. I'm too young to die!" Ignoring his pleas, the crowd gave one last heave and Ario was roughly pushed forward where he stumbled and landed at the feet of Festus.

The officer looked down at him like the repugnant pest Ario knew he was. With nothing more than an inconvenienced groan from Festus, two Winter officers seized Ario by the arms and began to drag him out of the factory.

Ario's face flooded with horror. He didn't know where they were taking him or what would become of him. He turned to the other Makers and begged, "Somebody help. Please, I tried my best!" But all he heard was a resounding chorus of boos and hisses. He was almost relieved when the Factory doors slammed shut behind him and he could hear them no more.

Ario sat huddled in the back of his cage as he once again found himself putt-putt-putting through the dreary streets of Winter City. Lost in his despair with his head burrowed in his knees, he had succumbed to the helplessness one feels when they no longer know hope. Hope is like breathing in a new morning full of happy promises and sunshine; Ario's heart was like the darkest night without even a solitary star to guide, and he had no idea how to make any of this right.

He became aware of the carriage slowing down and he raised his eyes slowly. They had come to a stop at a tall iron gate that barred entry to the looming and threatening palace he had seen yesterday. After an exchange between Festus and the palace guards, the gates clunked into action and began to open. Ario's gaze climbed the soaring turrets on either side of the gate all the way up large metal poles, which grandly displayed two blue flags. Up close, he could see the rich royal blue flags bore the emblem of stark white snowflakes as they flicked and flapped in the unyielding morning breeze.

The carriage passed under an icy smooth archway and entered an expansive square cobbled courtyard. When they came to their final stop, Ario's ears hung even lower; he felt like the loneliest Maker in the world. There, before him, was the Winter Palace. Its mountainous blue-gray frosty towers and turrets blocked the morning light and cast an ominous shadow over the bleak quad. Two snow beast ice sculptures snarled fiercely as they guarded the palace entry. They were poised on either side of a grand staircase, which was made of ice and glowed a frosty, baby blue. The steps rose wide and high to an imposing palace door constructed of iron and solid timber, and intricately carved with a flurry of snowflakes. All the way up the staircase were square, azure pillars, standing plainly and lined next to wrought iron lamps flickering blue flames. Ario had never before seen such magnificence or so many shades of blue.

Without a word, he was ousted from the carriage and marched through the courtyard by the Winter officers. He was becoming increasingly frustrated with their rough manhandling, but knew if he complained his treatment would be far worse. They followed Festus through a wooden side door in the wall surrounding the courtyard and disappeared into the bowels of the palace. Their footsteps echoed eerily as they passed along a seemingly endless series of sleeted passageways, dimly lit by glowing orbs of blue ice fixed upon the walls.

They eventually arrived at a long row of heavy wooden doors, at which they stopped. Festus stepped aside as a Winter officer opened one of the doors, roughly pushed Ario inside, and slammed the door shut. With a click of a key he was locked inside. Ario was met by a windowless glacial room, small in size with nothing but a large timber table and two timber chairs on either side. Outside, he heard Festus bark some orders then march off, leaving the other officers to stand guard. Ario stood anxiously in the middle of the room, unsure of what to do, so he sat in one of the oversized chairs and waited.

It wasn't long before he heard keys jangling outside the room. The door flung open and a fearsome Winter officer filled the doorframe. His neat short platinum white hair formed a severe peak in the middle of his forehead. It perfectly framed his cleanly shaven, middle aged face, which was chiseled in harsh angular lines with a deep dark blue scar that ran along his pale blue cheek. Ario shifted uncomfortably in his seat. The officer was clothed in the usual Winter attire, but his uniform was a subterranean sea blue. Ario noted with some concern that his coat was embellished with the fur and paws of a once formidable beast, which clawed down from both his shoulders. He was big—huge in fact—built out of solid bulking muscle that bulged and stretched under his well-fitted clothes.

The officer said nothing while he closed the door and walked across the room to the table. Ario swallowed uneasily as the officer slowly lowered himself onto the chair opposite and fixed a pair of stinging steel black eyes on him. Every fiber of Ario's being was seized tight in rock hard fear as he stared back at the officer, not daring to breathe or even blink.

The officer spoke with a low, calm voice. Every syllable that left his mouth was considered and measured. "I understand a lot of people are very upset with you, but don't worry. My name is Commander Lorcaan. I'm here to help."

Ario exhaled ever so slightly and gently relaxed his shoulders, for he felt he had finally found someone who would listen and help him fix this mess. Ario seized upon the goodwill, "Thank you, thank you Commander Lorcaan. This has all been one very big misunderstanding," he said.

The Commander's eyes squeezed ever so slightly as he nodded his head slowly a few times. "I'm sure. I'm sure," he said in guised empathy, but Ario was too caught up in the perceived benevolence to notice.

Unbeknownst to Ario, he was in fact in the presence of the most highly decorated and fierce officer of the Winter Armed Forces. Commanding Officer Lorcaan was responsible for the entire security and safety of Winter City. To him, this ridiculous Maker was nothing but a lizard or a mouse, and he was the soaring eagle ready to strike.

"Tell me, why did you stop the Making?" he asked in his low, even tone.

Without hesitation, Ario launched into his story. He shared what happened in the workshop, how he tried and tried, but with his poor musical ability nothing worked and how it was all just an unfortunate accident. Commander Lorcaan sat unmoving listening to the tale until Ario finished and slumped back in his chair, satisfied he had stated his case.

Lorcaan rose from his chair and walked to Ario. He stood towering over him with a now unmissable aura of menace. He spoke coolly, "So you're saying, that even though this cycle has gone uninterrupted for thousands of years, it suddenly stopped because of a... how did you put it... an accident?"

Ario helplessly shrugged, "Accidents happen I guess."

Lorcaan put his strong, thick, pale blue hands on Ario's shoulders and instantly emanated a freeze that cut to the bone and left the little Maker grimacing from the pain. Lorcaan's lips raised in a sneering smile. "Yes, yes, they do," he comforted with zero sincerity as ice particles began to form around Ario's shoulders.

Ario tried to wriggle and twist out of the hold, but the behemoth was too strong. Lorcaan went on, "This accident, however, will result in the extinction of your race and the end of our work force." Ario was dismayed by the course this conversation had taken. The only response he could muster was the chatter of his teeth as his entire body succumbed to waves of biting chills. Lorcaan's voice rose ever so slightly, "Either way, with no new Makers, we may not finish the machine in time, which means the volcano will kill us all." Ice crackled and splintered as he ripped his hands from Ario's shoulders. All Ario could do was hang his head and ears in guilt as he rubbed his shoulders to ease the burn. "Perhaps your Maker can shed some light on the matter," Lorcaan said callously as he exited the room.

Ario inhaled sharply, he hadn't considered how his actions may have dire consequences on his own Maker. His head pounded as he felt his world spinning even more out of control.

Ario was moved across the hallway to a large holding cell. Such was the chill in this part of the palace that glassy stalagmites rose high from the floor and stalactites hung low from the ceiling. Some of these growths met randomly to form chunky, frigid ice columns. Ario kicked off the jagged peak of one of the formations and used it as a stool; he sat and stared into space. He thought about the moment before he opened his eyes for the very first time. He was floating in a black peaceful nothingness when the most enchanting of sounds slowly crept into the void. It wafted upon sparkles of light—a kaleidoscope of color and harmony that called him into the world of the living. It was Melody; her music had infused his soul. When he opened his eyes and saw her looking back at him, there was such warmth and love that he immediately felt safe.

Footsteps and cries of distress brought Ario back to his cold, miserable reality. He scrambled to the solid wooden door and peered out of its small barred window. There was Melody. She helplessly struggled against two Winter officers as they pushed her inside his former interrogation room. Commander Lorcaan followed and closed the door behind him. Ario slunk back to his makeshift seat, ladened with guilt and remorse that she was now unwittingly mixed up in this mess.

After what seemed like forever, Ario's prison door swung open. Melody was flung inside and skidded across the floor to his feet as the door slammed shut. Melody's face was ragged and her eyes looked tired from crying and worry. Ario jumped to her attention and helped her up. With great concern, he asked, "Are you okay?"

Melody, though weary, was beyond furious and angrily shoved him with both arms. "What have you done!?" she yelled at him.

Ario was taken aback by her anger and recoiled, "I didn't mean it, it was an—"

"An accident?" she spat sarcastically while shaking with rage. "I've heard. You need to fix this," she roared at him with frustration, then kicked a nearby stalagmite for good measure.

Ario stood with a feeling of staggering isolation—every single Maker couldn't stand him, even the one who had made him. "I don't know how," he said with a meek shrug. Ario's ears twitched nervously as he watched Melody lividly pace back and forth, refusing to look at him.

Finally, she turned and fixed her turbulent blue eyes on him. "The other Makers are saying the Magnum Opus is the only one who can restart the Making. You need to find him!"

The weight of all that had happened and needed to happen bore down on him, his legs gave way and he slumped to the floor. His ears drooped low as he buried his head in his hands trying not to cry. "I have no idea how to do that. I'm useless, I can't even play a tune... why did you make me this way?" he asked in a wretched whisper.

Melody stared gobsmacked as his words hung heavy and true. Her part in this debacle now daylight clear. She felt her anger settle, if just a little, as she recalled how she made this creature with such love and passion. Never in a million moons did she consider that it could ever go so horribly wrong.

She folded her arms and scowled, not wanting to give up on her fury just yet. "I followed the book, I don't know why you turned out this way," she said curtly, then sighed and dropped to the floor next to him.

They sat in a stiff awkward silence as Melody began to realize ever so slowly, but no less overwhelmingly, that this was her prodigy. He was her creation and this debacle was now also her responsibility. The other Makers had started to point and look at her with haughty side glances. In their eyes, she was guilty by association, or worse, she was to blame for creating the worst Maker ever.

She sighed again, knowing that they were in this together and it was up to her to somehow remake this Maker. "So, exactly how unmusical are you?" she asked. Ario looked up at her, rolled his eyes and placed his head back in his hands. "Come on," she urged, " I have to know whether what I've heard is true."

Ario reluctantly lifted his head once more, flopped his ears to the right then to the left, took a deep breath, and both gently and earnestly, but with complete disharmony, attempted to sing a few notes. "Do, Re, Mi, Fa, So, LaaAAaa..."

"Stop!" Melody raised her palm calmly, but she couldn't contain her dismay at the assault her senses had just experienced. Ario's ears wilted and he dropped his head, defeated.

In that instant, Melody was filled by sadness and compassion for this Maker, her Maker. She saw that his heart so desperately wanted to sing, and she saw he so desperately needed to sing, but his body conspired against him. Surely where there is a will there is a way.

She stood up with a new found resolve, she knew what needed to be done, for this very moment anyway. "Okay, I'll teach you music," she said.

Ario lifted his head and arched an eyebrow, "You will?" he replied in disbelief.

He wasn't going to let himself be tempted with hope. While most of her anger had subsided, Melody still found her creation utterly annoying. Nevertheless, she tried to muster some enthusiasm in preparation for this formidable task. "We're kind of stuck in here with nothing better to do, just try and keep quiet so we aren't punished for making music as well as ending the existence of our kind," she said wryly.

Melody snapped off two stalagmite peaks and started to gently tap them against a another stalagmite. The impact of the ice let out a bright, well-rounded ting that delicately echoed through the cell.

"Your first lesson: music is all around you," Melody whispered as she proceeded to ever so softly drum out a hauntingly crystallized tune that caressed and warmed Ario's ears. It was as if he could see the sound as dancing ribbons of rainbows. He understood how each note vibrated and how each note interacted with the ice in the room.

An idea struck him and he jumped to his feet, "Wait... um I have an idea but it's probably not going to work." Melody stopped her playing in

CHRISTOPHER & CHRISTINE KEZELOS

anticipation, but Ario was too scared to say or do the wrong thing, on account of his limited but trying experiences of always saying and doing wrong things.

"Well?" asked Melody as Ario hesitated further. She impatiently tapped her foot, waiting for him to speak his mind, "Come on."

"No, it's stupid," he mumbled but Melody just glared. Fearful of igniting her wrath once more, Ario pointed to a succession of stalagmites. "I think you should play that same tune, but hit these ones here and here."

Melody frowned with slight annoyance, "That will sound awful," she said.

"I know, but..." Ario stopped and slumped in an utterly dejected heap on the floor again, "Don't worry about it," he said.

Melody rolled her eyes at the theatrics, but just to appease him and show him how bad a sound it would make and how much he had to learn, she played the tune anyway. Ding, ring, tink, CLINK. An entirely discordant and unpleasing high-pitched sound bounced throughout the cell. Melody held her ears and grimaced at Ario, but then... CRACK.

There was something about the depth and simultaneous shrill pitch of the notes that resonated at a frequency that sent a spiderweb of fractures across the far ice wall. Ario and Melody's jaws dropped in disbelief as they stood looking at the result.

"Oh my," she whispered as they peeked out one of the larger cracks and saw a Winter street. "We must be in an outer room of the palace," she said with growing delight.

They could hear muttering in the hallway and ran to the door to investigate. Commander Lorcaan was talking to Officer Festus in a low agitated voice. They couldn't clearly make out much, but Ario heard one clear and distinct word: "Compass."

Lorcaan yelled at Festus, "Go!" and he strode off down the hallway as Festus shuffled slowly behind him.

Ario gasped loudly and turned to Melody, "The compass!" he exclaimed. "What compass?" Melody asked confused. "It was in *The Making* book," he explained. "I accidentally brought it with me, but it was thrown out at the processing station."

"So what about it?" Melody said crinkling her forehead.

Ario's ears darted upright as his mind raced to piece together what little clues he had. "There was a message on it signed by the Magnum Opus. Maybe it's his?" He ventured further with uncertain conviction, "Maybe it leads to him?" he said with a shrug.

Melody's eyes widened; it seemed as plausible as it was implausible. "Well, it's all we have, and if you're right we have to get it before Winter does and get out of this city!"

Ario looked in awe at the creature before him, so bold and strong. He half smiled, "We?"

Melody was a 'cross each task off the checklist' type person and had no time for sentimentality. "I'm responsible for you, so I'll help you search for him," she said matter-of-factly.

Ario nodded, relieved to not bear this responsibility alone, "Thank you. But how?" he queried uncertainly.

Melody walked over to the cracked prison wall and sized up the damage. She took a deep breath and laid down on her back. Ario's ears perked to attention as he raised an eyebrow, this didn't seem like a good time for a rest. "What are you doing?" he asked, puzzled.

Melody started to kick the wall. "Come on," she ordered through a determined, clenched jaw. Ario nodded as her plan dawned on him and he enthusiastically joined her.

In a fearful, panicked, but exhilarated fury, they both kicked the wall again and again, as chips of ice began to break away. "One more!" Melody exclaimed. They both gave a final kick and a huge chunk of ice gave way, creating a hole big enough for them to crawl through. Cautiously, they peered out at the bright morning and surveyed the street lined with a number of Winter vehicles. Melody nudged Ario and pointed farther down the road at two Winter officers who were walking along. "Move now," she said as they both scuttled out of the hole and ran between two parked carriages. They held their breath as the officers strolled past, engaged in deep conversation about the precise method of extracting sneezleberry essence for use in cider.

Ario and Melody moved swiftly through the city streets heading towards the Maker Processing Plant. Melody had been on cleaning duty at the officers' barracks and knew it was located right next door. They kept their ears and heads down as to not attract any unwanted attention. Ario occasionally glanced at Melody in front of him; he admired her boldness and determination, but wondered how they were going to pull this off. Had any Maker ever made it beyond the Winter City wall? What was out there? What he did know was, if they did somehow make it out, surely what was out there couldn't be any worse than the horrors of horrors he was living within.

"Makers, stop!" a wheezy voice barked at them on the corner of a busy street, only a block from their destination. Ario froze as Melody nodded at him and forced a wide smile at the burly old Winter male they were trying to pass. He waved his walking stick while he eyed them both with an air of suspicion, "Where are you two off to in such a hurry?"

"Why, good morning, fine sir. We are off to the officers' barracks to finish our cleaning detail," Melody said with a solid mask of politeness.

He drew in a long rattling breath, then coughed and spluttered all over them, "Tie my boot straps, will you. They've come loose," he said.

Ario quickly obliged and dropped to his knees. He made several attempts at trying to join the straps, but his nervous fingers kept fumbling the buckle. Melody watched on, attempting to not look impatient. With a resolute grunt, Ario yanked the buckle tight and jumped up with a smile of accomplishment. Without warning, the old timer clocked Ario on the head with his walking stick. "Too slow!" he said, then turned and wheezed off down the street. Ario's smile dropped, he just didn't understand why people need to treat others like that.

"We have to move," Melody said as she grabbed Ario by the arm and dragged him forward through the streets.

They scanned the street, then cautiously ran up the steps of the Processing Plant to the front door. Melody kept watch as Ario tried the door handle. "It's locked," he said quietly, disappointed but undeterred, "lets try the side."

The Makers hurried into a narrow alleyway that ran between the Processing Plant and the looming frosty wall of the officers' barracks next door. As they snuck along the alleyway, they tried to open each window they passed, but they were all locked shut. Ario and Melody nodded at each other with excitement when they discovered one that was slightly ajar. After much heaving and pushing however, they realized it was properly stuck. Melody bent down and found a large rock on the ground. She wrapped it in her overcoat and began tapping the edge of the window frame, trying to loosen it. Low murmurings of Winter officers could be heard in the neighboring building. The Makers eyed each other worriedly as Melody continued to gently tap away at the pane and Ario repeatedly tried to push the window up. A large screech echoed down the alleyway as the window finally gave way and slid open. They held their breaths, eyes wide with fear. The conversations next door didn't miss a beat. "Go," Melody said softly.

Ario gave Melody a boost through the window, and, once inside, she reached down to help him up. She pulled him up a bit too forcefully and he tumbled and rolled inside, landing on the floor of the processing room. As Ario rose to his feet, he felt overwhelmed being back where it all began.

The air seemed to reek of Festus and his lunch. There was the huge desk and the levers poised ready to process the next poor unsuspecting Maker, his Maker, who may never arrive. He tried to shake off the doubt as he focused on what he was here to do and raced to the trash can near the desk. It was empty.

"Oh no," he exclaimed. They looked at each other perplexed at what to do next when they heard keys jangling at the front door.

"Shh," Melody motioned for silence then grabbed Ario and dragged him out the back door, just as the front door swung open. Officer Festus puffed and panted as he entered—the walk from his vehicle and up the steps to the front door had taken a lot out of him. He waddled his way to the trash can, but he too found it empty.

Ario and Melody absconded down the back stairs and nearly bowled over Fugue, a Maker trash collector, who was busy emptying trash cans into his cart. Ario had no time for civilities and verbally assailed him, "Hey, did you just empty the trash from in there?" he asked as he waved frantically at the Processing Plant.

Fugue looked blankly at the Maker flailing anxiously in front of him, "Uh huh," he said way too calmly and slowly for Ario's liking. Ario shoved him aside so he and Melody could peer into the cart's dumpster. They were hit with a wall of stench like that of a thousand fish heads, which it well could have been given that fish and their heads were also a staple of the Winter Citizen's diet.

Melody smiled so sweetly to Ario, "In you get."

Ario grimaced, he knew this had to be done, but boy oh boy, surely this task alone should count as full atonement for all his mistakes and any mistakes he would ever do. He took a deep breath, rolled up his sleeves, and dove in.

Melody kept an eye on the back door of the Processing Plant, while Fugue stood beside her and quizzically watched Ario as he rifled through the garbage. "What's he doing?" he asked.

"Looking for a compass," she said without taking her eyes off the door.

Fugue raised an eyebrow, "Really? What for?"

Melody had no desire to engage in small talk but curtly replied, "We think it may lead us to the Magnum Opus."

Fugue's eyeballs nearly exploded with excitement, "It does!?" he squealed as he pulled the missing compass out of his pocket and looked at it with new found admiration.

Melody turned around and with joyful relief saw the prize in his hand. Before he knew what was happening, she snatched it and pocketed it for herself. "Thank you," she said, but it was more of an order than a pleasantry. Fugue was disappointed; he loved the tales of the Magnum Opus and it would have been wonderful to possess such a relic, but he said nothing. There was something about these two Makers that suggested trouble.

At that moment, Officer Festus burst through the back door and saw Melody. "Freeze!" he barked and fumbled for his ice staff while simultaneously trying to lumber down the stairs. Melody knew there was not a moment to waste. She'd had some driving experience while on cleaning duty and now she was going to put it to the test. She barged past Fugue, jumped into the trash cart's cabin, and cranked the starter lever—hard. They hurtled off down the back alleyway at full speed.

"Stop!" Officer Festus bellowed as he fired at them. He missed and froze a collection of trash cans lined up on the side of the lane. He muttered angrily to himself as he waddled over to a vehicle, it was the epitome of Maker ingenuity sporting an engine fused to a sled-like base. He throttled the engine then sped off in high pursuit. Left behind was a very confused Fugue, whose observation on the character of those two Makers was now confirmed and whose most pressing concern was, how would he ever finish his trash round?

Taking advantage of Festus' awkward start, Melody was able to gain some distance as she zigzagged through the Winter City streets. She knew she had to make it to the north exit, which wasn't too far, and she had heard guards were rarely posted there. Festus, without his physical restrictions, proved to be quite dab at steering his sled as he ducked and weaved through the streets, quickly closing the gap. Ario, who, until then, had been neck high in trash, wondered what all the commotion was about as he was flung from left to right. He steadied himself and looked out the back of the cart. With a searing panic, he saw the Winter buildings whizzing by and Officer Festus not far behind, giving chase.

He waded through the trash to a small wooden sliding window that was at the back of the driver's cabin. He slid it open. "I can't find it, it's not here," he said despairingly to Melody. With eyes stuck to the road, Melody thrust up her hand holding the compass.

Ario was overcome with relief, "What? How'd you—"

"No time," she yelled and slammed the window shut. At that precise moment, a blast of ice missed Ario's head by a mere whisker and froze the sliding window over. Ario turned to see Festus only a vehicle length or so behind, wielding his ice staff and blasting at the trash cart in a frenzied rage. Ario dove in and out of the trash to avoid being hit as blast after blast left frozen patches splattered across their escape vehicle.

Ario made his way to the back of the cart to reach for a lever on the outside of the back panel. Guessing this would release the garbage, he hoped it would at the very least slow Festus down. The swerving of the trash cart combined with the bumps in the road made his task most difficult indeed. Festus wised up to Ario's plan, took aim, and froze the lever solid. Ario lunged for it regardless, but the freezing metal burned his hand. "Ow!" he exclaimed. Still dodging Festus' ice blast bombardment, he rifled through the trash and pulled out a suspect soggy rag. He wrapped his hand in it and gave the lever a hard pull, but the metal snapped right off. "Great!" he cried.

In absolute desperation, Ario lay down on the pile of garbage and began to kick at the back panel. He channeled all of the anger, all of the disappointment, and all of the frustration that he had amassed in such a short lifetime. There was no way he was going back, "No way!" he screamed to the sky. With one last roar and one humongous kick, the back panel snapped off its hinges from the force.

As it flung towards Festus, he skillfully swerved to avoid it. However, he was not so quick to notice that Ario had also pulled the tip mechanism on the cart's tray, which was now dumping its load in his path. Festus hollered in shock as he struck the debris and lost control of his sled. He was flung off his vehicle. Then, he bounced and rolled a few times before coming to a stop in the middle of the street. The two Makers continued to race through the streets of Winter, while a furious Festus was left behind, covered in an assortment of putrid garbage including a fish head or two, cursing the moment Maker 376890 had come into existence.

When they were a safe distance, Melody pulled the cart over into a side street, and jumped out of the cabin to give Ario a jubilant backslap, "Well done," she exclaimed. Ario flushed red and hung his head in embarrassment, he'd never received the slightest of praise before and had no idea what to do with it. Melody was quick to get back to business, "They'll sound the alarm any second, let's get out of here." Together they lowered the tip tray, then Ario joined Melody in the front cabin as they headed straight for the north gate. She sniffed the unpleasant odor that accompanied him, but chose not to say anything on account of his remarkable triumph over Festus.

Melody slowed the vehicle as they approached the north gate—an archway built into the imposing City wall. Blocking the exit was a boom gate attached to a small icy booth. Officer Jumino sat on a stool, deeply absorbed in the daily crossword. He heard the vehicle approach, but didn't bother to look up.

Ario froze in panic, "What are we going to do?"

"Don't worry, I've got this," Melody said.

Ario took comfort in the knowledge that Melody had a plan in the works. What story had she cooked up to convince the guard to open the gate? No doubt it would be a deliciously conniving lie that would see them casually continue on their path to freedom.

Melody steeled her eyes, took a deep breath, then tensely cranked the speed lever down hard. She drove the trash cart towards the boom gate at full capacity. Ario was totally confused as he grasped the dashboard in fear. "Too fast, too fast, too fast!" he screamed as they smashed through the gate.

Ario turned to look at the Officer as they passed. He too was somewhat bewildered by these events, so much so that he remained in his seat not sure exactly what to do. All Officer Jumino knew for sure was there was going to be *a lot* of paperwork. As they zoomed through the archway, alarm bells began to ring out across the city. Only then did the Officer find his senses and jump to his feet, watching the Makers as they hightailed it out of Winter City.

The Makers dared not look back; they drove in stunned silence until the gate was no longer in view. "Gadzooks! That was your brilliant plan?" Ario asked Melody incredulously.

Melody shrugged and smiled to herself without taking her eyes off the road. The trash cart barreled along at high speed as she tried to keep it from skidding off the icy, unpaved road. "It won't be long until they come after us, let's find that Magnum Opus," she said through gritted teeth.

Ario nodded solemnly and looked out the window at miles and miles of desolate snow covered plains. They were the result of many trees being felled over the years to support the expansion of Winter City. Many more miles away, a thick wide forest spread before them offering refuge. The sun hung a little low in the sky suggesting that nightfall was still a few hours away. Winter City grew smaller and smaller behind them.

# The Movement

# CHAPTER 6
## *The Forest*

With no more road to follow, the Makers had abandoned the trash cart and now found themselves at the edge of the forest. They had achieved what perhaps no Maker had ever achieved before them: they had fled Winter City. Now, the size and magnitude of the journey ahead loomed overwhelmingly.

For a moment, they stood in awe of the magnificently tall pine-like evergreens that burst through a carpet of soft, white snow. Each trunk stretched a hundred feet or more into the sky, with luscious, thick, green needles that protruded from knotted and gnarly branches.

Melody knew they couldn't wait any longer, so she reached into her overcoat pocket, pulled out the compass, and slapped it into Ario's hand. "Start searching," she said, trying to sound cheerful.

Ario held the solid silver compass and stared at it with uncertainty. They were placing all their faith in this instrument and it was the only lead they had. He opened the compass and saw the face was etched with Maker hieroglyphs depicting the four cardinal directions. For the first time, he noticed the compass had two needles. Unlike the workshop where the needles had spun around, seemingly out of control, one gold needle was now locked into a waypoint ten degrees west of true north. Ario pivoted and realized the silver needle tracked their position and how far they were off the waypoint. Slightly west of true north seemed to be the direction they needed to head. He took a deep breath, "Looking forward to making your acquaintance, Mr. Magnum Opus!" He and Melody took their first reluctant steps into the woods.

The compass was proving itself to be a good guide—every slight change in direction triggered the compass' silver needle, so Ario had to pay close attention to ensure they didn't stray off track. Looking at the compass more than the path he was walking, Ario tripped on a multitude of fallen branches and large rocks. He thanked Melody for consistently helping him up, but she could only muster a grim smile in response.

The Makers trekked silently through the snow for hours as birds sang and numerous forest critters chattered and called. The sun was still in the sky, but barely made it through the compact canopy overhead. When it did, it cast random long shadows across the snow-covered forest floor.

As they pressed on, Ario and Melody became lost deep in their own thoughts about the gravity of their situation, and the possibility of meeting the Magnum Opus. When they stumbled upon a small glade of brilliant white, they turned to each other and smiled. It was a little oasis that the sun was finally able to reach, and it did so in its full glory. Rays dazzled upon the snow-dusted needles of the tall trees that surrounded the open space. Throughout the clearing were saplings covered in frosted climbing vines that entwined and draped over their branches, glistening like tinsel.

Ario and Melody gasped in delight as a deer-like creature darted out from behind a nearby shrub; her fur shimmered with silver and her eyes were as dark and as sweet as molasses. The woodland creature reared gracefully on its nimble legs and nodded its delicate twisted horns at her visitors. She watched these strange beings for a moment, sensing they meant no harm, then, with a gentle snort, trotted off into the forest.

Just when Ario thought this moment couldn't be any more perfect, the finest flakes of snow started to fall. Ario raised his hands in the air to catch them and shouted with excitement, "Isn't this wonderful?" He needed no answer, but got one anyway when he was struck in the face with a snowball.

"Shh, someone will hear us!" Melody admonished with a loud whisper.

Ario eagerly wiped the snow from his face, he didn't want to contain this. "Look around, there's nobody out here," he said gleefully.

Ario was so overcome with the sense of freedom that surged through him that he threw his head back and sang, "We're freeeeeeeeeee!" Naturally, it held no detectable tune or pleasantness.

Melody was poised to throw another snowball, but something about the essence and intent of his tune made her lower her arm. The realization dawned on her. "We're free," she whispered. She allowed herself to soak in the beauty of their surroundings as she turned to Ario and beamed a wide smile. They had both been so focused on their escape that they hadn't stopped to truly experience their freedom. They had no one to answer to, they were no longer anyone's property, and they could sing if they damn well pleased.

Ario was delighted when Melody also threw her head back and let out the sweetest, joyful tune, which rang across the glade. She hadn't felt this happy since the moment she had met her Maker, or made Ario for that matter—*Thwack!* A snowball hit her right in the head. Ario laughed loudly as first shock and confusion, then pure mirth rolled over her face. She reached to the ground for fresh snow and returned fire. For a few precious moments, the two Makers chose to forget about the cruel city not too far behind them and the frightening unknown quest ahead. They chased each other through the meadow, throwing snowballs and singing songs until they collapsed on the ground, laughing and out of breath, looking up to the clear blue sky.

*Owooooo!* An unfamiliar and threatening howl echoed through the woods. They both sat upright, ears quivering and faces contorted with fear. Melody scrambled to her feet, "Come on, let's keep moving," she said nervously. Ario didn't need a second invitation, they walked quickly and quietly deeper into the forest.

Directly south, only two score and seven miles away, was the Winter Palace. Inside the throne room, Winter's ruler, Lord Crone, sat upon his royal seat that protruded with intimidating ice shards of all shapes and sizes. Crone was a hulk of a being, with muscles of brute strength and height that towered over all his subjects. He was in prime condition despite his significantly advanced age. His platinum white beard flowed wiry and wooly to his chest and was a stark contrast to the pools of piercing cold blackness that were his eyes. Upon Crone's head was a crown made out of luminous stalagmites that jutted out, sharply and aggressively. His robe was the shade of a starless midnight blue sky and was adorned with the paws of wildebeests that he had slain with his bare hands. A set of long, pale blue fingers clenched his regal ice staff—a solid silver spectre engraved with intricate patterns of snowflakes that spiraled up to reach a glowing blue ice crystal ball. His other hand rested on the arm of his throne as a Maker machine busied itself delivering a precise manicure. Another Maker contraception complete with roller gave him a deep tissue shoulder massage, while a third machine with mechanical fingers fed him a bowl of fresh sneezleberries.

Lord Crone was neither a vain or silly man. His lineage could be traced back thousands of years and he took great pride in his heritage and the responsibility his title bore. He had been raised as a true Winter warrior, trained in all aspects of military strategy and battle. As a mere boy, he was sent into the deepest, darkest ice caves of the barren wastelands and ordered not to return unless it was with the head of the deadly Occisaw beast that lived within. In an annual trial before the citizens of Winter, the young Lord was required to fight his combat mentor. Only upon slaying his teacher would he be considered a fierce warrior.

Like his father and his father before him, these harsh coming of age rituals were part of his preparation for ruling a kingdom, which he did both stoically and rigidly. He had no time for fluff; he was a man that appreciated directness of speech and firmness of action, but he could also appreciate well manicured hands. Crone was thoroughly enjoying this moment of solitude and pampering, it helped him unwind in between all of his lordship duties.

Commander Lorcaan entered the room and bowed low. Lord Crone merely raised one of his closed eyelids and waved a hand to summon him closer. Lorcaan moved forward and cleared his throat as he addressed his ruler, "Lord Crone. I'm afraid we've had an incident. The Maker responsible for ending the cycle has escaped the city with his Maker." Lorcaan was furious that he had to report this information and take responsibility for his subordinates' incompetence. *Festus will be demoted many times over for this,* he raged inwardly.

Lord Crone sat in silence, with both eyes now open and fixed soberly on Lorcaan—the calming effects of his pampering were rapidly diminishing. The Commander stared back with feigned composure, while he himself was a formidable character, Lorcaan followed everything by the book and always deferred to his ruler. He respected and strictly adhered to the chain of command and was also wise enough to know that he was no match for the sheer power that was Lord Crone, especially when he was in a rage.

The Commander continued. "We've learnt that they have a compass in their possession, they are using it to seek out their Magnum Opus to restart the Making."

"NO," he boomed in a voice that echoed across the room. He then viciously slapped the mechanical feeding arm away from his face, sending it flying across the room.

Commander Lorcaan was confused and questioned, "My Lord? We want them to restart the Making?"

Lord Crone shifted impatiently in his throne—he saw a bigger picture, "It's not the Making that concerns me," he thundered.

The Commander was confused and asked, "The Magnum Opus? He's but a fairy-tale."

Lord Crone took a deep breath and shook his head as he pressed a button on his throne to retract the various devices around him. He had avoided telling any of his subjects more than they needed to know, but now it was crucial. Lorcaan had proven himself time and time again and he would be needed in order to save them all. With a change of heart, Crone dropped his voice and calmly explained, "The Magnum Opus is a powerful Maker made once every few hundred years. It is a danger to our existence."

Lorcaan was surprised by Crone's concern, "A dangerous Maker?

I doubt we have to wor—" but Crone cut him off with a withering glance. Lorcaan knew better than to continue.

Crone pressed another button on his throne and the paneled floor at his feet began to slide open. Lorcaan raised an eyebrow ever so slightly. He had been privy to this hidden chamber a number of times, but he was always in awe when he was able to witness the full extent of his Lord's powers.

"The Makers are magical beings and should never be underestimated," Crone said. He rose with staff in hand and walked down the throne steps to the open floor. A large cloudy ice sphere began to slowly emerge from within. "Where were the prisoners last seen?" Crone asked.

"They escaped via the north exit," said Lorcaan. He paused recalling how Crone normally used his crystal ball. "But... my Lord, don't we need them alive?" Lorcaan asked.

"I just need that compass," Crone said with eyes that radiated with cool calculation. He knew that if the compass was important to those Makers, it was far more important to him. "The Makers must always remain in our control and this Magnum Opus destroyed... or our legacy will be lost forever," he said as he passed his hands over the dome. The cloudiness immediately evaporated, revealing a scaled replica of his Winter kingdom. From the treacherous mountain passages to the large expanse of forests and the almost endless barren fields that rolled to meet the eastern seas, Lorcaan watched with the faint hint of a smile on his lips, and Crone closed his eyes.

The energy that flows through worlds was again in play. While Crone was adept at its use, it was being channeled solely to further his own gain, to push his own agenda of fearful control. When it's used in this way, it's tainted. With a powerful thrust, Lord Crone struck his staff against the floor sending a pulse that Lorcaan felt move through his chest as it reverberated across the land.

On a long ridge high in the northern woods, a dappled black and gray bear-like creature with sharp tusks protruding from the side of its face hungrily devoured the carcass of his latest kill. It stopped. A shiver ran down its spine. It was no longer in control. The snow beast stood on its hind legs and sniffed the air. Detecting the faintest of smells and knowing what he sought was close, the savage beast licked its bloodstained jaw and let out an almighty roar as it charged deep into the forest.

Ario walked with compass in hand as Melody trekked beside him through the snow, "What do you think he looks like?" Ario asked.

Melody shrugged, "Old," she said.

"Do you really think he can help us?" he asked. He needed to hear that this plan could possibly work.

Melody shrugged again, she didn't like being asked questions she didn't have answers to. "He's the Magnum Opus," she said pointedly. Ario nodded and, taking the hint, returned to silence.

Melody stopped. Her ears ears pricked high. She grabbed Ario's arm, he had heard it too. The grunting of an animal and snow crunching under its feet. Something was drawing close, and fast. They heard a roar from behind and spun around to see the snow beast galloping towards them. Teeth bared and gnashing as saliva poured from its mouth in anticipation of its next meal.

"Run!" Melody screamed as she grabbed Ario's hand and they dashed with terror through the forest.

With the snow beast directly on their heels, they ducked and weaved over fallen branches and scrambled in between trees. Ario threw a large branch at the snarling beast, but it merely bounced off as it continued its charge. He grabbed another branch, and in doing so dropped the compass. He tried to retrieve it, but Melody kept a firm grip on his hand. "Leave it!" she yelled as she forced him to keep up the pace, knowing their survival was the priority.

They dove in between a clump of trees trying to seek cover, but hit an icy clearing that sent them sliding out of control. To their horror, they realized they were careening towards a cliff face that dropped sharply into a glacial ravine below. They were going too fast and struggled in vain to stop themselves, screaming in utter panic as they slid over the sheer drop. Ario managed to grab hold of a rock just under the edge of the cliff. His other hand still held Melody who now dangled precariously beneath him. Ario gripped the rock for dear life. The beast approached the edge of the cliff and started to swipe and snap at the Makers who were barely out of reach.

The beast snorted with frustration as it considered its problem, then it lay down on its sizable paunch and positioned itself for the final blow. Ario cowered in anticipation.

*Swoosh.*

*Thwack.*

The beast screeched and rolled over in pain as Ario looked up to see several arrows lodged in its back. The snow beast struggled to rise to its feet, lost its balance, and let out one last mighty roar as it tumbled past the hanging Makers, down into the ravine below.

Lord Crone's eyes snapped open and flickered with pure fury. These Makers were proving to be much more trouble than expected.

"My Lord?" Lorcaan asked, as he anxiously waited for his next instructions.

Crone turned to him and barked, "Track down the escapees. If they've found the Magnum Opus, have him restart the Making, then bring them all back for a public execution."

Lorcaan bowed, "Yes, my Lord." He turned to leave but suddenly stopped as he wanted to be sure, "And if there is no Magnum Opus?"

Lord Crone fumed, "Find another way to restart the Making cycle."

Lorcaan nodded, leaving Crone to mull over his miniature kingdom with unceasing agitation. The Commander was relieved to be excused, he made a quick exit and stormed down the palace corridor. He was infuriated that he would have to leave the sanctuary of Winter City and head into the formidable Winter terrain to bring those loathsome Makers home.

As Ario clung for dear life, several thoughts rushed through his head. *Where did those arrows come from? What do I do now? My arm is killing me. Do not drop Melody.* "Try and hold on," he grunted.

"I'm not going anywhere!" Melody yelled in reply.

He tried to swing her to safety, but Makers aren't known for their physical prowess. Their skinny arms were more suited to needlework and noodling instruments. "Okay, Plan B," he said. They hung helplessly, he looked down to the bottom of the ravine where the snow beast ended up and said sadly, "I have no Plan B."

Ario felt ice and snow fall on him from above. He looked up and saw a large head peer down over the edge of the cliff. "Arghhhh!" Ario shrieked with fear as its black eyes glared from behind a mask made from the skull of an animal.

"What is it?" Melody cried out as she felt his grip loosening.

Ario couldn't quite answer the question as he didn't quite know himself. Was this creature responsible for saving them from the beast? If so, did he want to make a trophy of them next? All he knew with certainty was that he couldn't hold Melody for much longer.

The creature extended a gloved hand. Ario had no other choice, he called to Melody, "Plan B." He seized the stranger's hand and wondered with dread, would the snow beast have been a far better fate?

Ario and Melody stood warily on the edge of the gorge before their savior. He towered over them, dressed from head to toe in animal pelts. The furs, which were various shades of white, gray, and black, were clearly hand stitched together without a Maker's finesse. Ario didn't want to think about how each unfortunate creature came to find itself as part of this cloak. The axe this stranger carried in his hand, however, provided a clue, as did the quiver and arrows that poked out from behind his imposing shoulders.

The stranger continued to stare at them anonymously from behind the menacing skull. Ario looked up at him and tried to force a smile in hope of easing the tense situation, "Thank you so much for saving us."

"We owe you our lives," Melody followed his lead trying to smile as her heart pounded.

The stranger merely stared in response; the silence made the Makers shift nervously on their feet. Ario, unsure of what to say next, babbled on, "So, I don't suppose you've seen... or know the Magnum Opus?"

The stranger said nothing, but he finally removed his mask. Ario couldn't stop a squeak of fear escaping from his throat, as both their faces dropped in horror. A Winter man complete with pale blue skin, white unruly beard, and black piercing eyes stood before them. With a deep voice, he growled, "I keep to myself." Ario and Melody took an uneasy step back in fear. The stranger's eyes narrowed, "If I wanted to harm you, I'd be wearing your skins by now."

This did nothing to calm the Makers as they started to edge backwards, casually looking for an escape. Ario, with as much calmness as he could muster, exclaimed rather unconvincingly, "Quite right, good sir. We won't take up any more of your time then."

Melody anxiously nudged Ario and tried to inconspicuously take sideward steps. Ario continued to blab with intent to distract, "Please. Carry on with whatever you were doing. Slaying wild beasts and what not." The Winter stranger shook his head at their shenanigans and reached into his pelted coat. The Makers froze with fear. "We'll do whatever you want, please don't make us a part of your wardrobe," Ario blurted out.

The man rolled his eyes and from his coat pulled out their compass. Ario breathed a sigh of relief, "Our compass!"

The Winter man held it out to Ario. "Take it," he said with a rumble.

Ario looked undecidedly at Melody who nodded quickly, so he carefully stepped forward and accepted the stranger's gift. He held his precious silver guide with such gratitude, he thought it was lost forever and it truly was the only hope he had.

Without warning, the wind picked up and a light snow began to swell around them. The stranger looked with concern to the sky, now heavy with dark clouds. "A storm approaches. You should follow me to shelter," he said.

Ario was conflicted. The stranger seemed to want to help, but he was one of them, one of their enslavers and his fear had the better of him. "Oh no, we wouldn't want to impose," he said politely as he waved the idea away.

The stranger paused and shrugged. "Fine, but you'll be dead by morning," he said bluntly as he turned and began to leave. The winds began to whip with as much sting as the stranger's words.

"He saved our lives, I think we can trust him," Melody said nervously, aware of the snowfall becoming heavier by the moment. Ario readily nodded in agreement. They had no shelter and there was no way they could continue their journey in a blizzard.

"What's your name?" Ario yelled out above the wind.

The stranger turned, "Tallac," he called back in his surly tone. Melody grabbed Ario's arm as they ran after him, trying to shield their faces from the harsh bite of the snowy gale.

𝄞

Later that evening, the blizzard was in full fury as it shrieked and pounded against the shuttered windows of Tallac's humble, but cozy wooden cabin. He had built his home just like himself, with a strong and sturdy exterior to withstand the harshness of the outside world. Utilizing the bounty of trees that surrounded him, almost everything within was also constructed from wood, from the chair and table to the bowls and cups—everything was finely carved by Tallac's rough hands.

Tallac and the Makers sat in a polite, but uncomfortable, silence. Ario was perched on a stool at a small stone fireplace, entrusted with stirring a snow rabbit stew. He changed stirring speeds every time the man looked at him, assuming he was messing this up too—after all, he had never cooked before. Melody sat on the floor beside him and kept herself occupied by whittling away at a piece of wood. She skillfully wielded a small, sharp knife and a delicate flute was beginning to take shape.

Ario occasionally took sly glances back at Tallac who sat in his large rocking chair, away from the heat with his eyes closed. His coat and boots were left at the door and he was now dressed in a woolen sweater, pants, and socks, which revealed his muscular physique. Tallac's wide open face was weathered from the harsh elements, but, overall, he exuded a great vitality from his active life outdoors.

Ario lifted the ladle to his lips and sampled his cooking, he still only had Winter spices to work with, but it wasn't bad. "Dinner's ready," Ario said as he served his first ever cooked meal into a bowl, a cup, and on a plate—the only dining ware the solitary Tallac had in his home. After such an eventful day, everyone ate gratefully and hungrily, enjoying the warmth and comfort the stew brought to their stomachs.

After dinner was cleared away, Tallac sat and looked at the Makers curiously. Having lived alone for so many years, he decided that if he had company, he was going to have conversation. "What brings you to the forest?" he asked gruffly.

Ario and Melody look at each other cautiously; they were still apprehensive about giving away too much to their generous but crusty

Winter host. "We were wondering the same about you?" Ario said as he tried to deflect the question.

Tallac raised an eyebrow and, while he sounded slightly amused, he gave no hint of a smile. "Still don't trust me eh? Very well. I will tell you," he sighed with a nod.

He sat back in his chair and began to slowly rock, "Many years ago, I was Lord Crone's commanding officer," he said.

"Whoa, whoa, whoa. You were the number two?" Ario gasped in surprise.

Tallac nodded as his eyes glazed over and he became lost in memories of a time long ago. "Yes. I was a loyal officer, enforcing the law by the book. One day, while patrolling the palace corridors, I heard an unusual noise. I followed it to a room and stood outside the door. Inside, a female Maker quietly sang to herself while she scrubbed the floor."

"Never before had I heard singing. With a heavy hand I had always ensured that it never happened, but then... It was the most beautiful sound my ears had ever known. I stood outside of that room, confused. I should have punished her, but I couldn't. A junior officer had also heard and entered the room from another door. He beat the Maker citing the law of Winter. As she cried in pain, I was conflicted. For the first time, I saw the Makers as so much more. I ran into the room, I grabbed that officer, and I hit him again and again. I couldn't stop myself.

"So, I made a choice that day. I saved the Maker, but I was forced to flee the city. I had to leave my home, my family, all I had ever known. I have remained hidden ever since." Tallac scowled into the fire.

The Makers looked at him with a fresh set of eyes, for they understood why this man was like he was. Their hearts over flowed with the gratitude and compassion they felt for him. Melody smiled at him with deep kindness, "Thank you, Tallac. Thank you for standing up for us," she said.

Tallac merely shrugged, it was in the past and no good had come from it. Not being the sentimental type, and not wanting to veer any further into his emotions, he quickly sought to change the topic. "Why do you seek the Magnum Opus?" he asked.

Ario and Melody looked at each other and she gave him a subtle nod.

Ario didn't know where to begin. "Well, I accidentally stopped the Making cycle," Ario said as he winced at the memory.

Tallac raised an eyebrow, "You stopped the Making?" he asked.

Ario shifted uncomfortably on his stool, "Yeah I'm really bad at music," he said.

Tallac frowned at him. "What sort of Maker can't play music?" he asked way too bluntly for the sensitive Maker.

Ario burned red with shame; that feeling of never being good enough was ever present and ever raw. Melody placed her hand on Ario's leg and continued for him. "We need the Magnum Opus to help us re-start it," she said.

Ario's mood brightened a little and he pulled out the compass to show Tallac, "We think this will lead us to him," he said.

Tallac looked at it for a moment and his eyebrows knitted with concern, "It's pointing to the Northern Forests, a very dangerous place," he said.

Ario was beginning to warm to this wild and wooly character, and thought that he would make a great chaperone. "Maybe you can come with us? Keep us out of trouble," he asked beaming with what he hoped was his most convincing smile.

Tallac's gruff exterior cooled even more. "I've stayed hidden for 20 years. I do not wish to be found when Winter comes looking for you," he said sharply.

Ario knew this man was perhaps the only person that could help him. "But how will we surv—" he started.

"That's fine, you've done enough already," Melody said to Tallac, then looked at Ario pointedly. She didn't want to upset their host. Ario reluctantly left the subject alone.

With a final flourish of her knife, Melody held up her finished flute as a welcome distraction. She took a deep breath to muster some patience. "Ready for your music lesson?" she asked.

"Sure," Ario replied half heartedly. He turned to Tallac, "You may want to cover your ears," he said.

Tallac sat back in his chair awaiting the demonstration absolutely intrigued.

"Come on, it's easy. Just listen to this, then try it yourself," Melody said with determined eyes.

She brought the flute to her lips and ever so gently began to play. It was a beautiful harmony that was reminiscent of the Making song. Tallac's face softened as the notes trilled and flitted throughout the snug log cabin—it reminded him of his childhood. He was there once more, with his friends, the wind in his face, racing sleds before school. With a final brilliant spiral of notes, Melody ended her demonstration. Tallac sighed as he returned to the room too soon.

Melody handed the flute to Ario. "Here goes nothing," he said.

He raised the flute to his mouth and attempted to repeat the tune. He started off-key and after that he scuttled and skittled along every other key never finding the right one. Tallac grimaced, this tune didn't take him away, but he wished it would—far away. He was unsure how a Maker could make a flute sound so bad. With Ario's final note he earned the unique distinction of being able to make his dainty flute honk like an angry goose. Tallac let out another sigh, but this time with relief.

Ario's ears and face dropped defeatedly as he tried to hand the flute back to Melody. "It's useless, I'll never learn," he said sadly.

Melody was not ready to give up and refused to take it. "Not with that attitude," she scolded. "This time, close your eyes and play what you feel in here," she said as she thumped him in the chest, perhaps with a little too much frustration mixed with passion.

"Ow!" he cried, but reluctantly lifted the flute to his lips once again.

Tallac coughed politely. "Do you mind?" he asked as he drew his hands to his ears for protection.

Ario shrugged, closed his eyes, and took a deep breath. As he blew into the flute he thought about his life so far. He remembered the joy of making Renaissance, the sadness he felt when the Maker supervisor shattered before his eyes, and he recalled how happy he was when he and Melody played in the forest. He breathed his sorrow and his joy into the instrument and in doing so, he colored the music with his heart and soul.

The tune didn't sound much better, but as the notes zigged and zagged rather discordantly, his audience became aware of an out of the ordinary warm breeze. It flowed through the cabin and began to spiral dust around Ario. Tallac raised a wary eyebrow and Melody looked at Ario quizzically, but he was lost in the music, despite its horridness.

As he played on, there was a crackle then a pop and a small spark flashed in the air. A dry brown maple leaf appeared out of nowhere and danced on the breeze. "Whoa!" Melody said quietly. Tallac jumped to his feet with fists raised, not quite sure what he was going to fight, but ready to fight nonetheless. Ario finished his tune and opened his eyes to see the leaf float softly to the ground and Melody and Tallac staring wide eyed back at him.

"How did you do that?" asked Melody.

"I did that? What is it?" Ario asked just as perplexed.

In their Winter world where all the trees were bare, bar the pine needles, none of them had ever seen a leaf before. Tallac picked it up and looked it over, "Vegetation of some kind," he said frowning intently. "I've seen this shape in the relics of the ancient ruins," he said as he looked to the Makers.

Ario leaned forward, "Can you show us?" he asked.

"We can't, we have to stick to the plan. We don't have much time, plus Tallac already told us he can't help," Melody said with pursed lips.

Tallac churned over the idea for a moment, while these Makers were a risk to have around, this event had piqued his curiosity. "The ruins are in the direction your compass points. I can protect you on this leg of the journey, then you're on your own," he said with a soft growl.

Ario smiled at Melody who now had no reason to disagree. "Thanks, we appreciate your company," Melody said, satisfied that it wouldn't hold up their mission.

"Alright, get some sleep. The blizzard will pass and we leave before first light," Tallac said in his gruff tone as he handed the Makers some blankets. The Makers snuggled under their covers, thankful that providence had brought them this crabby old Winter warrior. They soon fell into a deep, peaceful sleep, near the low burning hearth. As the blizzard roared furiously outside, Tallac lay in his bed, wide awake. He was rattled by the presence of his guests, who had brought with them mysterious events and painful memories of his past.

# CHAPTER 7
## *The Ruins*

On a small snow-covered hill, Ario and Melody stood in an awe inspired silence. Before them, the cool morning sun rose from behind the remains of a once magnificent palace, constructed of the purest of sandstone. Even now with the snow of ages piled high against them, the ruins could not be prevented from glittering wherever the sun's rays touched the blocks of golden sand. Strewn amongst the crumbled turrets and spires was a maze of wood and stone debris.

"What is this place?" Ario whispered. He felt a certain reverence as if he was in the midst of hallowed ground.

Tallac, who was not so inspired or respectful, kicked a nearby stone, "I don't know. It appeared about a year ago when the ice started melting."

Tallac beckoned for them to follow as he walked through the ruins to a large stone wall. He wiped away a layer of snow that had gathered on the surface and revealed a thick pane of ice. Underneath the distortion, the Makers could discern a colorful mosaic of pictures and symbols, but it was hard to decipher.

"There," said Tallac as he pointed to one of the fractured images.

Melody squinted, "It's too hard to make out," she said shaking her head.

Ario frowned, "Wait," he said as he looked to Tallac and held his hand out. "Mind if I borrow your axe?" he asked.

Tallac grumbled under his breath, but handed over his tool. Instead of hacking away at the ice, Ario placed his ear on it as he began to gently tap around the perimeter of the wall with the back of the axe. Melody and Tallac watched curiously as Ario strategically delivered one last forceful thump at the center. The entire ice surface broke away in a single piece then shattered at their feet to reveal a mosaic perfectly preserved in the ice. Tallac nodded with approval, noting this unmusical Maker still had a few tricks up his sleeve.

The Makers ran their hands over the kaleidoscope of colorful tiles that swirled around four distinct shapes. The familiar maple leaf, a snowflake, a flower, and a sun.

"What do you think it all means?" Ario asked, struck with its beauty and mystery.

Before anyone had a chance to respond, the sound of barking dogs could be heard in the distance. Tallac's face clouded with fury, "No!"

"What is it?" asked Ario fearfully.

"Winter officers," he said with a snarl. Ario and Melody gasped in horror. "Follow me," Tallac cried as he started to run.

The Makers hurried after him as they scrambled through the ruins, trying to put distance between themselves and the Winter search party.

They hadn't covered much ground before Tallac raised his palm. "Stop," he said. They halted in their tracks.

"Stop? Why stop?" asked Ario. He felt a rumble growing beneath his feet and his ears stood alert with concern. He turned to Melody and saw from the look on her face, that she too was scared. The earth moaned and the ground began to roll like waves as stones trundled and snow drifts collapsed around them. In the distance, the dogs howled.

"Look out!" Tallac roared as he dove at his smaller companions in an attempt to shield them from an avalanche of snow. The tremors abruptly subsided and the trio were completely covered. Without missing a beat, Tallac burst out from the snow with Ario firmly tucked under his arm. They were fine, but Melody was trapped neck high.

"Melody!" cried Ario. With his bare hands, he frantically tried to dig her out. The barking dogs grew louder and closer as they resumed their search.

"There's no time, you have to go," Melody pleaded.

Ario ignored her and looked around to see what he could find to assist him. He spied a couple of broken wooden panels a few feet away and grabbed them. He threw one to Tallac. "Help me," he said urgently.

Tallac looked to where the dogs would be coming from at any moment. The voices of officers could now also be heard approaching and he tossed the panel aside. He reached to his quiver for an arrow and placed it in the bow ready to draw, "I'll buy us some time," he said as he stealthily ran towards the danger.

Ario frantically started to dig Melody free. "Are you OK?" he asked between panting breaths.

She felt she was drowning in the cold, but tried to smile through chattering teeth. "I'm better than those officers are about to be," she said.

A blood curdling scream echoed over the ruins. Ario paused, eyes round and wide, he nodded to Melody in agreement. He returned to digging faster. "Almost done," he huffed.

Melody looked past Ario and screamed in terror, "Ario look out!"

Ario glanced over his shoulder to see a Winter officer descending upon them with his ice staff ready. Without a second thought, he spun around and whacked his panel squarely across the officer's face, knocking him out cold. Ario stood absolutely shocked by his accomplishment and turned to Melody, who could only shake her head in amazement.

Approaching footsteps crushed the snow and, with trembling hands, Ario raised his panel once more. He and Melody sighed with relief when Tallac bounded from around a crumbled stone wall. Tallac stopped and looked at Ario poised ready to strike, then at the officer spread-eagle on the ground. He raised an eyebrow at Ario who shrugged sheepishly, "I'm just as surprised as you," he said.

Ario returned to Melody immediately, and with a few final scoops he was able to pull her free. She was somewhat wobbly and weak as the snowy burial had numbed her legs, but she was otherwise fine. More Winter officers could be heard drawing near.

"We must keep moving," Tallac ordered.

"We can do this," he said with a smile as he grabbed Melody's hand. Melody held on tightly and returned the smile. She continued to be pleasantly surprised by her creation.

The small party dashed through the ruins and made their way across a snow-covered clearing surrounded by buried turrets, spires, and piles of wood and stone. As they passed over the center, there was a loud creaking beneath them. It was a different sound to the shifting of the earthquake, but still no less menacing. "Freeze," Tallac growled. They stopped not knowing that the old decayed wood hidden beneath their feet could no longer sustain their weight. It buckled and lurched. "Run!" yelled Tallac as they all tried to scramble to the safety of the piles of stones on the other side. But they weren't quick enough. With a final splintering crack, the snow and wood underneath them gave way. The trio cried out in terror as they plummeted fifty feet.

In those eternal microseconds, Ario's mind raged with clarity as he wondered, is this how it ends? Is this the total sum of my life? It couldn't, it mustn't end yet, he had to make it right. A crushing jolt hit his entire body as he hit a bed of snow with a dull thud. Clouds of soft snow plumed into the air, illuminated by the beam of light now pouring down from above. Ario lay there gasping for breath. All he could think about was the throbbing pain, but breathed a sigh of relief when he heard the groans of his companions.

Tallac was the first to gain his composure, "Ario? Melody?" he said in a low voice.

"I'm Okay," Ario whispered.

"Me too," said Melody softly.

They all slowly rose and dusted themselves off, a bit bruised and shaken, but glad that their free fall ordeal was over. The shaft of sunlight allowed them to see that they were in an massive underground cavern. Above them, the high wooden beams peaked to a cathedral arch that dripped with large stalagmites. Thick snow and chunks of ice covered the sandstone walls and lower flooring that, in its day, would have been a hall of outstanding regal beauty. Hoping for a possible exit, Tallac headed directly to one end of the room. Massive wooden doors with decorative wrought iron flourishes barred the way.

Melody explored a different part of the room. "Frozen phantasm! What is this thing?" she called out frantically.

Ario and Tallac rushed to join her and discovered an eight foot tall winged creature with a dog-like face trapped within a solid chunk of ice. They stood looking at this mystifying creature. "I've never seen anything like it," Tallac said as he shook his head confounded. After a decade or more of the same thing, life had changed far too much in a single day than he cared for. Though his isolation pained him at times, it was his normal, it was reliable. These Makers had brought nothing but danger and strange happenings into his life.

The barking dogs overhead reminded them of how much trouble they were in. They looked up to see the snarling pack circling the hole. Winter officers now also appeared and began blasting ice down at them. The Makers scrambled into the safety of the shadows while Tallac drew his bow and returned a succession of arrows. An officer let out a shriek of pain as an arrow found its mark. Satisfied, Tallac swiftly joined his companions out of view.

Commander Lorcaan appeared at the rim of the hole. "Makers, you have no way out," he called as his viperous voice boomed throughout the hall.

"It's him," Tallac said through a clenched jaw.

Ario looked up at Tallac, "Him who?" he asked.

"The junior officer. The reason I left Winter City," Tallac said with deep bitterness.

Ario and Melody's eyes widened in surprise at this revelation. Tallac's whole being seared with anger as he began to flex his bow, ready to strike. Melody gently placed her hand on his and Tallac's body softened slightly, but his face still blazed upwards.

"Tallac, you've been roughing it over the years," Lorcaan called out. Tallac took a deep breath and closed his eyes, he knew what was coming, his past had finally found him. "The dogs followed the Maker's scent directly to your cabin. Why does that not surprise me? Your little hut made a lovely fire for roasting breakfast on," Lorcaan said with delighted viciousness.

Ario's stomach reeled as he looked remorsefully to Tallac, "I'm so sorry," he said softly. He had never wanted to turn Tallac's life upside down, it seemed anyone that went near him had their life destroyed. The burden of his errors and failings weighed so heavy on his heart and he wondered if everyone would be better off without him. He looked up at Lorcaan. That man was a monster. He let his guilt give way to anger, which was a far more constructive emotion in these circumstances. He breathed deep as he steeled himself. He had to somehow find them a way out of this mess. He began looking around the cavern hoping for an exit strategy.

"Every time I look in the mirror, my scar reminds me of how you betrayed your people and fled like a coward," Lorcaan said from above.

Tallac could take it no longer, "I should have finished you when I had the chance," he roared as he stepped into the shaft of light shooting a wild arrow. It narrowly missed Lorcaan's head, but the commanding officer didn't flinch.

"That's incompetence for you," he said with a scoff.

"Don't worry, I always finish what I start," said Tallac as he quickly returned to the shadows, angry that he had blown his chance. Lorcaan responded with a hearty but nasty laugh that rang through the underground hall. He stepped away from the hole as the Winter officers resumed shooting icicles at the trio.

An artifact that was mounted on a nearby wall had caught Ario's eye and given him a superb idea. It was a large silver shield in the shape of a flower, burgeoning with gems and crystals that still shimmered despite being encased in layers of ice. He rushed over to investigate, but the shield was way too heavy and high for him to remove.

"What are you doing?" Melody asked.

Ario gave her a half-smile, knowing it was probably better to keep his plan to himself at this stage. "Help me get this down," he said to Tallac. Moments later, with a hefty strike of his axe, Tallac cleared the ice and was holding the shield.

"What are you up to Maker?" Tallac asked suspiciously.

Ario motioned to the overhead hole, "Move this under the light," he said.

Melody and Tallac took protection under the artifact and, like a dazzling tortoise, shuffled into the sun. Instantly, light reflected off the shield and blinded the Winter officers overhead. The officers were stunned and temporarily ceased fire, so Ario took the opportunity to join his friends.

"They've stopped firing," growled Tallac.

"Great plan," said Melody.

"That's not the plan" replied Ario. He quickly positioned the shield so the light now reflected a focused beam directly at the creature entombed in ice. The Winter officers regained their composure and resumed their attack from above, but their blasts immediately evaporated when they came into contact with the shield's intense heat. "Hold it there," Ario said to Melody and Tallac, then darted over to the frozen animal.

As the ice sizzled and steamed, Ario held his breath. *This is it, if this doesn't work...* he looked up to the Winter officers and shuddered. The ice melted rapidly and within moments the creature's head was exposed. Ario scanned its face, its eyes were closed and it had a long pointed muzzle covered in soft honey fur. He dared not blink, he waited for a sign. Then, the nose gave the slightest twitch. "Yes!" he cried. He looked to the others but they were hidden beneath the shield. A few moments later as more light flooded onto the beast, the nostrils of the rapidly defrosting creature began to flare. Ario's face burst into a full smile, "He's alive!" he yelled hopping from foot to foot.

Melody peeked from under the shield, "What's going on?" she yelled.

He raced over dodging ice blasts and crammed in next to them. "Wowee kazowee, it's working!" he said breathlessly.

"What's working?" Tallac asked with an annoyed rasp. He didn't have a clue why he was holding this ridiculously heavy artifact for so long, all he knew for sure was that he was getting a crick in his neck.

"The creature. It's waking. It's waking!" Ario exclaimed and without another word he cautiously dashed back to his station.

Melody looked out again, the creature's sleeping face was glowing from the light of the shield. Then slowly, the creature blinked, "Wowee kazowee indeed," she said, her eyes round and astonished.

The creature let out a huge yawn, which revealed sharp canine teeth and a large pink tongue. Still blinking with sleepiness, it let out an almighty sneeze as a small ball of fire shot from its nostrils. Ario screamed as the arm of his jacket caught on fire. Melody and Tallac peered out from under the shield to see Ario waving his burning arm around, then throwing himself onto the snow to extinguish the flame.

"Oh my gosh... Ario, are you alright?" Melody called out anxiously.

"Yep, just a singe," he said grinning down at his burnt sleeve. *This is incredible* he thought as he picked himself up and bounded back to the creature's side.

The beast was now fully awake, but still trapped in ice, it snorted and clawed at the snow with its defrosted front paws. Ario cautiously approached with an outstretched hand. "Easy, we're your friends," he said soothingly. He looked deep into the large almond eyes of brilliant green, framed by long flowing black lashes and saw that he was understood.

Above, Lorcaan was getting impatient with his progress. This sparkling object below was troubling and the fact that the escapees hadn't returned fire for a while meant they were up to something. "Prepare the men to enter the cavern," he said. The officers nodded as they scurried to ready ropes and harnesses for their descent.

Below, the creature had also grown impatient with its progress. It let out a hoarse roar then reared on its sturdy hind legs. The remainder of the ice shattered away and Ario was sent flying onto his back. He lay looking up in awe at the magnificent creature that was almost atop of him. He noticed that it was trying to spread its wings, but they were sopping wet and hung heavy.

"Point it at the wings! Point the light at the wings," Ario cried out to Melody and Tallac, who quickly obliged.

The wings fizzled and steamed, then the creature once again reared on its hind legs. This time, it stretched its muscular wings and flapped them with great vigor. They were as captivating as the wings of a butterfly, covered in the finest of fur that was colored like a swirling pastel flower garden. It was free and felt fantastic.

At the surface of the hole, the Winter officers stood harnessed with ropes secured to nearby blocks of stone. Lorcaan was just about to give orders for the drop when there was a thunderous roar from below. The officers looked at each other in confusion.

There was a second booming roar and the Commander's face clouded. "Back, back!" he yelled, but it was too late. A great flying beast burst out from the hole carrying the trio on its back, scattering terrified officers far and wide. Lorcaan dove for safety as the area surrounding the hole collapsed, swallowing a number of his men. Commander Lorcaan jumped to his feet and fired his ice staff to the sky, but it was in vain. Tallac turned back and gave him a mocking salute. Lorcaan had no idea what sort of cursed magic this was, but he could only stand soaked in a rage he had never known. He watched as the strange winged creature flew out of sight, carrying his prisoners to safety.

# CHAPTER 8
## *The Cave*

The winged creature flapped a steady rhythm as it flew high above the snow-dusted treetops. Ario rode at the front, straddled on the creature's shoulders with his arms clutching the neck; the rush of the chilly air across his face made him feel more free than he had ever thought possible. He checked his compass and saw that it pointed past the seemingly endless forest below to the mountain ridges that lay far ahead on the northern horizon. Ario leaned forward and spoke into the creature's ear, "Towards the mountains, my friend," he said as he pointed. The creature nodded and shot a small fireball out its nostrils in acknowledgement.

Melody sat behind Ario holding his waist, she too was lost in the grandeur of the flight and when Ario cried out, "Yipeeee, Magnum Opus, here we come!" she joined in laughing and hollering.

Tallac, however, was not impressed with this mode of transportation at all. He sat behind the Makers, gripping the creature's rump with white knuckles. When the creature let out a cough and a large snort of smoke, Tallac's body stiffened even more. He was all too aware that they were flying hundreds of feet in the air on a creature that, until not so long ago, had been frozen solid.

There was another large snort and a succession of coughs as the passengers felt the creature's body ripple with spasms underneath them. Fear sobered the faces of the Makers who were jolted back to reality.

"Great gosh almighty, are you Okay?" said Ario into the creature's ear. The creature rolled slightly to the left then started to dip in height. Tallac knew he should have gone with his first instinct that perhaps he was not made to fly. The creature snorted smoke once again and started to lose height fast. The trio cried out in fear. Tallac observed with great annoyance that this was not the first time he was falling from a great height that day. Ario spotted a small patch of snow between some trees, "There, there friend," he said to the creature as he pointed.

The creature continued to snort and cough as it began its rather ungraceful descent. It reached the treetops and beat its wings wildly trying to avoid the branches that whipped them as they passed. The companions screamed as they held on for dear life, their bodies petrified with fear. The ground approached all too swiftly. The creature clawed at the air, misjudged the distance to the ground then tripped over its own legs, sending everyone tumbling and crashing into the snow.

The creature whined as it stood and scratched at the snow, clearly unhappy with the way the cool substance felt on its paws. The trio helped each other up and patted themselves off, glad they had survived that ordeal unscathed.

Ario approached the agitated creature with an outstretched hand, "Thank you for helping us," he said gently as he gave it a scratch on its under belly. The creature chortled happily and nuzzled Ario with his cheek then gave him a huge wet lick across the face.

Ario giggled and Melody's heart melted, "Aww, cute as a button," she said.

Tallac was not so impressed, "Disgusting," he said as he walked to the back of the creature, he lifted her long tapered sandy colored tail and had a peek. "It's a girl by the way," he called out.

Ario noticed that the creature wore a leather woven collar around her muscular neck, he reached up and discovered a small silver flower tag and turned it over. "Look, her name is Lassar," he said, reading the inscription. The creature responded with a big snort of smoke.

Melody stepped forward and joined Ario in scratching her under the belly. "She must be somebody's pet," she said as she looked up into her big doleful eyes. Lassar whimpered softly in reply and lowered her head sadly. "She must have belonged to the people who lived in the ruins," Melody continued as she gave Lassar long strokes down the soft golden hair of her chest. She frowned, "Her fur is very thin," she said.

Ario also frowned as he patted her light coat, "Maybe it was warmer before she was frozen," he said with a shrug.

Tallac walked from behind Lassar with a raised eyebrow, "That makes no sense, Winter has been forever cold," he said. Lassar threw her head back, spread her wings and tried to breath fire, but only managed a croaky roar and puffs of steam.

Ario and Melody stepped back out of her way. "Well she sure doesn't like the cold air," said Ario.

Tallac placed his hands on his hips; he had grown impatient with this discussion on flying animal biology. "We should move. Officers will be searching for us," he said.

Melody looked at the big winged creature, "What about Lassar?" she asked.

Tallac waved his hand dismissively and started to walk away. "Leave her, she's too big. She'll give away our position," he said with a snarl.

Ario looked up into the gentle face, those eyes knew everything that was going on and he would hear nothing of the sort. "But she saved our lives. We owe her!" he criedw.

Tallac paused and turned back. He narrowed his eyes as he looked at the creature and conceded to himself that maybe this beast could be useful in the unknown journey ahead. He saw the two Makers were already ridiculously attached. "You don't know what she eats, you better hope it's not Makers," he said with a smileless chuckle, then he started to head farther into the forest.

Ario and Melody looked at each other with wide eyes, they grimly considered this possibility for a moment. When they looked at Lassar, she was happily snapping and pawing at vines dangling from a tree. They shook their heads and giggled, Ario gave a short sharp whistle, "Come on girl," he said as they raced to catch up to Tallac.

The sun was high in the sky as the group walked along the forest floor. Melody walked silently next to Ario as she thought about the way he had refused to abandon her at the ruins, and how he had devised their escape plan. She turned to him, "You were amazing back there," she said with a smile.

Ario stopped walking and pondered for a moment; he was proud that she said those words, but all he could think of were the things that he had done wrong. He hadn't been able to rid his mind of the image of Renaissance lying on the workshop bench. "That doesn't make up for why we're here in the first place," he said glumly.

Melody turned to Ario with eyes blazing as she threw her arms up in the air, "Heavens to ballywhack. You made one... BIG mistake, but if you're going to fix all of this, and I know you can, then you need to believe you can fix it. You saved all our lives and what you did was awesome. I'm saying thank you, so take it," she said.

With that, Melody turned her nose and walked off in a huff to join Tallac. Ario raised an eyebrow, he had wanted to make this right, he so very much needed to make it right, but did he really, truly think he could? He didn't know... but here was someone who believed he could. *Now that's a new perspective,* he smiled and happily whistled. Lassar didn't seem to mind the discordant tune at all, as they plodded along deeper into the forest.

Covering a lot of ground, the travelers walked all afternoon and well into the night until they came to a low stretch of softly rolling hills covered by towering evergreens. Nestled within the hills were a number of small caves. They found one big enough to comfortably shelter them all with room to spare. The north facing cave would also provide refuge from the harsh winds of the blizzard that would indeed blow sometime during the night. Inside, the Makers and Lassar huddled around a small campfire as it bounced shadows over the frosted rocky walls. On the journey, Tallac had caught a number of snow rodents and Ario was now roasting them on sticks over the open flames. Lassar curled up behind them being revitalized by the heat; she entertained herself by blowing small fireballs in between scoffing down the juicy meat portions that Ario threw her way. Tallac sat at the mouth of the cave preferring the cooler air and solitude.

Melody smiled at Ario as she pulled out her flute from a pocket, "Ario, play that tune from the other night, the one with the leaf," she said.

While still glowing from her praise and the successes of the day, the thought of having to play music when he was incapable made him feel instantly sad. He wasn't in the mood for a music lesson tonight and vehemently shook his head.

"You should, you'd play it better," he said.

Melody sensed the distress and decided not to push him tonight, she wrinkled up her nose as she tried to remember the notes. She recalled a few, but the whole tune alluded her. "I don't know it," she said with a shrug.

Ario paused for a moment and thought about the tune that he'd played just last night. As he did, the musical notes appeared in his mind like a picture, clear and precise on a sheet of music as they always did. He grabbed a nearby stick and drew musical staves onto the frosted dirt, then started to write the notes.

Melody watched him with a quizzical frown, "You can write music? That's rare for Makers."

This was true, while Makers were gifted in playing music by sight or working out a tune in their head, it was not common at all for them to sit and actually write out sheet music note for note.

Ario dropped his head, "I can see and hear the notes. I just can't play them."

Melody smiled at him consolingly then raised the flute to her mouth. Reading the notes on the ground, she gently played the piece beautifully— it danced and glided throughout the cozy cave. Lassar paused blowing fireballs and perked her ears as Tallac rested his head against the wall and once again felt the thrill of a sled racing down the hill.

As the tune reached a pleasant crescendo, just like the night before, warm air began to blow through the cave. Tallac sat up rigid and raised a cautious eyebrow as Ario excitedly clapped. "It's happening again, keep going," he said as he was inspired to scrawl more notes.

Melody nodded and continued to play, there was the same crackle and pop as the previous night, then a small spark flashed. When a crispy brown leaf once again appeared out of thin air, her stomach jumped with delight.

"You did it!" Ario gasped. He wanted to know how far this could go and motioned for her to go on. As Melody did, the air was charged with static as dusty orange, deep brown and golden yellow leaves materialized and floated on the warm air. Before they knew it, a flurry of rustic hues began to swirl around them. Ario jumped up and twirled about with the leaves, arms open wide as Melody played on with a sense of joyful trepidation. Lassar sniffed the air and tried to eat the leaves that blew her way.

Tallac slowly rose from his spot, sensing that something unusual was conjuring. A light as bright as a small sun flashed within the cave. They all jumped back in fear and shielded their eyes. When they were able to see again, a stranger stood in the center of the cave.

Melody's mouth dropped from shock and the flute fell to the ground. Ario could only manage a small squeak. The stranger stood a head above Tallac and was holding a garden rake with a long wooden handle and metal teeth. His gangly legs were dressed in light tan and brown pinstriped leggings, with chunky brown leather work boots on his feet. Hanging off his wiry frame was a snug fitted cropped jacket, decorated with a rich brown and orange leaf print which was accompanied by a cream undershirt and a deep earth orange scarf tied around his neck. He had a sweeping crown of thick dark brown hair, which rose like whipped cream to a peak. His long thin face was cocked to one side and his brown eyes sparkled with curiosity and surprise.

Before anyone had a chance to speak, Tallac bellowed, "Take cover!" and charged at the stranger with axe in hand. The stranger half smiled as he calmly raised his rake in self defense, deftly blocking a crushing swing from Tallac. Tallac used brute force and continued to strike again and again, but the stranger was nimble and, with his rake, was able to deflect each blow with an almost theatrical flair and an ever growing grin.

Tallac was becoming increasingly frustrated as he continued the attack, "What do you want!?" he roared.

The stranger appeared to be having fun—he executed a double pirouette and dodged another potentially fatal blow before he dramatically cried, "I want to live!"

The Makers and Lassar were pressed back against the cave wall trying to keep clear of the fight, not quite sure what to make of it all. The two clashed with their weapons and moved about the cave in evenly matched combat. Tallac swung again and the stranger swiftly stepped to the side.

Before Tallac could unleash more fury, the stranger reached out and stroked Tallac's beard. "You sir, have one fine bushy beard," he remarked.

Tallac exploded with rage and kicked burning logs at the stranger who frantically tried to pat out the embers that were threatening to set him on fire. Taking advantage of his distracted foe, Tallac shoulder charged him to the ground. The stranger tumbled as his rake flew from his hands and, for the first time, his face was overcome with concern, as Tallac positioned himself for his finishing blow.

Ario had been watching the stranger closely throughout and was certain that he was friendly and meant no harm, so he jumped in between the two men. "Wait!" he cried.

Tallac was reluctant and continued to hold his axe high and ready. Ario decided to try another approach to appease him. "He may know about the Magnum Opus. He may be able to help us," Ario pleaded.

The stranger on the floor merely shrugged his shoulders and shook his head, not sure what Ario was talking about, clearly the truth was more important to him than self preservation. Tallac growled and was about to lurch even with Ario in the way, but Ario cried, "I think he's friendly!"

The stranger found this to be agreeable and gave two thumbs up as he smiled and rapidly nodded. Tallac hesitated. He was hot tempered, but he was no fool and this stranger, though clearly some sort of imbecile, had only defended himself in the clash and had never been the aggressor. He snarled and angrily pulled back and returned to the mouth of the cave to cool down.

Ario sighed with relief. "We mean you no harm," he said as he extended his hand to the stranger.

The stranger, delighted by the news, broke into a wide grin full of shiny white teeth. "Wonderful!" he exclaimed as he sprang to his feet with Ario's assistance. His thin, reedy voice rose and dropped with dramatic inflections as he introduced himself with a deep bow and a flourish of his arm, "My name is Aquillo, delighted to make your acquaintance."

Ario was quite taken with the formality, and still even more confused by his sudden appearance "Where did you come from?" he asked.

Aquillo raised an eyebrow, "Funny, I was just about to ask how you odd folk arrived in Fall?"

Ario frowned, "What's Fall?"

Aquillo flung his head back and laughed hysterically, but as he looked at the blank faces around the cave he realized this was not a joke. "You really don't know?" he asked, also confused. Ario shook his head, this was beginning to become weirder and more weirder still.

Aquillo continued, "Why, Fall is one of the seasons. You know, first comes Summer, then comes Fall." He walked up to Tallac still moping at the entrance, as he put a hand on his shoulder and gave him a big smile and said, "Then comes Winter."

Tallac just rolled his shoulder to remove the hand and refused to look at him, but Aquillo was not easily offended. He was quite enjoying himself now, especially since he had a captive audience.

Aquillo skipped over to Lassar and waved his hands around him, as if presenting a prize, "Then comes Spring." Lassar seemed to like the stranger and licked his hand, Aquillo gave her a scratch under her chin then slid over to Ario and Melody. With a little frown he bowed low once more, "However, I have no idea what you two are ?" he said.

Melody was also enjoying Aquillo's elaborate high jinks, she smiled and performed a dainty curtsy as she introduced herself, "I'm Melody, this is Ario. We're Makers."

Aquillo rubbed his pointy chin as he took in these strange beings in front of him, "Makers eh? Nope. Never heard of you."

"And no one has ever heard of Fall. There is only Winter," he said growling as he pointed outside of the cave where a blizzard had begun to rage.

Aquillo's face dropped as he raced to the mouth of the cave, stricken with fear and deep concern to see thick white snow blurring any vision. "What in the—this is Winter?" he whispered meekly, the others nodded as all the pomp and drama drained from Aquillo's body. "Then how did I get here? I need to get back to my family," he cried as he slumped against the wall of the cave and slid to the floor, opposite Tallac. He was suddenly aware of the cold and pulled his jacket tight around him.

"I'm sure the Magnum Opus can tell us what's going on and help get you home," said Ario as he walked over and placed a reassuring hand on his shoulder.

"Magnum Opus. Makers. Blizzards. What's going on?" Aquillo wailed.

Ario looked down at Aquillo and felt a wave of sympathy. Once again, it was his actions that had turned someone's life upside down, now he had to fix this for him as well. "I don't know," he said apologetically. "But if you help us search for him, we may find out."

Aquillo waved his thumb towards Tallac with a cheeky smile, "Okay, but only if Happy over there joins us. He's the life of the party."

Ario and Melody tried to hide their smiles as they looked over at Tallac, who was staring out into the snow with brooding darkness. To him, this Aquillo annoyed him like no other, but he was a good fighter and he may prove useful yet.

Tallac turned to the others and growled, "I no longer have a home and just learned everything I believed in is somehow wrong. I too want to meet this Magnum Opus. Now sleep, we leave before light."

The embers of the fire were burning low as everyone was fast asleep, everyone except for Ario. His mind had been racing with his many worries and when he saw that the blizzard had ended, he went outside to get some fresh air and clear his mind.

On his stroll, he had seen the most spectacular sight and could think of no one else he would rather share it with. After returning to the cave, he tiptoed passed Tallac snoring on the ground and Aquillo who was cuddled up to Lassar's belly for extra warmth. He reached out to Melody who was huddled on Lassar's thigh and gently shook her, 'Melody," he whispered.

Melody awoke with a startle, "Ario... what is it?" Lassar stirred and grunted a little in her sleep.

Ario put his fingers to his lips, "Shhh, follow me," he said softly.

Silently, Ario led Melody through the forest and up a small hill with a number of trees towering on top. Ario pulled back some low hanging branches to reveal a small clearing. "Ta-da!" he said. In the distance lay a panoramic view of the forest. The valley below them swept deep and lush to the northern mountain ranges that were drawing closer.

They dusted off some rocks covered from the snowfall and sat side-by-side under the thick, starry sky as the glorious full moon cast a violet light over the land. A shooting star streaked across the night.

Melody gasped, "This is beautiful," she said with a smile.

She thought of all their kin currently huddled in the Winter City burrows, unaware that such beauty and liberty lay beyond those walls. She breathed that moment in for she knew it was such a huge responsibility that they were undertaking. "I wish all Makers could be this free forever," she said sadly.

Ario nodded solemnly, "Maybe the Magnum Opus can help with that?" he said with a sigh and pulled out the compass. He looked at the inscription on the back, "'Only together is life complete'. What do you suppose he means?"

Melody shrugged, "I don't know, why don't you ask him when we find him?"

Ario looked out over the land, he needed some reassurance, "Do you think we will?"

Melody nodded slowly but surely, "We have to believe we will, because if we don't... we have nothing." She turned to Ario and saw that tears had welled in his eyes and glistened in the moonlight. Her heart broke for this brave Maker who carried the pain and burden of them all. She placed her hand on his and looked him deep in the eyes, "I promise you, we'll find him." She had no idea how, but she believed with all her heart that they would. Ario took a deep breath and nodded, he felt much better. She was the most beautiful spirit he knew he would ever meet and he was so grateful he was on this journey with her.

Melody began to hum softly and sweetly, then she rose to her feet and took Ario by the hand. She curtsied and he followed suit, bowing with dramatic flair just as he had learned from their new friend. They both giggled. Ario took her in his arms and they waltzed around the small clearing to Melody's little tune. The moonlight captured the low hanging frosted vines that sparkled and shimmered. The wind whistled ever so softly and night creatures gently twittered in harmony. In that moment, there was absolute perfection in the universe, for the heavens smile upon those that know fear, but still follow their hope anyway.

As Melody and Ario stared intimately into each other's eyes, meteors and stars blazed trails across the darkness. The heavens do indeed celebrate when two souls regardless of their make and design realize that they are one and that their love is the treasure of this earth. As the two Makers' heads moved closer to steal the sweetest of kisses, the rustling of branches and crunches in the snow could be heard, their eyes opened wide with panic as they turned. Tallac stormed through the trees furious that he had found them missing and had to go looking for them.

"You shouldn't be out here, it's dangerous. Come back to the cave," he ordered.

As the Makers smiled at each other with disappointment, they took one last look out over the horizon, then followed Tallac back to camp. They left the heavens to shine as they always have and will... forever.

# CHAPTER 9
## *The River*

A vibrant golden sun was well over the horizon as Commander Lorcaan stood with his men on the same hill that Ario and Melody had stood the night before. Lorcaan, however, was not there to admire the beauty of the vista. For the past day, he and his men had been trudging through the snow without any sleep in hope of gaining ground on the prisoners. In his crazed bleariness, he was thinking of the many ways he would make his escapees suffer. The officers had tracked the party to their cave and then found a trail in the snow that had led them to the spot on the hill. The Commander crouched down to look at the small footprints in the snow and the booted larger ones.

An officer approached, "Sir, the dogs have picked up the Maker's scent, they're heading North towards the river."

Commander Lorcaan rose to his feet and narrowed his eyes as he looked over the far sweeping trees, "Send word to Crone."

Just behind Lorcaan, an officer stood with a large white bird perched on his arm. It was a striking blend of eagle and owl, with a streamlined muscular body and disc shaped eyes of black that glowed intensely underneath a feathered hood. The officer attached a small paper scroll onto a metal band above one of its razor sharp talons, then released it to the sky. The bird let out a high pitched screech as it flapped steady and strong and started its long flight south.

With compass in hand, Ario led the group through the forest valley full of towering trees that seemed to spread forever. Tallac and Lassar were at the rear while Melody walked side-by-side with Aquillo in the middle. Ario glanced shyly behind him and stole a glance at Melody, they had not spoken since their encounter last night. He saw her in deep conversation with Aquillo as she listened with such care and attention, which made him admire her even more. He quickly looked away, not wanting her to catch him, and focused on the long hike that lay before them.

Melody was curious to learn more about the strange fellow beside her. She saw that he liked to play the clown, but sensed there was something far deeper about him. "So what's Fall like?" she asked.

Aquillo paused as his face lit up, "Fall?" he replied. He didn't know where to begin, "How do you truly find the words to describe something that means everything to you?" But he started with the trees that burst with leaves of every shade of orange, brown, red and yellow. How there was coolness in the air, yet a warmth at the same time. Every full moon there was a huge festival where all the citizens would gather to celebrate. There were tournaments of jousting and arm-to-arm combat, which is where he learned to fight. Then there were the feasts! The food, oh the food. For almost always the harvest was good, every sort of fruit or vegetable that we know of or could possibly wish for. Every night families came together to simply celebrate being together and to share a meal that was always a sight to behold and a taste to experience; stews and pies and roasts and bakes and trifles and cakes. Aaah and the wine, so fruity and rich as it flowed for all. Melody's mouth salivated at the thought of such deliciousness that she had never known. On the coldest of evenings, his people would light bonfires and they would sing and dance and tell tales well into the night. There was nothing more he needed than his arm around his sweet Umalee and his two little ones curled asleep beside him. Melody could hear the excitement in his voice as he spoke of the place, and people, that he missed.

Melody looked at Aquillo sadly, "You miss them don't you?" His eyes darkened as shivers ran up and down his body, the bite of that Winter's morning seemed extra fierce and harsh. He nodded solemnly. He always tried to be lighthearted and fun, but the thought of never holding his family again was too much to bare. He gave her a downcast smile. Melody reached out and rubbed his shoulder as they continued walking together in silence.

After days of trekking through the forest, the trees finally came to an end. Stretched before the party of travelers was a frozen river bed. It was more than two hundred feet wide and covered with thousands of towering columns of ice that shot up at every angle in all directions. Ario looked at the compass, which pointed beyond the river. What lay on the other side was obscured by the opaque blue icy jungle before them.

"Through here," Ario said.

Tallac was at the edge cautiously tapping the river's surface, he shook his head, "It's too dangerous to cross. With the hotter weather, this ice may crack open at any time."

Aquillo couldn't resist a poke at Tallac, "So negative!" he said as he strutted confidently several feet out onto the ice. "See," he grandly gestured with his arms, "Nothing to worry abou—" but Aquillo slipped and landed with a hard thump.

Tallac's eyes gleamed with delight on his otherwise emotionless face as he watched Aquillo flounder trying to get to his feet. "I know how to stay alive," Tallac said with a sneer.

Aquillo gave up and lay on his side propping his head with his elbow, "I was right through, hard as a rock," he said rapping the ice with his knuckle.

Tallac paced the river bed. "It may be safe here, but we don't know what it's like out there," he said pointing out at the river. "We'll need to go around."

Ario looked up and down the river's path, it ran for miles and miles, "It'll take too long. We need to find a way to get us across... fast," he said with a frown.

"Whatever we do, can someone lend me a hand?" Aquillo asked.

Lassar carefully stepped onto the river and gripped the ice with her claws, and walked slowly towards Aquillo. She offered him her tail, which he quickly grabbed, and she flicked him back to land.

"If the ice can support Lassar's weight, we should be fine to cross," Ario said to Tallac.

"The beast has claws, the rest of us won't get very far—like this fool," Tallac said nodding towards Aquillo.

Aquillo just smiled. It would take a lot more than simple name calling from a grumpy old man to hurt his feelings.

Ario looked around for anything useful, and then his face lit up. He ran back into the forest without a word.

The others stood perplexed, "What's he doing?" Tallac asked.

Melody shrugged, but she knew it was going to be good, "Ario!?" she called after him, but there was no response.

Aquillo couldn't help himself, "Bathroom break?" he asked. Melody scooped up a snowball and threw it at his head in response.

After a few moments, Ario returned dragging tree branches and a bundle of vines. Melody's eye's lit up, "That's a great idea," she nodded approvingly. Tallac and Aquillo just looked at each other with blank faces.

Not long afterwards, the team was traveling across the frozen river on a makeshift sled. Ario and Melody had tightly woven the vines around the branches and then twisted more vines into a chest harness and reins for Lassar, who now cautiously pulled everyone behind her. Ario sat at the front of the sled steering, confident they would clear the ice in no time at all. Tallac and Melody sat huddled behind him, with Aquillo at the rear.

The Fall visitor casually looked down over the side of the moving sled to the frozen river. Something caught his eye. He frowned. He blinked. Then it was gone. He was sure he just saw what looked like a big black shadow move beneath the ice. "Hey. Did you see that? Underneath us?" he asked. The rest of the party looked down at the cloudy white ice all around them.

"See what?" Ario asked. Aquillo wasn't liking this one bit, he nervously shrugged.

"Black?" Tallac shook his head, "You have brain freeze," he said with a sneer.

As they continued on their way, Aquillo felt around his head for signs of brain freeze wondering if that was indeed a malady that could befall one in this sub zero world. Nevertheless, as Lassar zigged and zagged through the ice columns, he kept a sharp eye on the ice below.

There was more movement and Aquillo snapped his head to the left. "Arghhh," he screamed, his heart beating fast.

"What is?" Ario called with concern.

Aquillo looked again, but saw it was just the sun reflecting off an icy pillar. "Ummmm false alarm," he said sheepishly.

"You must have bumped your head when you fell," Tallac said.

Aquillo didn't say anything, but he did feel mighty jumpy that morning. He tried to calm himself with a menu of the feast he would prepare when he sat down for a meal with his family again. Pumpkin soup, of course, with crusty artisan bread, perhaps a sprinkle of... he inhaled sharply. Something had caught his eye again. He turned to look and with no doubt at all, he saw a black shadow moving slowly under them like a dark cloud across the sky. "Look, there it is!" Aquillo cried. By this time everyone was of the opinion that their Fall friend was becoming a little paranoid, but as they reluctantly looked down over the sled, they were surprised to see that there was indeed something big and black moving beneath them.

"He's right!" Ario exclaimed.

Lassar stopped walking, unsure of what to do as she sensed the rising fear within the others.

Melody squinted, "What is that?"

Tallac's mind raced as he tried to work it out, he tried to remember, and then it hit him. A childhood tale of great monsters that dwelled in rivers. "Oh no..." he gasped as his heart sank.

Aquillo wasn't liking where this was headed, "Is that short for "Oh nothing?" he asked with fading hope.

Underneath the ice, the black entity flipped open a lid and a giant, bright yellow eye with a black pupil bigger than their sled stared back at them through fractured ice. They all yelled in panic and fright except for Tallac, "Shh! Don't make a sound," he said, "Keep very, very still."

They all obeyed, not daring to move. The sea monster's eye remained unblinkingly focused on the group through the ice. Each traveler held their breath as they peeked over the side of the sled and watched carefully. They were all too aware that a layer of ice was the only thing between them and some sea beast possibly looking for its lunch.

*Whump.* The icy floor shifted underneath them as a giant tentacle full of suckers slammed into the ice. They all screamed with fright.

"Lassar, go!" Tallac yelled, but their trusty steed was already off dragging them at high speed. The ice began to crack in all directions as the monster used more of its enormous tentacle suckers to break through the surface. All around them, giant black limbs began to smash through the frozen river. Lassar dug her sharp claws into the ice as she weaved left and right trying to avoid the menacing arms and ice columns that started to crumble from above. The team desperately held onto the sled as they cried out in horror. *Crack.* A huge chunk of ice underneath them shattered and broke away. There was now only freezing waters and blackness below.

Lassar whipped the sled through the air as she flapped her wings frantically. Powered by sheer adrenaline and fear, she managed to fly herself and her passengers a short distance back to hard ice. Everyone that is, except for Aquillo—he was flung from the sled high into the air. Despite his overwhelming terror, Aquillo was able to maintain his reflexes. In mid flight, he swung his rake and impaled it firmly into the flesh of a slippery black tentacle. The tentacle writhed furiously in response. Aquillo saw the water approaching fast as he took the deepest breath possible before being dragged into the icy depths. Aquillo held that breath and the rake even tighter as the freezing waters seared his whole body in spasms of pain. Now he truly understood what brain freeze was. The beast momentarily halted its path of destruction as it thrashed him around underwater, frustrated at the the object now lodged in its skin.

Melody screamed, "We've lost Aquillo!"

Lassar stopped in her tracks as they all watched the churning dark waters, horrified and unsure what to do for their friend. They heard a deep gurgled roar beneath them, then a scream of terror as Aquillo emerged and was swung above the freezing waters, then pulled under again.

"We need to help him!" Ario cried out to Tallac.

"He'll be fine," Tallac muttered with false positivity. If there was one thing he hated more than flying, it was water.

The monster again raised its tentacle out of the water and tried to shake off Aquillo who flapped around like a flag in a storm. Aquillo let out another panicked cry as the tentacle rose higher in the air and slammed down into the water once more.

"We need to do something," Melody cried.

Tallac growled and reluctantly sprang into action knowing he had to be ready for the next time the fool resurfaced. He began to unravel a vine that was holding part of the sled together.

"No wait, it'll all come apart!" Ario said, hoping there was another way.

"Then you best hold on," said Tallac with a snarl as he quickly bundled up the vine then tied the end to one of his arrows. Aquillo screamed as he and the tentacle rose from the waters again. Tallac hurriedly placed the arrow in the bow and took aim.

The tentacle with Aquillo attached, swayed and rolled with agitation in the air. Aquillo panicked at the sight of the bow and arrow pointed at him, "Don't shoot me!" he cried.

"Don't tempt me," Tallac yelled as he let the arrow fly. It whizzed right past Aquillo into an ice column just above his head. "Grab the line!" Tallac ordered.

Aquillo hesitated, it was a long drop into the black waters below. "I want to live!" he wailed.

"Now!" Tallac knew they had not a second to waste.

Aquillo muttered a little prayer to the harvest gods as he placed both feet on the tentacle and pushed himself off while yanking his rake free. As he fell, he swung the rake with all his might and snagged the vine with the teeth of the rake. To everyone's delight, especially his own, Aquillo began to zip-line down the vine towards the sled. From the depths, the sea beast let out a gurgled roar and retreated into the water.

Tallac grimaced with pain as he held the rope taut with his bare hands. Aquillo hurtled towards the sled and Tallac tried to let the vine slack a little to slow him down, but there was no vine left. Tallac could no longer keep his grip and the vine slipped loose. With no traction at all, Aquillo flew the remaining distance through the air. Tallac turned to dive out of the way, but Aquillo bowled him over as the impact smashed the sled apart. Ario and Melody were also thrown, and they desperately hung onto parts of the sled as they were propelled at a high speed across the frozen river. They used their momentum to dodge and weave past the ice columns in their path while Lassar chased after her friends. Tallac ended belly down on a piece of wood with Aquillo clinging to him like a baby monkey as they too skidded along the ice.

"Thanks for saving me back there... and if you don't mind, could you keep on saving me now?" Aquillo said frantically into Tallac's ear. Tallac could only muster an annoyed growl as he focused on trying to steer them out of harm's way.

From behind, another sharp crack of ice could be heard. The party turned their heads to see a huge block of ice splinter into pieces as the monster's black balloon shaped head burst out of the water. The group let out a collective cry of panic as the water creature rose and towered stories high. Ario skidded across the ice alongside Lassar and he noticed her reigns were dangling behind her. He reached out and grabbed hold tightly. Lassar realized that she was now dragging Ario and immediately changed course towards Melody. "Grab the vine," Ario yelled to Melody. She reached out and snagged the other rein, holding it tight.

The monster's one bulging yellow eye glared menacingly. It let out a piercing screech from its beaked mouth and surged forward with tentacles lashing. Tallac and Aquillo were within reach and it made a grab for Aquillo's leg. "Yargh, not again!" Aquillo yelled in terror. With one arm still clinging to Tallac, he used the other to stab at the tentacle with his rake. "Back you bad beast. Back!" he cried as he struck it again and again. The monster shrieked and recoiled its limb in pain, but its other wild and flailing arms smashed at the icy columns in their path. It was not going to let its meal escape so easily.

Lassar saw her friends in trouble and changed course again towards Aquillo and Tallac.

"Grab on" Melody yelled to Tallac.

"To what?" Tallac replied not seeing any more vine.

"Me!" responded Melody.

Tallac reached out and grabbed Melody tightly by the ankle. "Apologies, Maker!" Melody grimaced from Tallac's tight grip, but kept a brave face.

Lassar was now dragging all her companions towards the other side of the river where the shoreline and trees were now in sight. The monster continued to lash at the ice columns as Lassar dodged through the smashed icy obstacle course. Lassar bounded up the embankment of the river with her companions in tow. They crashed into the snowy river's edge and rolled to a stop.

From the icy depths, the monster stretched its tentacles onto the shore in one last effort to snare his prey. The travelers cried out in panic as they scrambled over each other and ran into the safety of the woods that lay just beyond the river. The river beast let out a high pitched screech that echoed across the land as it slithered back into the murky depths from where it came. Then there was silence. The team lay exhausted and cold on the floor of the snow covered woods: wheezing, moaning, whimpering, hearts beating, looking up at the bright blue sky ever so grateful to be alive.

Thousands of miles north in the throne room of Winter City, Crone's eyes shot open. His iris' glowed a caustic yellow then clouded back to cruel, raging black. He let out an almighty roar that thundered through the palace. The white messenger bird that sat atop his ice staff flapped its wings and squawked with fear. Lost in his fury, Crone clenched his ice staff so hard that it blasted the unsuspecting bird solid. It toppled from its perch and shattered like diamonds across the throne room floor.

# CHAPTER 10
## *The Mountains*

Ario and the others had followed the compass to the other side of the woods. They reached an icy clearing and now stood at the foot of an expansive and unclimbable, snowy, rocky mountain range. The compass directed them through the only passage available—a treacherous mountain gully. It was a narrow chasm of craggy ice-covered rock walls that stretched hundreds of feet high. The path was barely wide enough to fit Lassar and they all peered in hesitantly.

Ario bowed before Melody, ushering her through with a sneaky smile. "Ladies before gentle—"

Melody raised her eyebrow, "Don't even think about it."

Ario took a deep breath and entered the gully first. Melody followed behind him smiling. Aquillo peered into the chasm, "Did I mention I'm claustrophobic?" he called after them.

Tallac shoulder charged passed him as he followed the Makers. "You can always stay behind," he said.

Aquillo looked back towards the woods, knowing that only sea monsters and those Winter officers the others seemed so worried about would welcome him there. He shrugged and followed Tallac in, as Lassar let out a worried whine and joined at the rear.

The gang walked quietly, still in shock from the horrors of the river and thoroughly enjoying the solid ground beneath their feet. Ario heard Melody humming a tune behind him; it had gusto to it, almost like a marching song. It inspired him and he picked up the pace—every step was fueled with determination to find the Magnus Opus. He turned to her, but she was staring at the ground in deep thought. He quickly turned back and looked ahead. There was so much he wanted to say, but she was so strong and sure, he would only fumble and stumble over his words. How could words truly convey what he felt, when he didn't know himself.

Ario sighed and gazed up at the towering gully walls, and saw that the sky wove like a cobalt snake above them. A deep moan could be heard underfoot. Ario stopped still. His ears stood erect and his whole body shivered with fear. Lassar whimpered. No one dared to breath. The gully walls began to sway like rolling waves.

"Earthquake!" Ario cried to his companions.

Melody held onto Ario tightly as the ground swell continued. Aquillo grabbed Tallac who just growled as he looked up and saw rocks and boulders begin to break free from the gully walls. "Run!" he roared and they all surged forward.

They ran for their lives, trying to shield their heads as rubble and stone tumbled down around them. Another huge tremor hit and they were flung to their knees. Lassar howled and raised a wing protecting her head while she spread the other over her friends. A thunderous crack echoed through the gully—then there was stillness. Only the coughing and spluttering of the travelers could be heard as the loose dirt filled their noses and mouths.

As the dust settled and they rose to their feet, they saw that a giant chasm of earth had opened before them. They were now trapped between a gaping hole and a towering wall of boulders and rocks behind them.

Aquillo was the first to his feet and looked over the edge of the hole; deep, dark and wide. He nodded and clapped his hands knowing this must be a piece of pumpkin cake for the Makers. He turned to Ario with a hopeful smile, "So what are you guys going to build, a bridge or a giant swing?"

Ario smiled. "No need," he said as he stood surveying the distance. He turned and looked at Lassar, "She's cold, but she should be able to jump it. We'll go two at a time to make it easy on her."

Aquillo nodded enthusiastically and started to climb on board. Tallac grabbed hold of his jacket and pulled him back down shaking his head. "The Makers fly first," he said. Aquillo reluctantly stepped aside as Ario and Melody scuttled onto Lassar's back and wrapped their arms around her. Ario gave her a reassuring pat, "Come on girl, you can do it," he whispered in her ear.

Lassar let out a hoarse roar as steam shot from her nose, then took a short run towards the crevice and leaped. She outstretched her front legs and tried to flap her wings, but all the elements were against her. The chasm was too wide, the gully too narrow and her strength waning under the freezing conditions. She clawed at the air and only just managed to catch the rocky ledge on the other side, saving them all from plummeting into the abyss. The Makers screamed as they were flung over Lassar's head, landing unceremoniously on the ground.

They stumbled to their feet dazed, then turned to see Lassar flapping furiously and clawing at the ledge, trying to lift her great weight up and over. They ran to her aid, but could do nothing but watch helplessly. Makers were not built to lift wild flailing winged creatures out of gaping holes.

"Come on Lassar!" Ario said.

"That's it girl, keep trying!" cried Melody.

Lassar snorted and grunted then gave one giant flap of her wings. It was just the momentum she needed to heave herself up and scramble to safety.

The mighty beast sat on the gully floor panting and whining softly. Melody ran to her side and lovingly wrapped her arms around Lassar's neck. Ario looked at Lassar slumped in exhaustion, then at the craggy walls of the gully.

"You'll have to climb across," Ario called to the others.

Aquillo turned to Tallac with a broad smile, "I think he just said you have to carry me across."

Tallac kicked some rubble off the edge of the chasm and they watched it fall into oblivion. Aquillo shifted nervously on his feet. "I'd be happy to," Tallac said with a sneer.

Aquillo swallowed and looked at the obstacle before him, he clenched his jaw determinedly, "You know what? I think I've got this." He started to limber up, stretching his legs and his arms while rolling his head. No sea beast, no mountain, no nothing was going to stop him from getting home.

Meanwhile, Tallac scanned the gully face and looked for jutting rocks that would be strong enough to carry him to the other side. He stepped out and carefully placed his foot onto a secure stone, then with an all-powerful swing cleaved it into the rock face. He took another step across as he used the axe as leverage.

Aquillo watched and nodded approvingly. He too stepped out from the ledge onto a rock, swung his rake back and slammed the teeth into the gully wall, then used his tool to hold him steady as he moved along.

The going was precarious at the very least as the icy rock face was unforgivingly slippery. Ario, Melody, and Lassar watched anxiously from the other side, not making a sound as their friends moved in a crab-like crawl across the wall. It was a painstakingly slow pace, but they were almost in reach of their friends when a low rumble could be felt beneath them.

Ario froze while Melody grabbed his arm in fear. Lassar whimpered. The climbers' stomachs lurched. "Hold on," Tallac called to Aquillo. The gully walls rolled once more as an aftershock rattled the earth. The tremor was short, but violent. Aquillo remained steady, but Tallac lost his footing and fell. He grunted heavily and swung his axe against the wall in an attempt to break his fall, snagging a rock in the process.

"Noooo!" Ario and Melody cried out in panic as they watched from the other side.

Tallac found himself dangling from his axe by one hand, but lost his bow and arrows as they plummeted into the chasm below. Tallac tried again and again to find a secure rock in the wall to place his feet, but they had been loosened by the quake and kept breaking away.

"Hang in there, Happy. I'd miss you if you fell," Aquillo said encouragingly as he started to scale the last part of the gully to the other side. With a final slam of his rake, Aquillo made it across into the arms of the waiting Makers.

"We need to help Tallac," Melody cried seeing that Tallac could not hold on for much longer.

"Fear not. I'm the man with a plan," he said with a dramatic point to the sky, then whistled to Lassar, "Hold me girl." Lassar snorted and wrapped her tail around his waist, then dug her claws deep into the ground. Aquillo stood on the edge of the precipice and held the head of his rake out to Tallac. "Don't be shy," Aquillo said with a grin.

Tallac scowled as he grabbed it with his free hand, then yanked his axe from the wall with the other. Lassar started to walk away from the edge, pulling Aquillo, who in turn pulled Tallac, all the way up to safe ground.

Tallac slowly rolled onto his back and let out a deep sigh. Ario kneeled over him and peered into his face with a look of concern, "Are you Okay? You had us worried."

Before Tallac could respond, Aquillo spun his rake in the air, struck it on the ground and leaned against the handle as he checked his nails. He beamed down at Tallac, "Now that we've saved each other's lives, we're like... best friends!"

Tallac growled as he jumped to his feet and stormed off ahead. Ario shrugged at Aquillo as he and Lassar followed behind. Melody turned to Aquillo and shook her head, "Too far," she said as she headed down the path. Aquillo frowned and filed in line at the rear, thinking perhaps he should have gone with 'best acquaintances'.

As they made their way along the winding and seemingly endless path, Aquillo was brainstorming all of the ways he could win the respect of his 'maybe one day' friend Tallac. Perhaps he could grow a beard? Maybe change his wardrobe to animal pelts? Or grunt more? Aquillo wondered why he could hear the sound of egg shells cracking. *Hmm a mushroom and bacon omelet would be perfect right now,* he thought as his mouth watered. He casually glanced around for the source of the noise. He stopped. He saw a web of fine cracks spreading rapidly along the gully wall. He frowned and looked closer—there was water trickling out.

"Hey guys, I think we're in trouble again," Aquillo called out, his voice about an octave higher than normal. The others stopped and turned, their eyes wide with concern.

"What's wrong?" asked Ario.

"It's probably nothing," he replied, "but—" a jet of water shot out of the wall and hit him full force in the side of the head.

Streams of water spurted from the walls behind Aquillo as crack after crack burst open. There was no other warning needed. The group turned and bolted through the gully passage. *Crack. Whoosh.* Aquillo looked over his shoulder. Horror gripped his chest. The wall had split wide open. A flood of water now rushed behind them through the gully.

"Water. Huge... copious... voluminous amounts ... of water!" Aquillo screamed.

The party pushed on in panic. Ario raced at the front, the passageway curved to reveal glaring daylight some thirty feet ahead. "There's an exit!" Ario cried with relief as they all raced towards the opening. He reached the end, but at the last moment he saw that the path turned into a cliff face. "Aargh," Ario shrieked as he tried to stop, but skidded and stumbled on loose stones and pebbles on the ground. He grappled for the walls but couldn't regain his balance and teetered at the edge.

Melody lunged at him, "I got you!" she said and yanked him back.

Ario peered down at the massive drop and thanked his lucky stars for Melody, then noticed a way out, "There's a ledge, come on," he yelled.

Everyone followed as they clambered onto the narrow ledge. Aquillo was the last to scurry around as the rampaging waters gushed over the edge in a magnificent waterfall.

Ario caught his breath and gasped, "Look," he said as he nudged Melody and pointed. Way below them was a sweeping canyon covered by ice and snow with pockets melted away to reveal an abandoned village buried in its belly, perhaps eons ago. Rows and rows of village streets lined with dilapidated buildings of stone and wood, spiraled to meet an amphitheater sitting as the crowning center piece. The theatre was partly crumbled—like a child had toppled over its tower of building blocks. Ario looked around to see that the mountain ledge they stood on was part of a ring of soaring snow capped rocky mountains. Directly across the ledge from where the travelers stood was another mountainous cliff which loomed hundreds of feet high. Neatly carved into its face were thousands of small burrow like holes.

"Are those Maker burrows?" Ario asked eyes wide and confused.

"They *were* Maker burrows," said Tallac solemnly. He then signaled along the ledge they stood on, it appeared to be a path that wound down the cliff face to the canyon floor. Filled with wonder and bewilderment, they all began the descent into the long forgotten Maker Village.

# CHAPTER 11
## *The Maker Village*

At the bottom of the mountain under layers of ice, a massive wooden wheel had fallen from its damaged frame and now leaned against the cliff wall. Ario looked straight up and saw a large hole in the cliff with a flow of water frozen mid-stream. He deduced that this contraption had perhaps once been a watermill. Right next to it was a collapsed wooden building that revealed a huge stone chimney oven. He guessed that this could have been a baker's cottage and the mill was used to crush the grain. His mouth watered at the thought of what sort of delicacies a Maker baker would have created.

Guided by his compass, Ario led the group along what would have once been the hustling and bustling streets of this Maker village. Peeking out from under the snow were broken pulleys and rigging, parts of contraptions and machines, capsized wooden vehicles, and crumbling edifices of stone buildings. Makers now long gone would have once walked down these very streets full of creativity and invention. Which Makers? How? When? Why weren't they here any more? His heart swelled with confusion and frustration.

Melody walked up to him and placed a hand on his arm, she too felt overwhelmed by what surrounded them, "What do you think happened here?" she asked.

Tallac was examining the ruinous buildings more closely and pointed to the blackened charred remains of a number of wooden beams that could be seen under thinning ice, "It appears the inhabitants were removed by force."

Ario and Melody shook their heads sadly. While his heart was heavy, Ario knew that they had come so far and now more than ever he had to find the one Maker who would know the answers to all these questions. The compass pointed to the middle of the town where the amphitheater stood.

"Come on, the compass says this way" said Ario.

"It's unlikely any Makers would remain" said Tallac in a solemn voice.

"While this compass still works, I'm not giving up on the Magnum Opus," Ario called behind him determinedly, as he ran ahead.

Melody gave chase and they ran to the center of the village, stopping in front of a damaged stone archway hand carved by a Maker mason. It was adorned with intricate stone carvings of musical notes and Maker hieroglyphics now indecipherable. Melody took Ario's hand and gave it a squeeze, they smiled sadly at each other as they walked through the archway and stepped into the amphitheater. While it had eroded over the years, the gloriousness of the structure had not been lost. Row upon row of stone steps climbed to form a now crumbled semicircle stadium surrounding a floor and stage. Ario knew instinctively that in a time long ago, this is where Makers of every shape and size would have gathered and performed unhindered and free. He stopped short. Where the orchestra pit would have once stood was a massive pile of smashed musical instruments preserved under ice. Ario felt a deep pang of sorrow at the sight of such beautiful instruments laid to waste and he now truly understood that something grave and terrible had happened here.

Melody wiped away a tear, "This doesn't look good," she said softly.

They walked up some side steps onto the raised stage of the amphitheater. As they made their way to the center, they noticed under the thin layer of ice, a deep circular impression carved into the stone. Ario kneeled down to study the shape.

"Does this look familiar to you?" he asked.

"Familiar how?" Melody replied.

"The processing station" Ario said.

"Oh," Melody said with surprise. "The disc we appear on when we first arrive!"

Ario nodded and rose to his feet then stood looking over the amphitheater. He remembered his wish of being welcomed with a marvelous celebration after he was made. Maybe this would have happened in a Maker world now lost.

Ario glanced at the compass once more and frowned—the compass needle was spinning out of control. There was a small *click* and the face of the compass sprung open to reveal a series of small delicately carved musical notes beneath.

"Baffle me bug-eyed," Ario cried to Melody, as he held the notes up for her to see.

"Is that music?" she asked as she squinted her eyes.

Ario was intrigued, "Play it! Play it!" he said.

Melody pulled out her flute from her coat and began to play the short, but sweet, tune. Even the destruction of the ages could do nothing to diminish the pleasant acoustics of the notes as they reverberated over the amphitheater. As she played, the rest of the gang joined them and listened contently to the performance. When she had finished, Tallac looked around with disappointment.

"Nothing," he said. He was expecting to see some sort of magical apparition at the very least.

"It sounded pretty though," Aquillo said supportively as he mimed playing the flute and parroted the tune.

"Shh... listen," Ario waved at them, as he focused on something that had caught his ear.

As they fell silent, they could hear the grinding of rock underground. The round impression at their feet began to develop cracks in the ice. Aquillo, who was developing quite a phobia of any sort of cracking sound, took a few steps backwards and stood fearfully behind Tallac.

"What's happening?" he whispered into Tallac's ear.

"Quiet, fool," Tallac said as he stood tall and tense. Ario knelt and enthusiastically pulled away the breaking ice to reveal a thick stone slab, sliding slowly to the side. It stopped. The party all crowded around and saw a large hole, with wide stone steps that disappeared down into darkness.

Ario jumped up in pure excitement, "This might be the entrance to the Magnum Opus' burrow!" Ario was about to step down into the entrance when they heard Lassar growl.

"What's up, girl?" Melody asked as she reached out and gave her a pat. Lassar turned her head and snarled ferociously at something beyond the amphitheater.

"It's an ambush," Tallac said in a low voice as he raised his axe.

Aquillo firmly gripped his rake at the ready. Officer after officer with ice staffs pointed emerged from hiding spots in every direction. The companions backed into a tight circle—they were surrounded.

There was a whistle and Winter dogs ran towards the group snarling and snapping at Lassar. She roared and flapped trying to take flight, but the officers shot multiple ice blasts at her feet. The weight grounded her, as she flapped her wings even more furiously, growling and snorting.

Commander Lorcaan walked through the archway and smiled up at them with a clear menace in his eyes, "I must say, I doubted the existence of your Magnum Opus, but now very much look forward to meeting him."

Ario was aghast and stepped forward boldly, "You leave him alone!"

"You're outnumbered and surrounded," Lorcaan raised his eyebrow as if amused and turned to Tallac. "You won't be running or flying away this time."

"I will kill you where you stand," Tallac said as he stepped forward and raised his axe at him.

Commander Lorcaan idly raised his hand and waved him away, "You and your friend will drop your weapons, or your precious Makers are ice." With these words, the officers all turned their staffs towards Ario and Melody.

Tallac grimaced then nodded to Aquillo as they both reluctantly lowered their weapons. "This isn't over," Tallac said with a defiant snarl.

The commander fixed him with a frosty glare. "Quite correct, you will be punished for your crimes," he said as he signaled to his men. Officers stormed the stage and took hold of Ario and Melody, then tied Tallac and

Aquillo to a nearby stone column. With teeth bared, the dogs surrounded Lassar who now lay on the ground exhausted and gave nothing more than a meek snort in response.

Lorcaan strode up to the stage. "Go ahead and scout the passage," he said to an officer. The officer saluted then disappeared down the stairs.

Everyone stood in uncertain silence, waiting. Moments later, the clunks and whir of machinery could be heard, followed by a chilling scream that echoed out the entrance and across the amphitheater. The officer's helmet catapulted out of the passageway and landed at Lorcaan's feet. A few Winter officers shifted uneasily, but Lorcaan's face registered nothing but stony coldness.

"Looks like you're not welcome," Ario said.

Commander Lorcaan glared at him. "Nonsense," he said with a scoff and kicked the helmet away. He walked over to Ario and Melody, grabbed them by the arms and dragged them towards the entrance. "I'll be your guest and you can lead the way," he said as he pushed them into the passageway. He signaled for two more officers who reluctantly followed.

The group descended down the steep stairway through an arched passage way, and as they turned a corner they were met with complete darkness. The officers at the rear raised their staffs, which emanated a soft blue light. They could now see a long, damp, arched tunnel, carved through the earth's bedrock. Most peculiarly, there were rails, cogs, springs, levers, and dials that formed latent mechanical contraptions that ran along the edge of the walls, as far as their eyes could see.

"This is incredible," Ario said quietly to Melody as they continued along the passageway.

She eagerly nodded in agreement, "Do you think it was built by the Magnum Opus?" she asked softly.

Ario smiled, "You can ask him yourself when we find him."

Lorcaan prodded them with his staff from behind and they said no more.

Knowing that this mysterious collection of odds and ends may have led to the demise of the previous Winter officer, the party warily pushed farther into the depths of the tunnel in silence. *Click.* Everyone froze. Ario looked down and saw that he had unwittingly stepped on a stone pressure plate. Instantly, a high pitched whirring could be heard.

"What's happening?" said Commander Lorcaan in a loud voice.

"I don't know!?" Ario remarked, trying to remain calm.

There was a succession of *clicks* and *clacks*, then dozens of round stones the size of billiard balls began to roll along multiple interweaving tracks. They wound down the tunnel wall in a seemingly random way, picking up momentum as they went. Ario and Melody watched the rocks and the pattern of their movement carefully, in the web of tracks they could see the path the balls would take. Ario looked at Melody and she nodded ever so slightly. The rocks disappeared into chutes, rattled along chambers, and then were shot with extreme force all over the tunnel. The two Makers anticipated their trajectory as they ducked and rolled to avoid the barrage of stones.

Lorcaan had been watching the Makers closely and shouted at them to get down, but the officers at the rear were too slow and took the full brunt of the flying stones, knocking them out cold.

Commander Lorcaan lunged at Melody and grabbed her by the ears pulling her back against his chest. "I'll be staying nice and close to your little friend, so I suggest you watch your step," he said to Ario as Melody trembled in his arms.

Ario looked at Melody with sorrow in his eyes as he nodded submissively; unfortunately, there was nothing more he could do. The trio walked on with Ario in the lead and the tunnel faintly lit by Lorcaan's ice staff. The journey proved to be a treacherous obstacle course, but Ario helped navigate the dangers. They avoided a trip wire that would have skewered them with wooden spears, a snare trap that would have dangled them like berries, and an inescapable pit trap cleverly concealed under a section of faux tunnel floor. Ario was astounded at the length the ancient Makers had taken to protect this entrance and wondered where it led. He looked back at Commander Lorcaan, who was still holding Melody roughly and pushing her along. Anger surged within him, and he became determined to find an opportunity to ensure this horrid man would never bother them again.

There was a curve in the tunnel and they were met by a stone wall that blocked the way. The wall had aged over the years and was covered with moss and mold. Carved upon the stones were lines and musical notes—like a big sheet of music. At each side of the tunnel were old pipes that looked like they had once been part of a grand old organ.

Ario stepped up to the wall and observed a rectangular stone at the center. "It looks like some kind of door," he said.

"Open it," Lorcaan replied.

Ario felt around for a handle or some sort of loose stone that could possibly be a button, but there was nothing. "I don't know how," he said with a furrowed brow.

Melody also studied the wall, "Maybe it'll open if I play the notes—like the compass?"

Ario frowned, "It's not going to play anything harmonious."

The Winter commander had had enough of chasing Makers through forests and mountains and now tunnels, he just wanted to find that wretched Magnum Opus and be on his way home. "Do it," he ordered as he released his tight grasp on Melody. She pulled out her flute and began to play.

As Ario predicted, the musical notes bounced discordantly through the tunnel walls. Melody finished the tune and frowned, expecting much more than nothing.

Lorcaan glowered, "Why didn't it work?"

Then the tunnel floor began to tremble.

"Uh oh," Ario said quietly.

Lorcaan's eyes flashed with concern, "What have you done?" he growled at Melody. A scraping sound of stone on stone could be heard followed by a huge thud from behind. They spun around to see a stone wall had dropped and they were now trapped in a narrow space. Unseen machinery clunked into action and the stone wall began to slide towards them.

The commander harnessed his ice staff and threw his hands up onto the wall as he tried to stop it, "Try something else. Now!" he bellowed.

"Ario?" Melody cried helplessly.

"I'm thinking. I'm thinking," he said as he paced anxiously looking at the carved musical notes. The wall was moving dangerously close and Lorcaan's attempt to stop it had no effect. Ario continued staring at the notes. He saw there was supposed to be a tune but the notes were wrong, the pattern was wrong... the pattern! *Yes that's it* he smiled to himself.

"It's a puzzle!" he cried excitedly. "I need to rearrange the notes so they make sense."

He rushed to the wall and grabbed the stone bricks, discovering they could be pulled out and interchanged. He studied the notes hard and fast and saw there were so many possibilities, for within a handful of any notes, a multitude of tunes can be constructed. Then it dawned on him, his face lit up, but of course there could only be one song. While he never got to play it, he had sung that tune in his head since the day he had first breathed life.

His hands moved quickly as he reordered the bricks. Their remaining space had shrunk down to only a few feet, "Hurry Maker!," Lorcaan said with a panic as he turned his back to the encroaching wall and pushed his legs against the other.

Ario didn't respond, he just kept rearranging bricks and finally inserted the last note into place. With a resounding *ka-chunk,* the wall stopped moving. They all heaved a sigh of relief and Melody hugged Ario, she had never been more proud or grateful that playing music and singing were never his talents.

A rush of cold wind could be felt and they froze, terrified of what would come next, but the wind blew through the organ pipes which now played a long middle C. The pipes then launched into a rousing rendition of the Making song with multiple harmonies and even a sweet bass line counter tune. Melody clapped as Ario beamed with pride. The song rose to a dramatic climax and finished with three short, sharp toots, then the stone door let out a sequence of clicks as the wall behind them began to slowly retract.

Melody laughed out loud, "You did it."

"I did it!" Ario found her joy contagious and laughed as well.

Commander Lorcaan shoved past them, unimpressed with their foolishness. He pushed open the heavy stone door and stepped through.

Excitedly, Ario and Melody followed behind into a small stone room lit by strings of tiny light bulbs zig zagging across the ceiling. A packed and dusty bookshelf ran the length of one of the walls and a cozy leather armchair sat in front of a long ago burnt out fireplace. They stopped cold. In a corner, slumped at a solid wooden desk with quill in hand, was the remains of a Maker. Tattered clothing hung off its skeleton of steel bones, cogs, and hinges. Beneath him lay a scroll that spilled onto the floor with rolls and rolls of paper, piling high all around.

With heavy hearts, Ario and Melody rushed over. "No, no no, don't tell me," Ario said softly. Melody gently freed the end of the scroll from the grasp of the skeletal hands and read the final entry.

*I leave you with this gift. My will is now yours - Magnum Opus.*

Tears streamed down her face. Ario felt like the room was spinning around him. This was it, he thought, the total sum of all we have journeyed. He's gone, there's no way of fixing anything or saving anyone. The only thing that's certain is punishment at the hands of Winter. Ario heaved a long, sad sigh, Melody reached out and took his hand. "What do we do now?" Ario whispered. He was more lost than he had ever known.

Commander Lorcaan was unmoved by the despair of these creatures; however, he was curious. What was so important that this Magnum Opus thought he should write until his last breath. "Read it," he instructed as he squeezed into the arm chair, "From the start."

Melody wiped away her tears and picked up the reams of scroll until she found the start. Ario put his arm around her as she took a deep breath and began.

*To whomever shall find me,*
*If you are reading, this I am gone. I have tried to show the Makers what they truly are, but they are ruled by their fear more than they have ever been ruled by Winter. My only hope lies in the Makers of the future, that they will open their eyes and hearts despite their fear. Listen and heed.*
*This world you inhabit is unbalanced. Ravaged by the cold hand of Winter. We toil and we labor in this inhospitable world. Forced into submission to obey*

*the will of our icy overlords. Know this my friend, it has not always been so, there exists three other seasons.*

Melody glanced up at Ario eyes wide, but Lorcaan glared at her and she hurriedly continued.

*The people of Spring once kissed this kingdom with flowers, rain showers, and rainbows. The Summer tribe basked in days filled with sunshine and welcome ocean breezes. The Fall folk were the merriest of us all and their harvest fed all. Of course, there was Winter, who once were a festive bunch and found much joy even in the long cold nights.*

*The people of the snowflake, flower, leaf, and sun once shared this land, but as I have found with my time amongst them, they struggled with a need for power and dominance. There raged a constant state of war. They misused the magic of this world and harnessed it to try and destroy one another. Fires, droughts, floods, wild winds, and snow blizzards wreaked havoc on our precious realm. Realizing that this world was facing imminent doom, the ruling Elders of the seasons formed a treaty, whereby they each agreed to take their turn to rule the earth, while the others waited—suspended in time.*

*To do so, they needed to create a guardian that would be responsible for ushering in one season after the next. A being that was more pure in heart than man and would carry out this sacred service with honor and reverence. Each Elder held aloft their magical staff and conjured the forces of all, a storm of fire, ice, air, and earth swirled, and from the eye of the storm a creature emerged. The Elders called it a 'Maker' and they bestowed upon this creature gifts that would ensure he would be a true guardian of the seasons.*

*He received knowledge of the world and the skills, creativity, and inventiveness of master craftsmen, which would enable the Maker to create whatever he dared to dream, including his next of kin. Most importantly, the Elders gave this Maker the gift of music. Music allowed him to breath his life and soul into the next Maker and together all Makers would use music to bring forth season after season.*

*This first Maker was magically hidden in a place that was secret to even the Elders themselves and their people were never told of their existence. The solitary Maker found himself on this very canyon floor and it was here the father of all Makers began his sacred mission. He created the next Maker and that Maker created the next and so on and so forth. In no time at all, they had worked together to create a flourishing Maker village. But their most important work was their role as guardians of the seasons. As the end of each season approached, the Makers of the village would gather in celebration and play a grand symphony, the notes and melodies of which reached the edges of the earth and resonated with the same joy that brings each new Maker into the world. A new season would arrive as the old was laid to rest. Each season embraced the change as they knew they would once again return to the land when it was their time. So was the way of the world for countless generations, Summer, Fall, Winter, Spring and the Makers, all in balance, all in perfect harmony.*

*That was until nearly a thousand years ago. A cruel and self centered Winter Lord wanted nothing more than to rule supreme. He had no desire to share his time or land, nor did he hold any qualms in betraying the other seasons and breaking their sacred oath. He led a quest to search for the Makers and to stop them from playing in Spring. Early one winter morning, the unthinkable happened. Just as the Makers had begun to play in Spring, Winter officers stormed the Maker village and shackled the Makers. Their musical instruments, the magical tools used for harnessing life and the cycles of the earth, were hardheartedly destroyed.*

*Thus, a forever winter fell upon the land, and the other seasons were helplessly frozen in time. The Makers, once the orchestrators of the seasons, were forced into slavery to serve Winter's every bidding. And so it has passed this way for many, many moons. The Makers lost their spark and too soon lost their knowledge and the ways of the old. No longer allowed to play their music, they have accepted what they believe is their fate.*

*Take heed, our world cannot sustain an endless Winter and will seek to restore balance with cataclysmic results. The Makers must unite, they must restart the seasons to heal our world—before it's too late.*

*I am old, I am withering both in heart and in body. I have tried again and again to change this tide, but alas with no avail. I have retreated to this room in hope that the day will come when our voices are heard once more.*

*You now know who you are.*

*I leave you with this gift. My will is now yours - Magnum Opus.*

Ario and Melody stood there stunned.

"We're not slaves?" she whispered as a singular tear glistened and rolled down her cheek.

Ario's eyes widened in realization, "The compass, that's what he meant with 'Only together is life complete'. Only when the Makers work together is life complete." A blast of ice shattered on the wall close to Ario's head.

"This changes nothing," the commander said with a sneer as he rose to his feet and began exploring the chamber. He felt enlightened, Lord Crone had kept this a secret over the years and now he understood what he meant when he said that Makers were dangerous creatures. Lorcaan began to feel around the book shelves looking for some sort of lever, there had to be more than just this room.

Melody was indignant, she couldn't grasp how these people could be so cold and callous, "What about the other seasons? You can't just leave them trapped," she said, standing with clenched fists watching him furiously.

Ario seized upon an idea, "The volcano! The melting ice!"

Melody frowned, she was not following, "What about it?" she asked.

He paced the room, "The Magnum Opus said the Earth will restore balance—it's heating up! We have to follow his instructions to stop the volcano from—"

Commander Lorcaan, who was busy tracing his hands across the wall had already thought of this and cut him off, "You need not worry—the machine you Makers are building will not only stop the volcano, but freeze the core of the Earth. It seems Lord Crone wants to ensure it remains Winter forever."

Ario and Melody were crushed by the realization of Winter's monstrous plan, "No. You can't," Ario cried out. His mind raced. Could it all be in vain, could it be that the Makers were unintentionally securing their own bondage for eternity.

There was a *click* and a *ka-chunk* as stone scraped against stone once more. The Makers looked at each other worriedly. Lorcaan had discovered a panel in the stone wall and as he pushed it, the wall slowly rotated to reveal a second room. He stood in the doorway grinning. "Finally, the secret Maker workshop," he said. Commander Lorcaan strode through the door fiendishly pleased by his unexpected discovery, there was no doubt Lord Crone would highly commend him for this.

There was the kiln now extinguished, the rows of shelves filled with books, jars and boxes, the overstuffed drawers, the tools, everything in the neat disarray that Ario had left just days before. The two Makers stood helplessly by a bookshelf at the back of the room while Lorcaan walked around roughly poking and prodding with keen interest. He showed total disrespect for the lineage, for the rich history that was contained within those hallowed walls. He approached the workbench where Renaissance lay lifeless and gave her a nudge, "You've done Winter a great service," he said gloating.

Ario and Melody's ears dropped as they lowered their heads with overwhelming guilt. Ario was grateful that they had found the workshop, but now that Winter knew where it was, he just couldn't bear to consider the possibilities. Once again, his actions would hurt so many. Ario cast his eyes sadly around the room, and as he passed over the bookshelf nearest him, one old bounded leather book caught his attention. He looked up at the commander who was at the workbench preoccupied with a drawer full of teeth, so he quietly removed the book and flipped through its frail yellowed pages. He stopped on one particular page and took a deep breath as an idea formed in his head. *This is it,* he calculated to himself and gently nudged Melody and showed her the page. She understood and gave him a quick but nervous nod as they moved into action.

Ario stood tall and strong, ears pricked, summoning all the courage he could muster. He held the book for Melody to see and gave a small cough as he cleared his throat.

"Winter fears what we're capable of," he said with a loud, clear voice.

Commander Lorcaan began to laugh as he turned to face the defiant Ario, but was distracted by Melody holding a violin-esque instrument with a flute for a neck. A dark mood shifted across Lorcaan's face. "Put that down," he said with a growl as he reached for his ice staff. Ario quickly nodded to Melody who played that instrument like her life depended on it, for, in fact, it did.

Ario had found the Book of Snowflake, Flower, Leaf, and Sun. It was the music sheets the Makers of long ago had used to beckon in the new seasons; the music that Melody now played was the movement of Spring. It was lush and bright—the music soared and danced ever so sweetly across the floor. Commander Lorcaan raised his ice staff, but before he could do anything, a burst of sunlight engulfed the room. The staff fell from his hands as he dropped to his knees and shielded his eyes. The warmth and brilliance was far too much for his cold loving winter constitution.

Ario was filled with his purpose, he understood the power of what Makers truly were. "This is a taste of the Spring to come," he said in a voice that boomed across the workshop.

Lorcaan growled in agony as the beams of light pained his body and the joy in the music seared his frozen heart. "We don't answer to Winter. Winter answers to us!" said Ario, as Melody lost in her tune continued to play beautifully and passionately.

Lorcaan tried to move against the force of the music, but with blinded eyes he fumbled on all fours searching for his ice staff. He knew this was his last chance before the overwhelming wall of sound rendered him useless. He grimaced in pain as he batted a stool away and then he felt it. He grabbed his staff and wildly blasted in the direction of the music. He hit a bookcase and the floor, but he also hit his mark knocking Melody off her feet. The music immediately stopped and the bright light vanished as the instrument cluttered onto the floor.

Ario rushed to her side, "Melody!" he cried, while he tried to assist her to her feet.

In a full rage, Lorcaan pounced on Ario who cried out in agony, as he was yanked off his feet by the ears. Lorcaan's cold hands sent excruciating chills through Ario's body before he was thrown to the floor in front of the workbench where his sleeping Maker lay.

"No more games, restart the Making... now," Lorcaan roared.

Ario covered his face in fear of a beating, "But only the Magnum Opus can restart the Making," he whimpered. Lorcaan was no longer in the mood to be trifled with and pointed his staff ready to blast Melody who was cold and groggy on the floor. "Please, no. I'll try!" Ario pleaded.

Ario stood and begrudgingly rotated the hourglass then watched with sadness as the sand began to fall. He picked up a guitar melded with an accordion from the wall and attempted to play the Making song. Even with his practice and lessons from Melody, there was no real improvement, his hands trembled in fear and did nothing to assist the discordant notes from finding a pleasing tune. Renaissance lay still, without life, just as before.

Commander Lorcaan was livid, "You are a worthless Maker and of no further use to me," he yelled as he blasted Ario with ice. Ario held up the instrument in his hand, which took the full force of the freeze. The searing chill burnt his hands and he dropped it as it shattered into hundreds of frozen pieces. With seething hatred, Lorcaan took aim again to finish the job.

"Stop!" Melody screamed as she rose shivering to her feet. "I'll do it. Just don't kill him," she said as she slowly shuffled to the workbench.

Ario shook his head, "No Melody, you can't trust—"

Commander Lorcaan pushed him to the ground, "If you fail, you both die," he said.

Melody nodded as she reached for the hourglass, and with a heavy heart she turned it in the opposite direction. It now began to spill back the small amount of sand that Ario had started. With a new instrument in hand, she stood poised at the music stand. Lorcaan stood near her with a watchful eye as she began to play. The tune was melancholy and echoed throughout the workshop with a somberness, it was the expression of her heart, but it was not the Making song. She smiled at Ario with tears in her eyes, "I believe in you, you'll make this right."

Ario was confused, there was such sadness in the way she said it and why wasn't she playing the Making song? He looked at the hourglass and realized the sand was about to end, he knew what she was planning. "Don't do it!" he howled, but it was too late, only a few grains remained. Melody started to dissolve and, before Lorcaan could work out what was happening, she grabbed hold of his arm. Commander Lorcaan roared in fury as he tried to shake her away, but it was too late, they were both whisked back to Winter City.

Ario stood alone as burning hot tears rolled down his cheek. "What have you done!?" he screamed to no one at all. She was the bravest, most noble being he had ever met and he now feared he may never see her again. Ario fell to the floor as an uncontrollable panic swelled like a fierce ocean within his heart, he gulped for air as tried to take a breath. The journey that stretched long and dark before him was overwhelming and filled him with such terror he was paralyzed. "What am I going to do?" he said sorrowfully, "What am I going to do, without you?"

# CHAPTER 12
## *The Return*

In the Maker amphitheater, Officer Stilano of the 22nd Regiment had been left in command. He shifted on his feet uneasily as he looked to the sky. The sun was going to set within the next few hours and no doubt another blizzard was brewing. It had been a cold torturous few days trying to capture these insolent offenders, and in moments like this he seriously doubted his career choice. He daydreamed about the simple life of a sneezleberry farmer. He looked anxiously at the tunnel entrance, Commander Lorcaan had been gone for some time now and they would need to address shelter very soon. He scanned the makeshift prisoner camp, the remaining Winter officers rested on the surrounding stone seats of the amphitheater, the flying beast had been properly secured with rope and the four dogs lay around it fast asleep. The two male captives were sitting on the ground with their hands tied around the column. The situation was contained, but it just didn't feel right. Much to his annoyance, the tall lanky prisoner had refused to be silent and it seemed he was not done yet.

"Don't you see," Aquillo said patiently to Officer Stilano, "Fall comes before Winter. I, Sir, have seniority here, now untie these ropes." Stilano just ignored him and continued standing at his post stoically.

Tallac, who had grown bored of waiting growled, "Don't waste your breath. They're mindless snow men, following orders is all they do."

Officer Stilano, who up until now had ignored everything the prisoners had said, took great offence to the comment. He promptly walked over to Tallac and angrily stood over him. He remembered Tallac from when he was a young officer, he had looked up to the brave and fair leader, but now he was nothing but a Maker sympathizer facing the wrath of Lord Crone.

"At least we're loyal," he said to Tallac and kicked snow in his face. Tallac's eyes brimmed with fury as he stared up at him. Officer Stilano glared back, he had to admit that what he saw in those eyes was deeply terrifying.

Aquillo raised an eyebrow, "Wow, I've never seen someone sign their own death warrant before." A *clank* echoed from deep within the tunnel and broke his gaze. He grunted at Tallac and returned to his post. He watched the tunnel intently, relieved that Commander Lorcaan would soon be here.

There was another *clank* and everyone turned to the entrance. *Clank, clank*. It sounded like some sort of machinery was picking up speed. The sound became louder and closer. The officers all rose to their feet with staffs pointed at the tunnel mouth, the dogs awoke and began to bark and the prisoners looked over with interest.

"Ahhh we're about to be saved," Aquillo said happily. There was silence. Then a series of slow rapid *clanks* echoed across the amphitheater as something climbed the passageway stairs. With one final *clank* a cat like mechanical contraption, minus the ears and tail, sprung out of the entrance. Its cogs and springs *whirred* as short but sturdy metal legs and feet propelled it along the ground.

Aquillo frowned at the size of the thing, "Not really the rescue party I was hoping for," he said.

The widget scurried across the amphitheater floor as the officers aimed and fired, but it was too quick so they gave chase. The dogs also ran after it and pounced, trying to rip it apart with their snarling teeth. *Ka-chink,* a net exploded outwards from the contraption and entrapped three of the hounds, who barked and growled ferociously as they tried to break free.

Aquillo was now enjoying the antics like a sporting event, he cheered and whooped, "Clearly I spoke too soon!"

Two Winter officers rushed to release the dogs while another blasted the contraption with ice. He crushed it with his boot to ensure it would create no further mischief. The officers were all distracted by the general chaos that they failed to see a certain Maker sneak out of the tunnel towards his captured friends.

"Snow men!" bellowed Tallac.

The Winter officers turned to discover Ario standing beside his untied friends, who were once again armed and ready to fight. Lassar roared as Tallac and Aquillo charged and the officers aimed and fired. Aquillo nimbly dodged the ice blasts then swung his rake artfully through the air, clocking an officer in the head and knocking him out. He turned and batted an ice staff from another officer's hand then planted the rake firmly in his leg. He finished with a high kick to the head, and the officer didn't stand a chance.

Not to be outdone, Tallac deflected each blast of ice with his axe as he set upon an officer and took him out with a powerful right hook. He turned to face Stilano, the last Officer standing. The younger man swallowed nervously, but raised his ice staff, ready to fire. Tallac wasted no time and, with a mighty swing, threw his axe. The last thing the officer thought before feeling the blow was that sneezleberry farming would definitely have been a far better career option.

Ario stood grimly surveying the scene; he wished it didn't have to come to this, but a thousand years under Winter's oppression was enough. He was going to take a stand if no one else would. He heard snarls and growls and turned to see the remaining dog running at him, savagely baring his teeth. The dog leaped. With no weapon to defend himself, Ario screamed and cowered in fear, but Lassar took two steps forward and snapped the mutt out of the air. With a great gulp she swallowed it whole, letting out a contented burp.

"Thank goodness for you, my friend," Ario said as he reached up and gave her a grateful pat.

As the others joined him, Aquillo looked around with concern, "Ario, where's Melody?" he asked, "And where's that particularly nasty Officer?"

Ario's ears flopped down as he took a breath and said quietly, "Boy do I have a lot to tell you."

Not long afterwards, daylight was still holding on. Ario was busy strapping a purpose built harness to Lassar, which he had fashioned out of leather and metal scraps found in the workshop. The harness was part of a saddle he had also made for three riders. With some adjustment, it fit snugly on her back then wrapped around her lower neck. It had a thick metal plate that spread across her chest and was adorned with a cursive letter 'L'.

Tallac watched him and pondered everything that had occurred in the Maker workshop—he did not like this plan at all. "Returning to Winter City is madness," he said.

Ario shrugged as he double checked the harness. He knew it too, but there was nothing else he could do. "I have to let the Makers know what I've learned. We have to restart the seasons," he said determinedly.

Tallac nodded but was still concerned for this brave but naive Maker, "Lorcaan will double security. You won't make it past the city walls."

Ario stopped. In his darkest moment alone in the workshop, when it all seemed beyond hopeless, he thought of Melody. She had never given up on him, she believed in him and he knew that he could never let her down. When he made that decision, that solemn personal vow to go on even when all seemed impossibly lost, that was when inspiration had struck. A plan began to bubble and boil and beg to be brought forth. He realized within the loneliest moments of his short and painful life, inspiration had never left him. The ability to create and to make, the gift that the Elders had bestowed upon the Makers, all those eons ago, once again showed him the way and Ario had to heed the call. He would somehow right all of this and he would somehow see Melody again.

He looked Tallac squarely in the eyes, "The volcano is going to erupt in two days. If they switch on that machine, we'll be stuck in Winter forever."

Aquillo did not need more than that to be convinced, "Forever is a long time. I've got a family to get back to. I'm coming with you Ario." Ario smiled at him with gratitude.

Tallac raised an eyebrow, no amount of Maker enthusiasm could convince him without a solid plan, "How will you even make it back in time?" he asked.

A black kettle hanging over a small fire began to whistle. Ario picked it up and carried it over to Lassar. Within the decorated chest plate of the saddle was a sealed metal container. Ario unlatched it and flipped the lid, then poured the boiling water inside. He looked up to Lassar and gave her a big neck rub and said, "There you go girl, how does that feel?" He latched the container closed and Lassar shook her neck a little as the warmth of the chest pack soothed her instantly. She began to snort, then she snorted harder as she felt her chest cavities warming. A few puffs of steam came out and the group cheered her on. Lassar took a deep breath and threw her head back, then let out an almighty roar as a flame shot out of her nose into the air. The gang broke into applause and she let out another celebratory fireball.

Ario laughed and turned to Tallac as he hoisted himself up onto Lassar's saddle, "Next stop, Winter City!"

Aquillo shook his head in amazement as he climbed onto Lassar. *These Winter goons better prepare to rumble,* he thought to himself.

Ario looked down at Tallac, "There's room for one more," he said hopefully, knowing that Tallac was instrumental to his plan.

Tallac thought for a moment, there was no way in all honesty he could leave this crazy Maker to take on an entire city by himself. And while he hated to admit it, he hadn't felt this alive in years. "I do have a debt to settle," he said as he climbed on board with agitation, trying to forget that he'd vowed never to fly again. They all held on tight as Lassar reared on her hind legs, gave a roar of fire, then bounded and leaped into the air, flapping her powerful wings.

They raced against the sun, which was performing its final act of the day, and a violet sky streaked with rays of gold. Helped along by a strong tailwind, the team rode with solemn resolve high above the treetops of the dense forest below. The journey that would have taken them days on foot was less than an hour as Lassar, fully invigorated with her chest plate, held a steady rhythm.

In the distance, Winter City was now in sight, it loomed gray and foreboding beyond the city walls. Tallac looked down over the land and spotted a Winter truck driving on the winding road, just beyond the edge of the forest. "Set down over there," he yelled over the rushing wind pointing well ahead of the truck. Ario nodded and tugged at the reigns signaling Lassar to begin their descent.

$$\text{\textflbassign}$$

Winter Officer Malcido was driving along his routine scout for the escaped Makers. He still had a number of miles to cover, so it would be some time before his shift was over. He was looking forward to dinner and he wanted to finish reading his book, *Snow Vixen of the Crypt* before bed that night. He slammed on the brakes and skidded to a stop. On the road in front of him stood a creature, a humongous creature. And what was that flapping, could it be… wings? The most worrisome part of this scenario for Malcido was the fact that this terrifying beast was blocking his path.

"What is that!?" he said loudly to himself. The truck door flew open and Tallac caught the officer by surprise.

"That… is a diversion," Tallac said with a matter of fact grimace before he punched the Officer in the nose, knocking him out cold.

Ario and Aquillo ran from their hiding place behind the trees and helped undress the unconscious Officer. Tallac then put on the oversized uniform, which was a bit loose on account of the previous owner's distaste for any sort of physical activity and a particular fondness for sneezleberry pie. Wielding his axe, Tallac got busy chopping down and stripping a number of trees as Ario and Aquillo assisted by loading the logs into the back of the truck. Lassar was more interested in a wood rat that had foolishly crossed her path. She bounced around trying to catch it, batting it with her paws, but the terrified critter was proving quite the challenge.

After the truck was loaded up, Ario whistled for Lassar who happily bounded over, having secured herself a tasty rat treat for her evening meal. Ario packed her chest plate with snow, then stood back as Lassar breathed fire onto it making the metal red-hot.

Ario looked up into her sweet black eyes, "I'm afraid you're too big to come along, you'll give us away."

Lassar made a soft whimpering sound. She understood what her tiny friend was saying and she didn't like it. Ario pulled a short, thin cylinder from his back pack, "You need to stay hidden big girl, but don't worry, I'll signal you with this flare if we need your help." He pointed to the horizon where the silhouette of Winter City stood ominously against the now starry night. "Keep an eye out for it," Ario said.

Lassar nodded and snorted then gave Ario a big lick across his face. Ario smiled as he wiped away the kiss and slipped the flare deep within a concealed pocket on the inside of his jacket. Tallac, who was in the driver's seat, had grown impatient by then and honked the horn. Ario gave Lassar one last scratch then ran to the back of the truck and jumped in next to Aquillo. With a heavy foot on the accelerator, they sped off for the Winter City limits. Lassar watched them sadly as they disappeared, but she heard a rustling in a nearby hedge and was off again to find herself some more food.

The west checkpoint was being manned by Officer Filmo and Officer Hedian, who were were in the middle of a board game known as *White Out*. It was a game of strategy where the object was to entrap your opponent's castle using giants, snow beasts, warriors, and ultimately wiping them out with a snow storm. Much to their annoyance, they were interrupted by an unexpected truck that pulled to a stop at the booth. It was Filmo's turn to complete the security check, but he didn't trust Hedian to be left alone with the game, so he motioned for him to follow.

With clipboard in hand, Filmo stepped up to the driver's side window, while Hedian waited behind him. "I didn't expect you to return so soon." He stopped short for it was not the Winter Officer he was expecting.

Hedian had also noticed the driver was not the normal scout, "Hey... who are you?" Hedian queried, confused.

"I was ordered to take over this shift," Tallac said with a shrug.

"On whose authority?" Filmo asked with rising suspicion.

"Commander Lorcaan's," Tallac said nonchalantly.

Officer Hedian frowned as he looked over his clipboard containing all the leaves and passes for the day. He shook his head, "I have no record of this—"

"Are you questioning Commander Lorcaan's authority?" Tallac said with a growl, sensing this wasn't going to be the easy access they had planned.

Hedian was becoming flustered as he had no desire to upset Lorcaan, "No I just…"

"Then let me proceed," said Tallac.

The officers looked at each other for a moment, Filmo gave a slight shake of his head and Hedian nodded. Officer Filmo stepped forward, "Out of the vehicle."

Tallac sighed, "You're making a mistake," he said.

Filmo drew his staff and pointed it at Tallac who complied with hands raised as he climbed out of the truck. "Check the cargo," Filmo said to Hedian while keeping a wary eye on Tallac. Officer Hedian walked to the back of the vehicle and flung open the door. He was shocked to discover one of the missing Makers peeking out from behind a tall lanky man with wild brown hair and strange clothing, the likes of which he had never seen. Before he could say anything or trigger his ice staff, Aquillo jabbed him in the face with his rake. Aquillo winced, "That's gonna leave a mark." Hedian now understood the term 'seeing stars' and roared as he randomly fired his ice staff. With the commotion in the rear underway, Tallac pounced on the distracted Filmo as they both wrestled for his staff.

Meanwhile, Aquillo and Ario dove from the back of the truck, narrowly avoiding the officer's icy volley that would have made them both life sized ice blocks. Hedian was again seeing clearly and able to successfully dodge a second attack from Aquillo's rake, but the attempt did manage to knock the staff from his hand. Aquillo swung again, but the officer raised his arm and caught the rake. With an almighty heave, Hedian whipped it around locking Aquillo in a choke hold. At the same time, Filmo charged at Tallac and headbutted him in the nose. Tallac stumbled back momentarily stunned. He growled as he shook it off and pulled out his axe, but Filmo stood firm pointing his staff at hm.

"Hey snowmen," a voice cried.

Both officers looked over to see Ario determinedly pointing at them with Hedian's ice staff. Without hesitation, Ario blasted the officers who instantly turned into ice. Tallac and Aquillo nodded in appreciation, greatly impressed by this Maker's spirit in battle. They turned back to their foes and smashed the officers to pieces with their tools.

As they drove through the Winter City streets, Ario peeked through a gap in the truck's sideboard. It seemed like an eternity since he'd driven along these streets, but today he did so in entirely different circumstances. Then, he was considered nothing more than property, a slave, his soul handcuffed to a world where music was not allowed. Now, he was a free person; he couldn't play music, but he knew its awesome power, now that he knew the truth.

He noticed with great concern that even at night there was an increased number of Winter officers patrolling the streets and Makers being stopped and questioned as they went about their business. Before he was created, the Makers had enjoyed some autonomy, but now... he took a deep breath. He could not succumb to his guilt or negativity. With all his willpower he vowed that he would do all he could to make sure Makers would never be ruled in this way ever again. He would use the truth as a key to free every single Maker from Winter's cruel, cold hand.

# CHAPTER 13
## *The Plan*

allac reversed his truck into the factory loading dock and drew in a long, calming breath as a Winter officer approached his window. He gave Tallac a curt nod and reached out his hand, "Paperwork."

Tallac nodded, "Sure," then thumbed to the dock. "Just let me park. Can you show me how far back I can go?"

The officer obliged and walked around to the rear of the vehicle. Tallac looked into the side mirror and saw the officer wave and call, "Okay. Nice and slow."

Tallac knew he was beyond the point of no return. While these were his kinsmen, he knew what his people were doing was wrong. He had to do all he could to assist Ario and the other seasons; he could no longer be holed up in the forest, hiding from his past. He somberly moved his gearstick into reverse then stepped hard and fast on the pedal.

When the Maker formerly known as 367890 walked into the front office of the factory with two terrifying strangers, the Maker scout was at a loss of what to do or say. He was so concerned for his own life that he just followed Ario mutely inside as the strangers waited behind. Ario stood and surveyed the proceedings, the factory was no longer busy and bustling, it was in fact bursting and busting with organized chaos. An uncountable number of Makers swarmed all over the work floor and up the surrounding scaffolding and ladders.

Much ground had been made in the past few days and the Freeze Machine now towered to the full height of the factory ceiling. In order to beat the impending disaster, all non-essential Winter City duties had been suspended and every available Maker had been forced to work in the factory around the clock. Sleep was sacrificed as the full blown campaign to complete the machine in time was underway. They tinkered and soldered, they screwed and hammered, and they tightened and tested and retested again. Time was stretched fine indeed, there could be no mistake and no delay, the future safety of all depended on this—or so they believed.

Ario saw all of them so frantic, so focused on completing this monstrous machine that would only ensure their subservience forever. He picked up a large spanner and walked to the nearest pipe. He stood straight, raised his head, then banged the pipe slowly and purposefully five times. With each strike, Maker after Maker turned. By the fifth ring there was a silence over the factory as every single Maker stared at Ario in shock.

Ario stood his ground and gazed over all the faces before him, locking eyes with a few. He was not the same Maker that had left here and he wanted them to see that. He was about to speak when someone cried from the third floor, "It's the one who doomed us all!" This was all the others needed, a palatable swell of anger erupted across the room and more Makers joined the chorus. A number of Makers booed, "You're not welcome here!" someone else hollered.

Ario put up his hands to quiet them. He knew the reception would be hostile and he was undeterred, "Wait. I come with important news from the Magnum Opus."

There was another hush over the room as the Makers muttered and whispered to each other. "You spoke with the Magnum Opus?" a nearby Maker called out, as all the Makers waited for the answer.

"Well, no. He was dead when I found him…" the Makers gasped in horror and before Ario could finish, they resumed their angry chatter. "But he left a message!" Ario cried out hoping this would be the hook and bait that was needed, but the Makers weren't interested.

"Why should we believe anything you tell us?" a Maker bellowed from the sixth story scaffolding.

Ario turned to the factory exit door and motioned for Tallac and Aquillo who were waiting. "Because I can prove every word," he said boldly as they walked in.

The Makers were instantly seized by panic when they saw Tallac dressed in a Winter Officer's uniform. His brown haired skinny companion also sent chills down their spines, as they scrambled over each other to return to their work.

"No! Wait, they're on our side," Ario said to the Makers, but they ignored him and continued working. To the majority it was quite clear, it was not too long ago that this very Maker had brought so much trouble upon each and every one of them. They couldn't believe the audacity of Ario and had no desire to be drawn into his world of bad luck, poor choices, and offensive musical skills.

Ario's ears flopped defeated, he turned to his friends, "I don't know what to do," he said as he looked over the factory despondently.

During this time, an old Maker named Hymn had hobbled to the front of the crowd to take a closer look at the spectacle. Since he was made nearly a century ago, he had been enchanted by the stories of the Magnum Opus. Every morning, when he rose from his burrow, he had made a silent wish that the Magnum Opus would one day come and free them all. He was not going to miss an opportunity of a lifetime to speak to someone who had news from his hero. Hymn looked up at the peculiar fellow with sweeping brown hair and frowned, wondering where on all planets known and unknown this creature had come from. Then he turned to peer into the Winter man's face, his heart skipped with excitement as he remembered.

Hymn winked at Ario as he took the spanner from his hand and then loudly rapped the same pipe as he called out in a surprisingly strong voice, "Makers. Makers... I recognize this officer." Everyone stopped work and turned around, for Hymn was one of the last remaining

Elders and was respected by all. "He was second in command, but fled the city years ago. A Maker sympathizer they called him," he said as he smiled up at Tallac.

Ario saw the captivated audience and seized the opportunity, "Yes, yes and he's here to help."

Hymn turned to Ario and searched his face, *this Maker has really been a menace, but he keeps slipping out of Winter's cold fingers. Maybe there is something more to him.* "What wisdom did the Magnum Opus bestow upon you?" he asked, his copper brown eyes glistening intensely.

Ario stood tall again, "Winter is not the only season. There are others. There is one called Summer, it's the opposite of Winter where all the snow has melted away and the days are long and warm." Ario then pointed at Aquillo, "Our friend here comes from a season known as Fall where they grow and harvest food of every kind." Aquillo gave a huge grin then bowed low with his customary arm flourishes. "Tomorrow morning we must gather and play a grand symphony to welcome in Spring, another season where warm winds blow and flowers bloom." Ario stepped forward with urgency in his voice, "Our world depends on it!"

Hymn's eyes widened at the revelation, but then his heart sank. "But music is forbidden," he shook his head.

"Only because it gives us the power to control Winter!" Ario shouted defiantly. Those words hit the heart of every single Maker and the floor exploded in excited chatter.

"We control Winter!?" someone called from the rafters.

"That's why they wouldn't let us play," another Maker yelled.

"Yes, yes! Of course," another said.

Hymn hollered over the top of everyone, "We have no instruments."

Ario smiled at the old Maker so warmly and gratefully, he had helped his message be heard and he just wanted to hug him. "We have all that we need. Gather around and I'll tell you everything." A hush fell over the floor as all the Makers leaned in.

Tallac walked out to the loading dock to stand guard. He was pleased the Makers were able to see the truth. A chilly wind blew down the long street. He took a sharpening stone from his pocket and started to grind his axe to a solid razor point. He knew the plan had only just begun, soon Winter would come calling and he had to be ready.

The timber logs Ario had brought from the forest were now being used by all the Makers to fashion their own musical instruments. The rich scent of the fresh pine wafted through the factory, along with the voices of the Makers. There was no monotony, no routine—for once they truly had a purpose that was their own. For the first time ever, they had tasted freedom, even if it was only in their minds. This meaning informed their hands and their voices, and they sang from their souls. None of them had ever truly known such a thing as hope before.

Hymn sat amongst his fellow workers, humming in his low baritone. He felt an emotion swell inside himself, profound and deep. He had only ever known it fleetingly—it was happiness. He actually felt happy. He smiled broadly as he lovingly carved the piece of wood in his hand.

Ario sat at a makeshift desk made from crates, scribing from memory the musical notations for the Spring symphony. His plan was to print hundreds of copies of the sheet music which they would all use to play. The work on the Freeze Machine had halted and now a few Makers were in the process of repurposing the said machine into a printing press that would make copies of the symphony for everyone.

The Maker supervisor approached Ario, "Workers in the Winter palace have sent word of Melody."

Ario's stomach lurched, "Where are they keeping her?" he asked.

"The North Tower," the supervisor responded. "But it's being heavily guarded. There's no way in or out."

Ario nodded slowly as his eyes glazed over, "Thank you," but the supervisor was already gone.

Ario paused and looked out at the throng of Makers intently focused on the craftsmanship of their instruments. They sang a gentle song filled with buoyancy; it floated, it danced, and it promised happy endings. He smiled, Melody would be so proud. He knew he couldn't break her out of prison to see this, but was confident that tomorrow would be Spring and they would all be free. But he longed to see her, to see if she was alright. A plan began to form. The rest of the Makers had this under control and they wouldn't miss him for the short time he would be gone. He scribbled down the last bar of the music and walked it over to the Makers at the almost finished printing press.

Looking casual, he then gathered the tools and equipment he would need to carry out his idea. He found himself a quiet corner tucked out of sight and, as he worked on the contraptions he required, he looked around for a suitable exit. He couldn't use the factory entrance for there was no way Tallac would agree to such a plan. He noticed a window at the back of the factory, out of view from most. When he had finished, he gathered up his things in a knapsack and without a second thought he slipped away.

The city clock struck three as a light snow dusted the deserted streets. Ario moved from shadow to shadow, avoiding the officer patrols that passed him by. In no time at all he found himself at the foot of the North Tower, a soaring structure attached to the outer palace wall. He glanced up and down the empty street behind him, then pulled out the equipment from his knapsack: a set of gloves and two foot harnesses that strapped over his boots. Fitted with multiple metal hooks that had been sharpened into points, he put them on his hands and feet and then slammed his hand into the tower wall. Ario smiled, it latched on perfectly. With each strike of his hands and feet, he was able to slowly spider his way up the icy facade.

The frigid night winds flapped his coat and chilled him to the bone, but he worked steadily and surely rising higher and higher. He knew a foot wrong would send him crashing to the street below. He had just pried a hand off the wall when he felt the tower begin to tremble. His heart raced as he slammed his hand back into the ice. Ario's eyes bulged in fear as cracks began to form in the wall around his gloved hands. As the tremors increased, pieces of the tower began to break away around him and the once sturdy tower heaved under the violent shudders of the earthquake. Ario clung tightly as he rode the waves until they subsided. He was now high enough to see beyond the city walls, and in the distance the volcano spewed smoke and shot flames. The earth was furious and was simply letting them all know. Ario breathed a sigh of relief, then pulled his glove out from the wall and thrust it hard above his head, as he continued to scale the tower.

As the snow and winds whipped all around, he finally reached a single small window right at the top of the tower, heavily fortified with thick iron bars. "Melody? Melody?" he softly called.

Melody instantly appeared at the window. "Ario! What are you doing here?" she cried, unable to contain her joy and relief.

Ario pulled off a glove and reached for her hand, "Are you Okay? They haven't hurt you have they?"

She squeezed his hand. "Nothing I can't handle," she smiled sadly, looking weary and extremely disheveled.

"The Makers are secretly building instruments. In the morning we'll play in Spring—then we can be together." Tears began to well in Melody's eyes and Ario reached for her face, "No tears," he comforted her.

She nodded and smiled, they held hands through the bars and together they began to sing. They sang of their dreams and wishes, imagined welcomed Summer breezes and dry golden leaves crunching under their feet. They saw themselves dancing through meadows bursting with flowers and though snowflakes would fall again, it would never be as it was. They knew that together they would see so many seasons and there would never ever be a reason to be apart again. Their little song of hope and love danced upon the freezing Winter wind and was carried to a place where hopes and wishes go to await their time.

"I knew you would save us all," she whispered to him. When she left him in the workshop she believed that they would meet again, but then again she never really knew.

Ario nodded sadly, but determinedly, "I have to go, but I'll see you again soon." He gave her hand one final squeeze and put his glove back on.

Melody smiled, "Be careful!" she called as Ario began his descent.

A hundred feet below on the desolate Winter street, Commander Lorcaan stepped out of the shadows and put his monocular back into his coat pocket. Anger seethed and fueled his vision of vengeance. He smiled thinly and cruelly, then turned on his heel as he hastened towards the palace chambers.

# CHAPTER 14
## *The Slow Freeze*

irst light softly glowed against the crisp silhouetted city, which had only just begun to stir. Inside the factory, the atmosphere was subdued, yet optimistic. The instruments were now completed and what an array there was to behold. There were countless combinations that fused woodwind, percussion, strings, and brass. Every Maker had created his own unique design with distinct flair in honor of such a momentous occasion, carving each with flowers, leaves, suns, and even the occasional snowflake, heralding the new seasons that would come. All the available Makers were assembled from floor to rafters, the sheet music was distributed, and they were all now quietly tuning their instruments in preparation to play in Spring.

For the fifth time that morning at least, Ario paced up to the supervisor, "What's our status?" he asked.

The supervisor wrung his hands nervously, even though things were going smoothly, "We'll be ready to play in a few minutes."

Ario tried to smile, "Great."

"Where's your instrument?" he asked, noticing Ario's empty hands.

"I think it's best I sit this one out. I have a knack for ruining things," Ario said in a low voice as he shuffled away.

He heard something outside and stopped. The distinct stomping of many boots. His heart was wrenched with devastation. He turned to the factory doors as they flew open. Commander Lorcaan stormed onto the factory floor with more than a dozen officers in tow. The Makers screamed in terror unsure of what to do, they had nowhere to hide and no excuses to give. They looked at each other bewildered, knowing they were now at the mercy of their Winter masters. Ario stood frozen and unprepared. He couldn't look at the other Makers, he could only whisper, "No, no, no!" as all their dreams lay trampled and crushed.

Lorcaan strode to the center of the floor and stared over the Makers with a look of smugness. His black eyes bore cold fear into the heart of every Maker as a raw dread rippled over the factory. He waited a few moments more, soaking in the uneasy and uncomfortable silence.

"Destroy those weapons against Winter," he roared.

Without a word, Winter officers systematically swept through the Maker crowd. A cacophony of malicious destruction echoed across the factory. The *plucks* and *plings* of the instruments reverberated over stifled cries and sorrowful sniffles, as every single instrument was ripped and snatched from its helpless creator. A relentless staccato of *crashes, bangs, clinks,* and *plunks* punctuated the air. It was as if each instrument cried out as it was smashed beyond repair on the stone floor. Ario watched and cringed at every slam and split of wood. It was not the symphony he had hoped or wished for on this Wintery morning. As he looked at the shattered instruments that now began to pile high in the center of the factory, he believed this was it. It was over, he didn't even try to hide as there was nothing he could do.

Aquillo perched on a ledge high up on the Freeze Machine as he watched the events unfold. His heart sank along with the Makers as his hope of being reunited with his family faded. He knew his only chance to ever see them again was to survive to fight another day. He decided to remain hidden and quickly shuffled to the other side of the machine. In his haste, he lost his footing, slipped, and bumped his head. With all the chaos in the factory, no one saw an unconscious Aquillo tumble and disappear into one of the machine's many pipes.

Satisfied that all the instruments were destroyed, Commander Lorcaan now searched for his prime target amongst the crowd. The surrounding Makers had fearfully inched away from Ario, so he wasn't hard to find. Lorcaan approached him with zealously cruel intent. Self preservation kicked in as Ario tried to run, but the Commander grabbed him by his ears, lifted him off his feet, and held him high like a trophy.

"Makers!" his voice boomed. The silence was thick with a terror you could definitely taste. "You have taken a great risk by defying Winter's law."

The factory doors flung open and Ario saw two officers enter, dragging Tallac. They threw him at Lorcaan's feet. Tallac looked up at Ario apologetically—he had taken a beating with cuts and bruises all over his face. Ario grabbed Lorcann's hands around his ears and kicked furiously trying to free himself, but fell limp when he realized his efforts were in vain. *I should have never dragged him into this mess,* Ario thought guiltily. .

Commander Lorcaan continued, "One that may have paid off, had this foolish Maker not visited his precious Maker girlfriend last night."

A murmuring tidal wave of rage swelled across the floor. Ario closed his eyes in disbelief, it wasn't like that at all, his actions had been totally misconstrued. Then a pang of shameful realisation hit him, he now saw that if it had been a good idea, he wouldn't have been so secretive. He had put his feelings for Melody above the freedom of them all.

A Maker standing mid way up the machine screamed down at Ario, "You've doomed us again!"

Lorcaan fixed a steely eye on the Maker, casually raised his staff then shot him. He instantly froze and toppled to the ground, the echo of splintering ice shards silenced the Maker's unrest. Commander Lorcaan looked over the floor, his annoyed eyes dared anyone to be next, "I don't care for interruptions. Yet, this Maker was correct. The punishment for the crime you've all committed is death."

A frantic communal whimper echoed as the consequences of their actions became harshly evident. Lorcaan paused dramatically, then in a tone dripping with feigned benevolence he continued, "However, Lord

Crone is a compassionate ruler and may consider forgiving your crimes, should you resume work and complete the machine ahead of schedule."

Ario was seized by sheer panic, this could never happen. By their own hands, they would ensure their slavery forever. "Don't do it, he's just trying to—" Lorcaan yanked Ario by the ears harder and he cried out as pain shot through his scalp and spine.

Commander Lorcaan dangled him close to his face and whispered, "If Lord Crone didn't want you alive, I would have snapped your belligerent neck long ago. Quiet or I'll have your tongue." He smiled thinly to the Makers, "My men will oversee your progress."

Lorcaan then froze the nearby Maker supervisor solid, snapped off his helmet and placed it on the head of one of his officers. The officer stood to attention and roared, "Get to work!" The Makers did not need to be told twice.

Lord Crone stood at his favorite window in his throne room. It opened onto a view of the distant forests and mountain peaks, with the volcano billowing smoke in the distance. He remembered just before he had come of age, his father had stood with him at this very window and reminded him of all he would inherit. It was this same day that his father had revealed to him the true history of their great Wintery kingdom and warned of the dangers of the Makers and their music. Crone agreed with his father that Winter should continue to reign supreme. A ruler must look after his people and never bow to some pact or treaty that does serve his own. He had vowed to his father then and there that he would pass on this legacy to his own son one day. His father had nodded proudly. Crone's lineage went back as far as time itself, each generation of his family had built upon this grand kingdom. There was no way he would let it be threatened by one measly Maker.

The hair on the back of Crone's neck raised in a chill as the metal chandeliers overhead began to tinkle. He wasn't afraid of the tremors about to hit, but knew what they represented if the Makers didn't finish the machine in time. He stood firm as his palace and city began to shake. The volcano in the distance spewed more fire and smoke, taunting him just like that one Maker. He comforted himself with the thought that he would soon be back in control of everything.

Crone walked purposefully up the steps to his throne and settled himself into a regal pose with ice staff in hand and he pressed a button on his armrest. A loud gong echoed through the halls and the large throne room doors flew open as the procession of the prisoners commenced. An Officer led Melody down the carpet of the great hall with his ice staff pointed at her back. Melody gulped at the life-sized paintings hanging from the walls of past Winter Lords whose eyes seemed to follow her along with glaring disapproval. Two officers escorted a stoic Tallac and, finally, Ario walked in with Lorcaan hulking over him and pushing him along with his ice staff from behind. The prisoners were presented to Crone at the base of the throne platform as more officers filed in and took positions around the room with ice staffs drawn.

Ario leaned over to Melody, "Are you alright?" he whispered with concern.

Commander Lorcaan pushed Ario to his knees. "Silence," he said loudly.

Ario looked up into Lord Crone's piercing holes of blackness and shuddered, he could feel his stare chill his bones. Crone slowly shook his head, "It's hard to imagine, one insignificant Maker, could cause so much trouble," he said in a low voice laced with underlying brutality.

Though trembling, Ario mustered the courage to speak, "We know about our past. About the unbalance you've brought to our world."

Lord Crone was clearly amused at the audacity of this Maker and waved him away, "Fear not, at sunrise the Freeze Machine will be activated and the Earth will be frozen for eternity."

Ario was aghast at their wanton disrespect for the ways of this world. "But the other seasons... they'll be wiped out forever!"

Lord Crone shrugged callously, "And you will soon join in that fate."

Lord Crone rose out of his chair and descended the steps to tower over a trembling Ario. He looked down at him with a menacing calmness, "You are a defective Maker who broke the Making cycle and jeopardized the lives of your kin." His words cut Ario sharp and deep as his ears and head dropped in shame.

Tallac could no longer contain himself, he had once held Lord Crone in the highest esteem, but not now. "You are a coward! Hiding behind a secret, terrorizing these benevolent creatures."

Lord Crone haughtily turned his head to face Tallac and stared for a moment. This was the man he had once groomed from a budding officer into a fierce warrior. A man that he had trusted above everyone. His voice lowered even more, "You cast aspersions of cowardice, yet are not man enough to face your own crimes," he said with a snarl.

Overcome by anger, Tallac's breath was hard and fast as he tried to keep a measured tone, "My only crime was not finishing Lorcaan all those years ago."

Commander Lorcaan growled as he pointed his ice staff ready to finish him, but Crone casually raised his palm and Lorcaan backed down. He nodded his head almost sadly, "You are a disappointment, Tallac, and you will be punished alongside your little friends." Lord Crone signaled to his officers who began to bind and gag the prisoners.

Ario struggled desperately, "No wait, what you're doing is wro—" but the gag tightened and all he could muster were grunts and moans. Crone picked Ario up off the floor by his neck. Crone's icy touch immediately sent an abrupt and frightening cold though Ario's body as crystals formed around his eyes and mouth. Crone pulled him close as his frosty breath chilled Ario's face and his black eyes gleamed with unrestrained loathing. "The Makers have no voice and will always be our slaves," Crone said in a whisper, as a cruel smile played on his lips.

The cool afternoon sun had begun to cast long shadows over the Winter City town square, which stretched before the entrance of the Winter Palace gates. Various lanes and city streets ran to meet the expansive cobblestone area, which was a popular location for dining and entertainment for Winter citizens. There was a multitude of shops and restaurants running along the sides of the square, with small, thick glass windows set within gray ice facades. The windows were framed by plain awnings with hanging glass oil lamps in wrought iron enclosures, which lit neatly placed table and chairs set for sub zero alfresco dining.

Opposite the Palace entry, at the south of the square was a paved promenade that wove for miles alongside a wide frozen lake. The people of Winter once ice-skated on the lake as a form of recreation, but with the warmer climate and thinning ice it was no longer recommended. Throughout history, the Winter Citizens had gathered here to honor the major events of the Family of Lords: their coronations, births, deaths, and marriages. It was here that each ruling Lord would address his people and this was such a day.

A large turnout of curious Winter folk had arrived at the square to see what punishment would be dealt to the rebel Makers and the Winter sympathizer. All Makers not needed on that day's Freeze Machine shift, had been forced to attend, to witness the repercussion of civil disobedience.

With the Winter Palace as a backdrop, a makeshift wooden stage had been erected. It had a raised deck and a tall arch that stretched overhead and was adorned with blue flags emblazoned with white snowflakes, that flapped in the cool breeze. On the stage stood three thick vertical timber poles. Each were a few feet apart and positioned underneath a maze of pipes, gutters, and cogs that coiled and wrapped around the arch. Lord Crone stood center stage flanked by Commander Lorcaan and Lord Festus, who was extremely chuffed to be a part of the proceedings. He gleefully waited for his retribution on the Maker who had brought him severe embarrassment and a cancelled vacation.

A silence fell over the crowd as the prisoners were somberly marched by Winter officers up the stage steps. They were lined up against a wooden pole, then their feet were blasted with ice to freeze them into place. Lord Crone stepped forward as his sobering voice boomed across the square, "It brings me great sadness when one of our own betrays us. Yet when this occurs, there can only be one punishment." Winter citizens cheered in response, as a guard began to tie Tallac's hands behind his pole. Lord Crone continued, "Makers, these prisoners before you have led you astray." With a heavy heart, Ario looked out at the sea of disapproving faces that glared back. "In doing so," he thundered, "they have revealed to us your hidden workshop which is now under our control." He paused for optimal dramatic effect as the Makers gasped and whispered amongst themselves, then raised his hand for silence, which his subjects obeyed. "Let it be known that if any other Makers defy Winter or incite music, they too will meet this fate," he roared with sadistic certainty.

Lord Crone turned to face the prisoners, "I hereby sentence you to the SLOW FREEZE."

An Officer stepped forward to tie Ario, but he desperately struggled free and ripped the gag from his mouth. "You won't get away with this!" he cried and pulled the flare from deep within his jacket pocket, hoping that he could alert Lassar and turn the tide. He ripped off the cap, but before he had a chance to pull its cord Officer Festus shot his hand with an ice blast. The freeze was so biting that Ario dropped the flare and watched in dismay as it rolled off the stage.

The Winter officer re-tied the gag and resumed securing Ario and Melody's hands behind their poles. Officer Festus walked up to Ario and sneered, "I told you what would happen if you broke the rules." Festus then walked over to a large lever at the bottom of the guttering facade and gave it a hard yank.

The surrounding cogs began to *whirr* and *clank* and a rush of water could be heard filling the pipes as the death machine sprang into action. At the behest of a Winter Lord long ago, the Makers had been required to create this contraption of punishment, which was saved for only the most notorious of Winter City transgressors. Water would funnel into the multiple gutters suspended over each prisoner, then slowly drip onto the blocks of ice that encased their feet.

Festus walked back to Ario and wheezed in his face, "As the water drips, the ice will rise, freezing you solid. If the cold doesn't finish you, at sunrise these hammers will fall, smashing you to pieces," he said with an unsettling cheeriness.

Ario, Melody, and Tallac looked up to see a large hour glass at the center of the arch, rigged to three raised hammers with long arms. Their eyes widened with fear as Officer Festus' big belly laugh rang through the square as he walked away. The crowd now satisfied with the carriage of justice, began to disperse.

The light of a luminous full moon cast a shadowy blue glow over the deserted square. The prisoners were slumped upright upon the stage, half-frozen and unconscious—the ice had now climbed to their waists. Ario tossed his head as he slowly became lucid once more, he turned to Melody and Tallac beside him. He tried calling out to them, but the harsh cold air froze his larynx and only a barely audible grunt could be heard through the gag. He felt as if he stood on the edge of the deepest of sleeps, yet the most vivid of awakes. He could go now if he wanted. He could pass. He felt heavy, like eyelids yearning to dream, yet he was as light as a feather floating free on a warm sweet breeze. A tear rolled from his eye and froze solid on his cheek. With the last energy he had left, he struggled to break free, but to no avail. He gave up and slipped back into unconsciousness.

It was in that place that Ario felt like he had left his body. He floated above the dreary Winter City, high into the chalky clouds. A flash of light filled the sky and he viewed his small seemingly insignificant life, as if watching a film. There he was with Melody in the ice prison as she picked up the stalagmite. *Your first lesson, music is all around you.*

The crack of the ice prison wall deafeningly reverberated through his mind. He was back in the mountain cave far in the Northern forest scribing musical notations in the dirt. *I can see and hear the notes in my head. I just can't play them.* He heard a voice boom the words of the Magnum Opus across the sky, *Only together is life complete.* He felt Lord Crones icy breath chill his bones once more. *The Makers have no voice.* There was another brilliant flash of light then he was surrounded by a darkness of pure raven black. He heard Melody's sweet voice, *Music is all around you... music is all around you.* Her words echoed into an eternity.

Ario's eyes snapped open and he saw in that moment, all that he was and all he could be. He was not what others said he was, but rather, he was what his heart yearned and knew to be his truth. He was not any one thing that he had done, but he was the culmination of every single thing that led him to this now. It was from this clear and cloudless present that he knew where he needed to go. He thought of his musical ineptness and for the first time in what he had thought had been a miserable little life, he felt not one ounce or drop of sadness. For he finally understood. Yes, his voice may not dance and soar and grace the ear. True, his fingers may not be able to artfully caress an instrument like that of his brothers and sisters, but music flowed through him and flushed him full of life itself. He could see it, he could feel it, he was music and he understood music like no other. Even when there was no music to be heard, it still played in his inner ears. The Makers would try once more, they would gather to play in Spring, but this time he would take his rightful place in the Orchestra. He would lead his kin in the grand symphony of the Seasons. He was the leader of the band, he was the conductor. Just as he had finally awoken, so too would the other seasons rise.

He looked over to Melody, but she was unconscious. Despite the paralyzing coldness that pervaded his body, he had to get to her. As always, inspiration and providence never left him, especially when he opened himself to their gifts. A plan fizzed and frothed and unfolded with delicious glee, for when you know who you are are, there is nothing or no one that can stop you.

He had to act quickly, a Winter patrol would pass soon enough and discover him. With his tied hands, he felt around behind the pole, and, to his sheer delight, he discovered a stalagmite forming. He wiggled determinedly until he could jam its point into his bindings. He grunted as he wiggled some more and, finally, with rising excitement, he managed to loosen the rope enough to free his hands. He ripped off his gag and called hoarsely to Melody and Tallac, but there was no reply.

Ario used the rope that had bound his hands and tied it into a lasso. He looked overhead to the guttering and narrowed his eyes with concentration, then he threw the loop snagging the edge of the gutter. He yanked it and yanked it harder still. With one last determined pull, he snapped it clean off and it cluttered to the ground. He then carefully reeled the gutter into his hands. Wielding it like a shovel, he used it to hack away the ice that encased his body. With every fervent chip, he could only think of poor Melody next to him. He kept a steady pace until he reached the final hack and was able to kick the remaining ice away.

His whole body was hindered by numbness, but that didn't stop him. He stumbled to Melody and began to desperately chip at her ice prison. Tears welled in his eyes—she was unresponsive. He hacked away at the final ice casing and she slumped into his arms, lifeless. Tears now streamed down his cheeks as he looked into her face. "Melody. Melody, wake up," he said as he gently shook her, but she remained heavy and still. His voice became more desperate as he shook her harder, "Come on, don't leave me again." He felt for her pulse, but no life remained in that slight delicate body. "Please!" begged Ario as he sat rocking her.

Snowflakes lightly fell around them. His whole being was weighted in the most ravaging of sadnesses, a devastating emptiness that you never really understand until you lose that someone who is most dearest to you.

He whispered in her ear, "I know what to do to stop Winter. I wish you were here to help me." He sobbed ever so softly. This was not how it was suppose to be, none of this. He cried out in anguish, overwhelmed by a crushing sense of loneliness at the thought of having to go on without her.

Ario didn't know what else to do, but he knew all he had was music. He began to ever so gently sing to Melody. Of course, he was not pitch perfect, not by far, but he sang a tune colored by his pure heart and his pure intent. The song was the "Making Song' but in his grief and desperation, he found words that were a mirror to his soul.

*I am you, you are me, only together is life complete*
*I need you, you need me, please, please stay with me.*

Lost in his music, Ario now appreciated the true essence of what the Magnum Opus had meant with his inscription on the compass. There was no closer bond than the bond of love and it should be honored above all else. No gadget or kingdom means anything unless you can share the experience of real love and connection with another.

Tallac stirred into consciousness and turned to see Ario cradling Melody in front of him. While cold and entombed in ice, Tallac cared nothing for himself. His heart broke—he knew the burden and responsibility that Ario had carried and understood all that he had lost. Despite its imperfection, he thought Ario's song to be the most profoundly perfect song he had ever heard.

*You are the maker of my magic*
*You bring power to my dreams*
*Giving my life its purpose*

*Filling my world with love*
*Only together can we be free*
*Please please stay here with me.*

Tallac gasped, the magic of these creatures had never ceased to amaze him. As Ario continued to sing his gentle discordant lullaby, misty rainbow hued tendrils began to swirl around him and Melody. Ario's eyes were closed, just like Melody had shown him, and he had become the song. This was no wish or hope or dream, he was expressing his deepest love and his deepest belief that they could not yet be over. They still had more of the journey to go. By laying his soul bare, he saw beyond his fears, and he saw the gifts that her life had brought him. From this place of gratitude, he had awoken the magical energy that lights the sun and throws meteors across the sky.

*If all is perfect in design*
*Then this will not be goodbye*
*I am you, you are me*
*Only together is life complete*
*I need you, you need me*
*Please, please stay with me*
*Only with you is my life complete.*

Ario's voice trailed off and he opened his eyes and gently kissed her on the forehead. He looked into Melody's face, so pale, so peaceful. Unbounded tears flowed down his cheeks. He stopped short and took a sharp breath. His heart skipped. He wasn't sure, but then yes, there it was again. Her eyelids gently fluttered. "Melody..." Ario cried with overwhelming happiness. Melody looked into his eyes and smiled. "I taught you well," she said with soft, cracked voice. He pulled her close to him, so tight and strong as he made a silent oath that they would never be apart again. Ario relaxed his hold and they gazed into each other's eyes as he reached his hand out to Melody's face. They leant in and kissed each other ever so softly, the tenderness and bliss melted away any remaining Winter chill. In that embrace they felt the promise of each new day to come, and no matter what happened from here, together they were in accord with the whole universe and everything was perfect.

While Ario could have stayed in that embrace forever, he knew they had much to do before they could rest. He gently pulled away and helped Melody to her feet, "We don't need instruments to play in Spring. We can use our voices—and I'll be the conductor who leads the symphony." Melody smiled, she didn't know if she could be any prouder.

Tallac gave a little self conscious cough, hoping the moonlight would not reflect on his face and reveal his tears. "It won't be long before we're discovered. We need to move."

Ario obliged and after he untied his Winter friend he began to dig him out with the gutter. With each slam of the ice, Tallac considered what he had just seen. Now he knew that miracles truly do happen and he had a feeling these Makers had a few more up their sleeves.

# The Great Crescendo

# CHAPTER 15
## *The New Plan*

I t was still in the small hours of the night. A light snow gently dusted the city as Ario, Melody, and Tallac took refuge in the shadows of an alley only a few blocks from the town square. They discussed their next move, knowing it wouldn't be long before their escape was discovered.

"We have to get to the supply shed—there's some things we'll need," Ario whispered, not wanting to stir the occupants snoring in the townhouse bedroom directly above their heads.

Tallac, as always, saw the flaws of any plan, "Not a good idea, we'll have to pass the Officer's barracks to get there."

Ario had preempted this exact line of questioning, "We'll sneak through the troll cages on the opposite side of the road."

While Tallac had always thought of himself as fearless and strong, he knew better than to voluntarily put himself in harm's way. "Do you know what will happen to you if you wake a sleeping troll?" he said with a shudder.

Ario smiled, "I'll take my chances with trolls over Winter officers any day."

The muffled laughter of a small group of officers could be heard as they sat outside the barracks playing cards and enjoying a few bottles of sneezleberry ale after their shift.

On the other side of the otherwise deserted street, Ario, Melody, and Tallac quietly slipped through the bars at the side of the first troll cage and began to tiptoe through, keeping an unwavering eye on the officers. A patrol vehicle passed and they dropped to the floor, hiding behind a troll. When all was clear, they continued to sneak between the cages. All proceeded without incident until there was a huge *clank*, then a rattling of *clunks* that echoed across the silent night.

Tallac realized that he'd accidently kicked a tin can and grumbled something best not heard under his breath. The trolls stirred in their sleep and the trio once again dropped to the floor in fear of being discovered. The commotion caught the attention of the Winter officers across the street and they flicked on a huge spotlight. They scanned the cages only to find the trolls sound asleep.

"Stupid beasts," an officer sneered. They all laughed in agreement as they turned off the light and resumed their game.

The gang remained on the floor and exhaled with relief. Tallac signaled for them to continue, but paused when he heard Ario gasp in fear. He and Melody turned to see a big hairy clawed hand around Ario's arm. Melody and Tallac looked at him in horror, not sure what to do, especially when the troll sat up and pulled Ario towards him. Their concern however, was soon replaced with surprise when the the troll gave Ario a juicy lick across the face with his huge bumpy tongue.

Ario softly chuckled under the ticklish shower of drool, "Hey, I know you."

The troll gently released his paw and replied with a small grunt as he nuzzled Ario's cheek with his head. The troll softly cooed as Ario stroked his matted woolly coat. "I missed you too," Ario said in a comforting voice.

Melody and Tallac looked at each other in disbelief.

"How do you two know each other?" Melody asked Ario.

"I shoveled her dung once," Ario said with a smile.

Ario, Melody, and Tallac finally made it to the end of the troll enclosure and out of the direct line of sight of the officers' barracks. They quickly crept next door into the supply shed, which was a small square building that stored all the necessary equipment for the city's Maker maintenance crew. Even with the light of the moon, the darkness was a hindrance in their search for supplies.

Melody rifled through a shelf and called over to Ario, "What are we looking for?"

"Paint. Brushes. Some buckets," came the muffled reply, as Ario dangled head first in a large supply container.

"I can't see a thing," Tallac grumbled as he knocked his shin on a hard, unseen object.

Melody was pleased when her hands come across a flashlight. She switched it on, "How about now?" she asked accidentally shining it in his eyes. He raised his hand to block the light and growled with frustration. "Oops sorry," Melody said as she moved the light.

Tallac's mood quickly brightened, just beside him hanging on a hook was his favorite tool of all—a trusty axe.

Tallac then heard a patrol vehicle pull up and peered through the front window, "We've been discovered... hide!" he said softly.

Ario's mind raced as he grabbed a bucket and rope. "Help me with this first!" he replied.

Officer Heplok had finished his last patrol of the western quadrant of the city and was grateful to return to the barracks and call it a night. As he drove past the supply shed, he noticed a flashlight moving about. With everything that had been going on, he was suspicious of anything out of the norm, and lights in the supply shed were definitely unusual. He pulled over to investigate.

Not sure what to expect, Officer Heplok drew his ice staff as he slowly opened the shed door. He was surprised to find a light swinging back and forth in the middle of the room. He stepped inside and walked cautiously towards it, nervously pointing his ice staff left and right. As he reached the bright pendulum, he discovered it was just a bucket suspended by rope with a flashlight inside. He wondered what to make of this curious discovery and pulled down on the rope.

His inquisitive moment was short lived. The rope was attached to a precariously balanced metal toolbox sitting on an overhead beam, which promptly came crashing down on him. Ario, Melody, and Tallac stepped out of hiding and looked down at the the flattened officer covered in an assortment of tools.

Tallac was impressed he didn't need to lift a finger and shook his head at Ario, "Remind me to never, ever cross you."

The officers were still engaged in their game of cards and didn't look twice when a patrol vehicle drove past the barracks. "Heplok off to see his missy I take it," one of the Officers joked as the others chortled.

Tallac grasped the steering wheel and kept his eyes straight ahead as Ario and Melody popped out out of hiding.

"We did it!" Ario exclaimed.

"Indeed," Tallac replied without relaxing one bit.

The trio drove across town as Tallac tried to remember all the shortcuts from his days in the city.

"Hey. What happened to Aquillo?" Melody asked.

"I'm not his keeper," Tallac said as he focused on the road.

Ario paused with a frown, "Last time I remember seeing him was in the factory," he said.

"Where ever he is, he appears to have evaded capture," said Tallac.

Melody looked out the window a little worried for her Fall friend, she wished there was time to look for him.

They had just passed a deserted cross street when they heard a low groan. The Makers looked at each other as Tallac gripped the steering wheel tight. The earth rumbled beneath them and the ground rippled with waves. Tallac swerved all over the road trying to maintain control of the vehicle. A thunderous crack roared from below the earth as the road in front of them split in two.

"Look out!" Melody shrieked, but they were going too fast to stop.

Tallac pulled the steering wheel in a hard right and narrowly missed the gorge. Both Ario and Melody screamed as he locked the wheel to the left and accelerated to avoid a tree that had just toppled in the quake. The tires screeched as the vehicle fishtailed down the road. Tallac wrestled with the steering wheel, finally gaining control as the tremors abated. He pulled over and they all sat in silence for a moment breathing hard and fast. They all knew that these tremors were going to get worse unless the symphony was performed.

Ario spoke up, "We have to hurry, it won't be long before Winter switches on the machine." Tallac nodded in agreement and with a rev of the motor, they sped off to the sleeping burrows.

The full moon was beginning to dip behind the looming mountain cliff, but it still offered some subdued lighting for the task at hand. Ario, Melody, and Tallac stood at the foot of the Makers' burrows, armed with brushes and cans of paint. The burrows were empty with the entire Maker population at the factory, working on the machine.

Melody looked to Ario and smiled, "What now?"

Ario beamed back at her, pleased at how the stages of his plan were progressing. He pointed his flashlight illuminating the burrow's portals. "Now we paint," he said dramatically as Tallac raised an intrigued eyebrow.

The moon had fallen way below the western cliff face as two officers stood guard outside the factory. Inside was chaos, so they were glad to enjoy the stillness of the night. A large rattle of metal and the scuffle of feet broke the quiet. Suspecting it was some animal, but needing to sure, they drew their ice staffs and followed the noise towards the corner of the factory. Tallac crept from behind a nearby dumpster and with the blunt edge of his axe, clocked the unsuspecting officers from behind, knocking them to the ground. Tallac gave a low whistle and Ario and Melody peeked from around the factory corner.

All work in the factory had halted. Throughout the cramped factory floor, Makers stood alongside a number of Winter officers, waiting in an uncomfortable silence for the next update. Commander Lorcaan was in deep conversation with the supervising officer and a few key Makers at the base of the machine. He nodded regularly and seemed pleased with the discourse.

With a final nod he turned to address the expectant crowd, "Makers. Your hard work and vigilance has paid off. The machine is ready. We will be saved from the volcano."

The Makers offered no response and only stood gravely as the burden of their actions weighed on each and every one of them. Lorcaan drew breath to continue his celebratory monologue when a cry of terror pierced the silence. An officer's limp body slid across the floor and landed at the Commander's feet. No one dared to say a word as Lorcaan's face contorted with fury. All eyes followed the path along the floor the body had taken to see Ario, head high and ears bristling as he stood on a wooden crate flanked by Melody and Tallac.

"Don't turn on the machine!" Ario yelled, "It's not too late to do the right thing."

Nervous chatter broke out amongst the Makers; they were amazed at how these rebels continued to defy Winter again and again, and were terrified at what consequences awaited them now.

Commander Lorcaan fixed the latecomers with a withering glare, "You've arrived just in time to witness history in the making," he said as he moved towards the machine.

"No, wait!" Ario cried.

It was no use. The commander exuded great joy in pulling down lever after lever to the halfway point. The dials began to flick, the cogs *whirred*, and the machinery started to *putter* and fire up. Satisfied the cooling sequence had commenced, Commander Lorcaan turned and bellowed to his officers, "Finish them!"

Three officers wielding ice staffs began to fire. Makers all over the floor dove for cover to avoid being caught in the crossfire. Tallac swung his axe deflecting the ice blasts as he charged with a clear, focused rage. He made short change of two officers, knocking them to the ground, then lunged at the remaining Officer with a right hook followed by a crushing kick to the chest. Tallac swooped down and seized one of their staffs and with one fluid movement blasted ice through a narrow gap in the Maker crowd, freezing an unsuspecting Lorcaan on the other side of the factory floor.

Ario and Melody pushed through the Maker throng and made their way to the Freeze Machine. Ario seized the levers and pushed them up one by one until they were all turned off. The machine steamed and puffed then chugged to a stop.

Ario and Melody clambered up some metal stairs to a platform high on the machine in view of all. "Makers," he called, "It's not too late to change the seasons and restore balance to this world."

There was a buzz all around, the majority of Makers were terrified, if Crone discovered that Commander Lorcaan had been frozen and the Freeze Machine had been stopped, who knew what he would do.

"We listened to you once and we were almost killed for it," a Maker yelled out from the crowd.

"There's nothing we can do," another called.

The whole floor erupted into chaos as Maker after Maker in their anguish and fear, screamed over each other to be heard. Ario yelled to try and get their attention, but Melody raised her hand.

"Listen," she bellowed in a voice so loud and large, she surprised everyone into silence, including Ario. "You must listen to him, he is the new Magnum Opus." There was a roar of disbelief as the Makers laughed and heckled the notion that Ario, who couldn't play an instrument let alone sing, could be a Magnum Opus.

Ario turned to Melody, "Why did you just say that?" he frowned confused and embarrassed. Melody just smiled warmly at him and turned back to the factory.

"Silence," Melody yelled at the crowd again. "I have seen the signs." She went on to explain each remarkable feat Ario had performed as they journeyed to find the Magnum Opus. Ario fidgeted self consciously as she shared how it was his resourcefulness and understanding of sound and music that had gotten them out of trouble time and time again. "If it wasn't for Ario, we Makers would never be where we are today, knowing what we now know. We'd never be so close to freedom for all. He may not be able to play an instrument, but he knows more about music than any of us... he's a conductor! Maker lore says, the Magnum Opus can sing with 100 instruments in unison. Ario can make hundreds of instruments sing at once!" The Makers chattered amongst themselves still not entirely convinced.

Melody shook her head a little exasperated, but she had one more thing up her sleeve. It was the one thing that had always niggled at the back of her mind. She turned and smiled at Ario as she reached in her pocket and pulled out a handkerchief. She leant in and with a bit of spit and elbow grease, used it to rub off the f-hole symbol from his forehead—the one she painted on a lifetime ago. The Makers gasped in surprise as Melody turned to them and roared, "The Magnum Opus looks unlike any other Maker!"

An electrifying level of elation broke out across the floor as the Maker's gushed excitedly amongst themselves. Melody turned to Ario, grabbed his hand and looked at him proudly, "You are my greatest work of all," she smiled.

They reached out to embrace, but the factory lurched and the walls buckled. Ario grabbed Melody and tightly held onto the railing. Screams filled the air. The earth groaned underneath them. Ladders toppled and Makers dangled from platforms, as stairs threatened to give way. This quake was more fearsome and violent than the tremors that had passed before. The volcano was unleashing a growing fury across the land. After what felt like forever, the tremors slowly subsided.

Ario knew they could no longer delay singing in Spring, but he wanted to show them one final wonder. He needed them to truly understand.

"Sing the Spring symphony," Ario said to Melody and she nodded eagerly.

Ario whistled loudly to get the attention of the factory. He raised his hand to count her in, then his hands gently rose and fell as he guided her through the Spring song in acapella.

*Spring has begun.*
*The new season has come.*
*All is one.*
*Leaf, snowflake, flower, sun.*
*Spring has begun.*

Her beautiful voice resonated across the factory, floating and cascading and soothing the audience who listened intently. A warm wind began to blow through the factory and the sweet smell of jasmine filled the air. Soon, the Makers started to nudge each other and point. Just above the heads of the crowd on the factory floor, a swirling golden light sprinkled with rainbow shimmers appeared. Gasps of awe broke out as flowers burst from its center, blushed with sweet hues of red, pinks, and yellows. The Makers raised their hands in wonderment, catching the floral rain as Melody and Ario brought the song to a gentle end.

Ario smiled at Melody with a grin as the spring shower ended. He turned to the crowd. "That was just a glimpse of Spring. This is what one voice can do. Imagine what we can do together, as one! Let's restart the seasons and be free of Winter's tyranny forever!"

The Makers finally saw that this crazy, troublesome Maker had actually spoken the truth and they cheered for him with wild unabandoned support, now truly understanding the power of the music that flowed through each and every one of them. Finally, after generation upon generation of Makers suffering, they all felt emboldened and worthy—they were finally whole. But in their heart of hearts, every Maker always knew how powerful and magical they truly were, they just needed a little reminder.

"Makers," Ario cried. "Assemble at the burrows. It is there we will play our symphony… Only together is life complete!"

"Only together is life complete!" The Makers roared in unison.

The sound of shattering ice interrupted their cheers. The miraculous display of Spring had melted enough of Lorcaan's ice to allow him to break free from his icy prison. He threw his head back and screamed in a crazed rage, "Remain where you are!"

The inspired Makers ignored Commander Lorcaan, and, in a bid to arm themselves, grabbed whatever tools and pipes they could find and began to swarm out of the factory. Lorcaan marched over to the levers of the machine and pulled them down to maximum capacity.

Ario and Melody looked at each other with horror then dashed along the platform out of the commander's line of sight. The machine kicked into action and the dials, cogs, and pipes rattled, hummed, and blew steam. Ario and Melody slid down a pole to the floor then scuttled through the crowd of Makers to find Tallac on the other side of the factory.

Without his ice staff to protect himself, Lorcaan picked up an industrial spanner the size of his arm. He was outnumbered and unsure how to make these creatures obey him, but his priority was to keep this machine running. He roared in fury then ran to a nearby wall, where he thumped a big red button to activate an alarm. As it rang out, he barged his way back to the Freeze Machine, sending Makers scuttling and flying as he went. Commander Lorcaan then stood guard at the levers as he stared at the factory door, waiting for backup to arrive.

The group of officers at the barracks were still outside playing cards when they heard the emergency alarm sound. They looked at each other grimly then sprung into action.

In a corner of the factory out of view, Ario, Melody, and Tallac huddled with Presto, a Maker engineer who was now downloading all he knew about the machine. "At its current momentum, there's only a short amount of time before the earth's core is permanently frozen," said Presto.

Ario turned to the Tallac, "My friend, you need to stay behind to shut this machine down."

Tallac snorted knowing full well he was a timber and ice type of man. "I have no experience with Maker technology," he said with a frown.

"Presto, is it just the four levers to turn this thing off?" Ario asked.

"Yes, just pull them down," Presto replied with a nod.

Tallac raised an eyebrow in surprise, "That's it?" he asked. He was sure that saving the world from eternal freeze would be much harder.

"Keep an eye on the dials—you want those needles to stay in the white, if they reach the blue zone, well, you only have a few minutes before..." Presto said with a half shrug.

Tallac cocked his head slightly, "So, that's it?" he asked with a rising sense of self assurance, he thought this should be a breeze.

Presto looked past Tallac and gulped, "Well, you have to get past those officers first."

Tallac spun around to see Commander Lorcaan's call for reinforcement had been answered. Three burly Winter officers who were all determined that the earth's core would be frozen today, had entered the factory.

"Good luck," Presto said as he forced a toothy smile and scooted off to join the last of the Maker exodus to the burrows.

Keeping an eye on the menacing Winter forces approaching, Tallac turned to Ario, "You better get going too."

Ario stepped forward and held his arm for a moment. "The Makers are indebted to you, brave Tallac," Ario said solemnly, then he grabbed Melody's hand as they too raced out of the factory, the last Makers to leave.

Tallac watched them go, as a bittersweetness tugged at his heart; he knew it was in fact he that owed everything to them.

Tallac's face darkened as he returned to the task at hand. His moment of reckoning had arrived. He walked to the center of the factory floor and faced his foes as he assumed a defensive stance. His feet felt sturdy and sure, he rolled his shoulders and then his head from side to side, and his bones gave some long, satisfying cracks.

With eyes ablaze, Lorcaan walked over with his spanner clenched in hand and stood in front of him only a few feet away. "I've waited a long time for this," the commanding officer said with a vicious growl.

Tallac wholeheartedly agreed, as he raised his axe. "Then let us wait no more," he said low and ready.

The three officers charged with ice staffs firing fast and furious. Tallac skillfully swung his axe and deflected the frosty volley as he moved forward with agile speed. He was upon his opponents swiftly and lunged at the first officer with his axe. The axe connected with the officer's arm and he shrieked in pain. Tallac then ducked low to miss an ice blast from the third officer.

He continued the onslaught on the first with a left hook to the side of the head, then threw him with full force into the second. The officer's ice staff tumbled to the ground and Tallac quickly scooped it up and blasted them both. With another swing of the axe, he smashed the pair into a thousand crystal shards.

Tallac roared as he ran at the third, who fired furiously in defense. Tallac dive-rolled on the floor to evade the assault then jumped to his feet. Wielding his axe, he chopped the top of the ice staff clean off, then, with his full body weight, he delivered a well placed kick to the head. Tallac landed on his knee and blasted the officer with his staff, as he fell and exploded into nothing but icy remnants on the floor.

The adrenalin pumped through Tallac's veins as he rose to his feet and wiped the dripping sweat from his brow.

"Bravo," Commander Lorcaan said. Tallac turned to see him standing at the levers. "But I never expected them to stop you, just waste your time," Lorcaan said with a sneer.

Tallac anxiously looked at the machine's gauges, the needles had now reached the blue zone. There was only minutes remaining before the machine would complete its full freeze.

Tallac gritted his teeth and raised his axe, and then rushed at Lorcaan. The commander deftly blocked the onslaught with his spanner. The two adversaries went blow for blow in evenly matched combat. Strike after strike, axe and spanner connected. Years of anger mixed with visions of revenge fueled the fray.

Tallac dodged yet another strike of the spanner from Lorcaan. He immediately responded with a swing of his own weapon then followed up with a quick jab to the chest, causing Lorcaan to stumble back. Tallac seized the opportunity and delivered a devastating blow to Lorcaan's cheek with the back of his axe. Commander Lorcaan crashed to the floor, momentarily stunned. Tallac dashed over to the levers and started to yank them up. With each lever, the machine dropped a gear in its rumbling and the dials returned back to white. He heaved a sigh of relief.

From the floor, Lorcaan shook off his daze. He gripped his spanner and snuck up on the otherwise occupied Tallac. As Tallac reached for the final lever, Lorcaan swung the spanner and cracked him over the head. Tallac dropped his axe and fell to the floor.

The commander stood over him, "A valiant effort for such an old man."

Knocked speechless, Tallac lay on the ground writhing in pain. Lorcaan kept a mindful eye on his nemesis as he restored the levers to full capacity. The machine once again kicked into overdrive and the needles flicked back to blue.

Lorcaan then picked up Tallac's axe and began to hack at the levers, chopping them clean to the base. He smiled smugly, "We've now reached the end of our reunion."

Lorcaan roughly picked up Tallac by the collar and dragged him a few feet across to the Freeze Machine's engine. It was fully exposed with giant metal cogs that spun noisily and teeth that could easily crush anything that had the misfortune of coming between them. He grabbed Tallac's head and started to push him into the jaws of the machine.

The commander's eyes flickered with raw hatred, "It's fitting that your demise will come through a machine made by your pets," he said.

Tallac could feel the spinning cogs nip at his hair, but was not about to let it end this way. He summoned his last remaining strength to push back against the brute force of Lorcaan's full body weight.

*Clunk.* Steam shot from the machine's joints as it began to shudder with an odd clanking noise, and the dials fluctuated wildly between white and blue. Tallac thought it was all part of the design, but out of the corner of his eye he saw Aquillo ejected from within the machine down into one of its transparent snow-filled pipes. The pipe Aquillo had landed in was one of many that was funneling snow and blue liquid deep into the core of the Earth. Tallac had no idea how that crazy man had ended up in there, but saw that Aquillo was unconscious and on a one-way downward path. Now that its blockage was cleared, the machine accelerated its operation and the dial snapped back to blue.

Tallac took a deep breath as he looked Lorcaan in the eyes. He steeled his whole body and roared, "I. Want. To. Live." Tallac caught the commander off-guard by seizing his shoulders and delivering a powerful headbutt to the nose. With an all or nothing heave, he swung a disorientated Lorcaan around, straight into the cogs. Commander Lorcaan let out a scream of terror as he was dragged into the belly of the machine

Tallac closed his eyes astounded and relieved. It was over, once and for all. He stood for a moment and silently acknowledged the death of a powerful and courageous warrior, who, unfortunately, could not rise above his limited view of the world. His eyes flashed open, *Aquillo!* He ran to the broken levers, but there was nothing to hold onto. The needle had been on blue for too long. He looked at Aquillo, he looked at the machine, to and fro with no idea how to save him or stop the freeze. He saw that Aquillo was about to disappear down the pipe, deep into the earth. He grunted in annoyance and picked up his axe from the floor and prepared to do the only thing he knew how to do—he began to chop hard and fast into the pipe.

The machine clunked once more as its operation kicked into final gear and the needle remained so far into the blue that there was no hope of bringing it back to white. Tallac swung even more furiously as the axe slowly cut away at the tough clear casing, causing ice and blue freeze liquid to spill out. Aquillo was nearly out of sight. With a final blow he made a hole big enough and grabbed Aquillo by the leg, then pulled him out of the pipe. Tallac lay him on the floor and knelt over him as he slapped his face.

"Wake up. Wake up!" Tallac yelled in a panic, fearing the worst.

He shook his head with annoyance as he considered his only remaining option. With a grimace he leaned down and pinched Aquillo's nose, ready to resuscitate him. He looked at his mouth and growled hesitantly, then slowly moved in.

Aquillo's eyes fluttered then opened, "No, no, nooo," he said with chattering teeth. Tallac jumped back in surprise. "I know you missed me," Aquillo said as he sat up and hugged himself for warmth, "But I'm a married man."

Tallac replied with a growl.

Aquillo held his face for a moment, "Why does my face hurt and what's going on?" he asked.

Not wanting him to sense his relief, Tallac quickly hid behind a dour face. "I'm stuck with you forever in Winter," he replied.

The machine began to shudder as the needles flicked between blue and white. Heavy clouds of steam blew from the hole Tallac had chopped. Tallac's eyes brightened, "Maybe not!" he said as he raised his axe and rushed to the next pipe. "Go find something and start chopping."

Aquillo dashed away and returned within moments with a long handled shovel. "I prefer rakes, but I'm good with a variety of garden tools," Aquillo said as he slammed his shovel hard into the pipe alongside Tallac.

They worked in unison as they pounded and battered each pipe until it cracked wide open, then moved onto the next. With each pipe destroyed, the machine slowly lost more and more pressure as it heaved and blew smoke. The duo didn't stop until all five pipes had huge, gaping holes.

Tallac and Aquillo stood trying to catch their breath as blue liquid and ice pooled around their feet. The Freeze Machine gave one last dying sputter as it shut down for good. The dials rested on white and all was still. Tallac saw a wildebeest's claw from Lorcaan's coat on the factory floor. He picked it up and put it in his pocket, a poignant reminder of how close an irreversible winter actually came.

"We did it!" Aquillo cried out, the possibility of him being reunited with his family was still alive. He threw his arms around Tallac and gave him a giant hug before the Winter man could stop him.

Unaccustomed to public displays of affection, Tallac went rigid, unsure of what to do. He did pause as he noted that Aquillo was right—they had done it. Lorcaan was gone and the Great Freeze Machine would never harm the earth again. He growled and pushed Aquillo away, that was more than enough. Now they just had to somehow stop Crone, play in Spring, and then they could finally send Aquillo back to his family, so he would never be pestered by him again.

# CHAPTER 16
## *The Rebellion*

rone stood uneasy at the throne room window. In the distance, the volcano heaved and puffed as it glowed threateningly against the stark black of the night. He was unable to sleep; his life's work was reaching a culmination and shortly he would receive word that this land would be forever his. He looked proudly at the faces of his ancestors who lined the wall—this victory was for all of them. A clock chime echoed four times across the room, and Crone frowned as he wondered what was keeping Lorcaan.

Officer Droslo hesitated nervously outside the throne room doors. He knew this would go terribly for him—Lord Crone did not receive bad news well. He took a deep breath, exhaled, and pushed the heavy wooden doors open then strode purposefully down the aisle. He bowed low in front of Crone whose forehead furrowed with confusion. Droslo decided to take the short and direct approach. He rose straight and tall to attention then fixed his eyes on the wall just behind Crone's head, not daring to look directly at him.

"My Lord," he said. "The Magnum Opus has returned and the Makers are rebelling!"

Lord Crone's face bled of all color, "What!? Where's Commander Lorcaan?"

Too anxious to even blink, Droslo replied, "Killed... and the Freeze Machine has been destroyed!"

Crone reeled backwards as every degree and nuance of rage flowed through his body. "The Makers must not be allowed to gather and play music!" he roared at the officer. He stormed out of the throne room and down the hallway, the survival of his kingdom now rested solely on him.

Droslo kept a safe distance behind as he hastened after him. He was somewhat surprised and relieved that he survived the encounter without so much as a spot of frostbite.

$$\oint$$

Darkness still spread thick across the city and the light snowfall had all but ceased. Normally, the city would be lost in slumber, but this, of course, was no normal morning. The ringing of alarms combined with the hoops and hollers of Makers as they scattered through the streets towards the burrows caused the city to stir. Lights flickered on across homes as the sleepy occupants wondered what incarnations was going on.

Amongst a large group of Makers, Ario and Melody held hands and ran for dear life. Ario smiled at her, what ever happened from here, he would die a happy Maker. He knew who he was and he knew who he loved and he knew that he was fighting alongside his own kind for a better world. Herein lies the source of true power, there is nothing more potent than someone who has created their path of destiny, there is nothing more brilliant or more magical, and no one more unstoppable.

Hundreds of Makers reached the town square and suddenly stopped. Under the dim glow of the street lamps stood rows of Winter officers, all blocking the alleys and streets leading to the burrows. The Makers looked at each other with wide horrified eyes, as a murmur of fear rippled over them. The officers' ice staffs were aimed and ready. A chilly breeze whistled through the square as Makers and officers faced each other in a tense silence steeped in equal resolve.

"Fire!" an Officer's voice echoed across the square.

The icy assault bombarded the Makers as the officers furiously blasted with their staffs. The Makers shielded themselves with trash can lids and deflected the blasts with what tools they had as they continued to move forward.

"Melody, look out!" Ario screamed. He yanked her back as an ice blast hit the ground at her feet.

"Thanks!" she said gratefully.

Despite their determination, the Maker's numbers began to dwindle as many of them were frozen in their tracks. Ario would not lose hope—not yet—they had come too far, he screamed in his mind as he ducked and weaved through the glacial barrage.

On top of a little hill with a prime view of the sprawling Winter city, sat Lassar. She was feeling lonely and abandoned; She had waited obediently and passed the time snacking on snow rodents and heating her chest plate, but now she was growing impatient. Lassar watched the sky keen for her little friends to send a sign. She sniffed the air—something was amiss. Her heart raced faster. She sensed a deep rumbling in the ground beneath her. Her claws clenched the snow with overwhelming fear as a violent jolt shook the whole earth.

Lassar jumped to her feet and whined as a loud, aggressive boom thundered across the land and echoed through the sky. She turned her head to the east; there, amongst the yonder mountains, the volcano finally delivered on its threats and erupted in a massive explosion. Volcanic debris in a brilliant display of glowing red and orange sprayed across the night. The gusty wind carried burning chunks of ember and flaming ash, which it rained down on Winter City. Lassar whimpered softly, unsure as to how she would see Ario's flare now.

The ferocity of the blast rocked the earth and the accompanying fire rain sent everyone in the town square scattering, as they ran for cover. The officers halted their freeze attack. Ario and Melody dove under a bench seat as fireballs hit the ground around them. Ario looked out at the snow, dotted with sizzling craters. Just in front of them stood the slow freeze stage where only a few hours a go they had stared death in the face. But now, it was taking a pounding from red hot volcanic rocks. He spotted his frozen flare on the ground where it had rolled off the stage the day before.

"The flare!" Ario said as he pointed.

"Be careful," Melody replied as she watched Ario scramble out into the open to grab it. He was forced to retreat when a nearby officer fired on him.

Melody took a deep breath, "I'll distract him," she said and immediately ran in the opposite direction. Ario followed her queue and dive-rolled across the snowy, cobbled ground. He picked up his frozen flare then dashed under the slow freeze stage for cover. Ario scoured the square and saw Melody running, then saw the officer fire his staff.

"Melody!" Ario screamed, but it was too late. The officer blasted Melody, freezing her solid mid stride. His heart sank, every fiber of his being wanted to run to her, but even in the midst of his despair he knew he needed to keep going.

He smashed the flare with fury against the ground, the ice encasing broke away exposing the preserved unused flare inside. He rolled out from under the stage and looked skywards as his eyes gleamed. "C'mon Lassar, we need you!" he yelled to the heavens. He pulled the trigger cord and a small flame shot up into the air then burst into a vivid glowing orange fireball, but it was simply lost amongst the volcanic flashes that streaked the night. Ario's forehead puckered in thought, *I need a bigger flare!* as his eyes darted across the square searching for inspiration.

An old metal trash can outside a storefront caught his attention. As he rose to his feet a Winter officer came lumbering his way and opened fire. Ario dodged the blasts, but slipped on the ice underfoot and fell to the ground with a heavy thud. He lay on his back and looked up as the smug officer stood over him about to fire. A heavy fear that he may not see his plans through to the end rose in Ario's throat and threatened to choke him.

The officer hesitated. His finger twitched, his face convulsed, and his eyes bulged as he groaned and tumbled forward. Ario quickly rolled away as the officer crashed to the ground almost on top of him. He looked up and saw Tallac step into view and extend his hand to help him up. Ario's eyes welled with tears; never had he been so happy to see this man.

"Tallac!" he cried as he took his hand and jumped to his feet, immediately throwing his arms around him in a hug. Tallac's solemn demeanor thawed just a little, he was not used to all this spontaneous affection, but he was beginning to feel it was something he could get used to.

"Did you stop the machine?" asked Ario.

Tallac nodded, "I did, with a little help." He pointed further back in the square where Aquillo was surrounded by a number of Winter officers, artfully battling with his shovel. He was blocking ice blasts, avoiding volcanic debris and having a jolly old time knocking the officers about.

Ario squealed with excitement, "Aquillo!" He turned to Tallac, "We have to break Winter's defense."

"But of course," Tallac replied. In one fluid motion, he bent over the unfortunate fallen officer to retrieve his axe from his back, then swung it into the air smashing a falling ember hurtling towards them. Without a second thought, he bounded off to join the melee.

Ario turned to gaze at Melody and took a deep breath; he couldn't imagine playing in Spring without her. He looked at the trash can again, then ran over to it and unlatched the lid. With his bare hands, he scooped a pile of snow into the can, then tore down a long strip of material awning from a store front. He grabbed three burning oil lamps hanging outside the store and tied them with the awning, then threw them into the trash can hard. They smashed into a fiery blaze. Ario slammed down the lid, then latched it closed. The can trembled and steam hissed as the pressure started to build.

Ario turned and ran straight towards an approaching officer who lowered his ice staff slightly puzzled. He couldn't understand why this Maker was running directly at him instead of in the opposite direction. Before he had a chance to work it out, Ario dove for cover head first into a pile of snow in front of him. The trash can exploded with an almighty boom as glass and metal shrapnel sprayed the surrounding area, taking out the officer and two others nearby.

Ario lay dazed in the snow, his ears rang from the blast. He rolled over onto his back and watched with a growing smile as the fiery oil lamps shot into the sky. The flaming awning trailed behind like a shooting star far larger than any of the random embers still streaking the night. Ario waited, lying still, searching the sky as a tiring Tallac and Aquillo continued to battle through the remaining officers.

"Come on, come on," he whispered through a clenched jaw. His eyes squinted as shadowy shapes in the darkness tricked him again and again. Then his heart skipped. He finally saw the unmistakable silhouette of Lassar gracefully flying through the sky. "Yeah!" Ario cheered as he jumped to his feet.

An enthusiastic Lassar swooped down breathing fire at terrified Winter officers, who unsuccessfully tried to outrun her. Lassar saw the rows of frozen Makers and flew back around as she skillfully shot each of them with tiny fireballs in rapid succession, immediately defrosting them. The Makers saw that Aquillo and Tallac had cleared a path through the officers and they resumed their dash to the burrows.

Ario ran over to Melody and whistled to Lassar, "Over here!" he called and waved. Lassar hovered mid air, flapping her wings as she shot a small fireball that hit Melody square in the chest. The ice melted instantly, "Woohoo!" Ario hooted, as he hugged a soaking Melody. "Are you OK?" he asked concerned as he looked her over carefully.

"What happened?" she replied, a bit groggy and confused.

"Our backup just arrived!" Ario excitedly pointed to Lassar, who roared flames all over the square as she dominated from the sky.

Only a handful of Winter officers remained and they were now at risk of being overpowered by Tallac, Aquillo, and the rebellious Makers.

Melody's heart fluttered with hope as she smiled at Ario. "Let's get to the burrows," he cried as he led her by the hand.

They ran across the square when an ear splitting roar from above halted them in their tracks. They looked up to see Lassar flapping vigorously, struggling to stay in the air. She'd been struck in the chest by a blast of glowing blue ice.

"Oh no!" Ario cried.

Ario and Melody spun around to see an enraged Lord Crone standing at the back of the town square with his ice-staff raised menacingly in the air. Lassar attempted to breathe fire onto her frozen vest, but she could only manage a snort of steam. Cold and weak, she spiraled out of control and crash landed in a heap of snow.

Satisfied that he'd contained the threat of the flying beast, Crone turned his attention on the rest of the square. He frowned with overwhelming displeasure. He saw the Makers had largely gained the upper hand and were now escaping at the far end of the square. He fiercely raised his staff towards their exit and blasted a large steady stream of his brilliant blue ice. A number of Makers screamed, but their cries were snapped to silence as they were caught in the glacier burst, while many others ran to hide. Crone whipped his staff upright and snarled with content as he observed his handy work. An ice-barrier now sealed off the square and blocked the path of the Makers, and his remaining officers could now round them up. Crone cast his vengeful eye over the square calculating his next move.

Tallac had witnessed the arrival of Crone and growled as he pummeled an officer into the snow. "I've got Crone, you stick to the plan," he bellowed to Ario who nodded anxiously.

Ario watched as Tallac raised his axe, grimacing with fury, and charged towards Crone. Out of the corner of his eye, Ario caught sight of a sled vehicle racing directly at him. He reeled around to see Officer Festus at the helm. With his target in sight, Festus pressed a button on the dashboard that fired a net from the front compartment of the chassis.

"Look out!" Ario yelled as he pushed Melody aside, but he wasn't fast enough to save himself. The net ensnared his whole body. Festus zoomed by yanking Ario off his feet.

"Let's see you slip out of this one Maker," Festus cackled. He drove off down a side street dragging his prized catch along the ground behind him. Melody chased after the sled in panic, but all she could do was watch Ario scream as the sled whipped him from side to side until they disappeared.

Ario's troll friend had heard the chaos coming from the town square and across the road in the barracks, and had been pacing in his cage for some time now. He was highly agitated, unsure of what was going on. He stopped and sniffed the air—a familiar scent was carried on the wind. He grunted as he heard the screams coming closer and closer. Finally, Festus' sled came into view and he saw his Maker friend being roughly hauled along from behind.

The troll roared and shook his cage door in outrage as Festus sped past the cages, spun his sled around, and began to drive back down the street. The troll was furious. This Winter officer had always been cruel to him and he was now causing pain to the creature that had only ever been kind to him.

Empowered by his anger, the troll repeatedly rammed against the cage door. As he did, the large steel hinges began to buckle under the pressure. With an all powerful roar that filled the streets, he gave one final slam and the door burst clean from its hinges. The troll boldly bounded towards the oncoming sled. Festus' stomach dropped as he saw the crazed troll headed directly towards him. He knew he was in trouble; his jaw tightened as he fearfully locked eyes with the beast. The troll didn't flinch as he shoulder charged the sled coming at him at full throttle. The sled toppled over, sending Festus flying onto the snow-covered streets.

The troll raced to Ario and tore open the net, picked him up, and cradled him in his arms like an infant. The other five trolls howled and roared as they shook their cages in excitement. Ario was dazed, grazed, and bruised, but altogether fine considering he had just been dragged through the streets of Winter City.

He placed his hand on the side of the troll's face and looked warmly into his eyes, "Thanks big guy, you saved my life." The troll snorted in reply and gave him a nuzzle, so glad his little friend was alright now. Ario looked at the caged trolls and back at his friend, then his eyes widened. "Hey, can I ask a favor?" he asked. The troll nodded and snorted in response. "Our rebellion against Winter could use your help."

Without hesitation, the troll grunted then hoisted Ario up on his shoulders and stomped back down the street. He stopped at the head of the troll cages and yanked a big metal lever, opening all the cage doors at once—he had wanted to do that ever since he was a youngling. The troll threw his head back and roared at his fellow trolls who stepped out of their cages and roared deep and loud in reply. With Ario and his friend in the lead, the newly inducted reinforcements stormed back to the town square, but not before one of the trolls broke away to wallop and stomp Festus deeper into the snow.

The first rays of daylight were starting to color the horizon with golden hues. The volcano still spewed molten lava, which glowed red hot and shot sporadic chunks of rock across the land. The earth itself gave out an almost constant rumble, low and deep as the earth underfoot continued to buckle randomly under the mounting pressure.

In the town square, an exhausted Lassar was surrounded by a small group of Winter officers, who cruelly took turns zapping her with their staffs. Aquillo, who had finally overpowered his last officer, raced to her aid. "It's okay, I'm here now," Aquillo shouted to the winged creature who could barely lift her head.

With his shovel held aloft, Aquillo ascended on one officer smacking him square in the face. Without turning, he jammed the long handle behind him knocking the wind out of another. Then, with a delicate pirouette, landed a not so gentle roundhouse kick to the head of the third, who fell fast and heavy to the ground.

Lassar had no fight left and whimpered as steam snorted from her nose. Aquillo saw that her chest warmer was frozen over, so he raised his shovel once again and stabbed at the plate until the ice cracked away.

"Don't worry, I'll find something," Aquillo said. He frantically looked around in a panic, "Boiling water. Boiling water. Boiling wa..." A fireball from the volcano hit the ground nearby, the snow hissed and steamed, instantly evaporating the snow and ice. "Molten rock!" Aquillo said with a cheer. He scooped up a pile of the volcanic debris with his shovel, flipped open Lassar's chest warmer, and stocked it full.

Lassar snorted with pleasure from the jolt of heat as warm steam shot out of her nostrils. She rose on her hind legs, instantly feeling stronger, then with another snort small flames flickered from her nose. Her ears perked up as she began to feel invigorated and she let out a belly deep roar and blew a fireball. The flames nipped at Aquillo's feet as he hastily buried his toes in the snow to keep himself from catching on fire.

"Now you're cookin'!" he exclaimed.

Aquillo turned to survey the rest of the square. With Crone's giant ice wall blocking the path to the burrows, the Makers had scattered trying to evade capture from the remaining officers. Aquillo wondered whether they still had any chance. He spotted Tallac at the back of the square facing off against Lord Crone. He knew he couldn't stay in this wintery hell hole and was not going to give up the fight just yet.

"C'mon," he cried to Lassar, "We've got to help Happy."

♪

Tallac stood before Crone, even though he was a tall well built man, he looked almost diminutive in the presence of the towering and all powerful Lord.

"You don't stand a chance against me," Crone raged with bitter intensity.

Tallac narrowed his eyes as he recounted the words of another fallen officer. "I don't expect to stop you, just waste your time," he taunted.

Crone raised his staff to blast him, but a cacophony of howls and roars caught his attention. His face tightened as he looked over Tallac's head. "No!" Crone bellowed.

Ario rode astride the shoulders of a troll, followed by five more trolls entering the town square. The much needed back-up began to effortlessly squash his last remaining officers. If there was one thing Crone hated more than Makers, it was those disgusting trolls, but he would have to deal with that situation later. He returned his attention to the issue at hand: Tallac.

Tallac looked directly into Crone's eyes, "I served you, I believed in you, but now I see the error of your ways," he said.

Crone just shook his head and sneered, raised his staff and blasted a torrent of ice aimed directly at Tallac's chest. Tallac deflected it with a blow from his axe, but the force pushed him back a few steps. Crone blasted again and again. Tallac smashed the ice beams before they struck him, but his swings were growing weary.

"It won't be long before your rule comes to an end," Tallac said as he puffed angrily from under the heavy barrage.

"Never!" Crone thundered as he changed tact and bore down on Tallac with his long staff. Tallac swung his axe in defense and ducked and weaved as the much stronger Winter man held the upper hand. With a low sweep of his staff, Crone knocked Tallac's legs out from under him then batted his axe away.

Lord Crone smiled cruelly as he stood over his former deputy and pushed his boot into his chest. He pointed his ice staff at Tallac's face and slowly squeezed the handle, the blue tip illuminating as a massive blast began to swell. Tallac closed his eyes. He was not afraid to die knowing he had fought with bravery and that the Makers were more than capable of finishing the rebellion themselves.

As Crone fired, a fireball from Lassar streaked across the square hitting Crone and his staff. Boiling water exploded as both men balked under the piercing heat. Crone growled in frustration as he grappled with his searing staff. Tallac took advantage of the distraction to grab his axe and scramble to his feet. Aquillo ran to his side with shovel raised, and Lassar roared as she leapt to his other side. The trio stood together, eyes blazing with sheer determination, ready for whatever the Winter Lord had in store.

Ario surveyed the icy barricade created by Crone. His head was held high and his ears stood erect flooded with adrenalin. He pointed to the wall and called to the trolls, "Charge the wall!" The trolls beat their chests and roared. They then ran at full speed, batting away any officers foolish enough to get in their way before furiously ramming into the icy wall.

Ario and the Makers cheered them on as the trolls slammed the blockade over and over again. The trolls finally had an outlet for the anger they felt from being mistreated for generations; the wall didn't stand a chance against their fury. They could see they were close to a life without shackles, and they wouldn't give up on that hope.

Ario looked at the cracks spread across the wall and saw they were near the breaking point. With a final few blows from the trolls, a section of the wall crumbled and shattered into hundreds of pieces. The Makers and the trolls cheered and roared in celebration.

Ario took Melody by the hands and squeezed them reassuringly. "You go ahead, prepare the symphony. I'll stay back and make sure everyone gets through," he said to her.

"Be careful; the Makers need their Magnum Opus," Melody replied. They gave each other a warm embrace then Melody hurried off. Ario yelled to the Makers at the top of his voice, "To the burrows!"

With no remaining Winter officers to slow them down, the Makers began to pour through the opening and run down the street. Ario approached the trolls. "Brave trolls. Please follow them. Protect them." The trolls snorted in agreement and gave chase, but Ario's troll friend stayed behind. Ario turned to him, "Why aren't you going?"

The troll pointed to his own chest, then to Ario's.

Ario smiled and placed his hand on the troll's arm, "Thank you," he said.

Ario looked over the town square. Bodies of the fallen, both Makers and Winter, were strewn everywhere. Craters dimpled and scorched the cobblestone as the volcanic rock still sizzled and steamed. Ario felt the heaviest weight on his chest. This needed to end. He didn't want to fight, but what do you do when your words and songs aren't enough? A tremor suddenly and forcefully shook the square. He knew there was so much at stake. Sometimes a fight is the only way to make it through to the other side.

Flashes of fire and blue ice from across the square caught Ario's eye, and his face clouded with concern. Tallac, Lassar, and Aquillo were locked in a fierce skirmish with Lord Crone. The men swung and jabbed at the Winter ruler while Lassar shot fire balls that Crone easily deflected with freeze blasts. It was evident to Ario that the trio was growing weary. Tallac and Aquillo's weapons began to weigh heavy, caked under a thick layer of ice. Lassar's fireballs were rapidly diminishing as she took the icy brunt of many of Crone's attacks. Despite their best efforts, they were no match for Lord Crone, who was centuries old and imbued with the forces of Winter. A succession of savage ice blasts pushed the trio back onto the dangerously thin surface of the frozen lake.

Crone raised his staff by the edge of the frozen water then struck it hard against the ice. Ario gasped. Cracks raced towards his friends as they tried to scramble out of harm's way. He heard their cries as the frozen lake shattered beneath them. Tallac and Aquillo plunged into the depths. Lassar flapped her wings fiercely and hovered above the lake. She grasped her flailing friends with her hind claws and started to pull them out, but Crone narrowed his eyes and shot at her with a solid blast of ice that clipped her wing. Lassar howled with agony as she too dropped into the icy waters.

Crone watched by the edge of the lake as the trio floundered. The sides of his mouth curved with deep satisfaction. He turned his attention back to the other side of the square and saw that the Makers were escaping. Crone growled in anger, realizing he should have just snapped that Maker's neck when he had the chance. He began to stride across the square brandishing his staff.

Ario's eyes flashed with fear as Crone approached. He looked at his friends in the lake and every fiber of his being wanted to help them. If he did, he would risk ruining everything, just like when he snuck away to see Melody. With the heavy heart of a leader, he was forced to choose the good of all. With the last of the Makers now out of the square, he looked up to his Troll friend and cried, "Let's go!"

The troll grunted in agreement. He picked up Ario and placed him on his shoulders, then started to bound towards the burrows.

Tallac, Aquillo, and Lassar waded to the edge of the lake, then crawled out and slumped in the snow, exhausted and shivering with cold. They saw a wrathful Crone chase Ario out of the town square, ice staff glowing blue. Tallac jumped to his feet and put his hand out to a teeth chattering Aquillo. "It's not over just yet," he growled.

Aquillo nodded wearily as he shakily rose to his feet. Lassar let out a small, miserable whimper and snorted a puff of steam, then she stretched her legs and shook her head—she too was ready. They looked at each other and nodded solemnly as they raced off behind Crone into the Winter City streets.

# CHAPTER 17
## *The Grand Symphony*

ore and more Makers began to arrive at the burrows, and each gasped with wonder as they looked up at the cliff face. The rose gold rays of the morning sunlight illuminated Ario, Tallac, and Melody's handiwork from the night before. Numerous burrow windows had been painted black, their circular shape forming the head of large musical notes. All the other necessary flourishes of musical notation had also been added. The stark black score was arranged against the dull grey stone, forming the sheet music of the grand Spring symphony.

The Makers eagerly chattered amongst themselves, excited by the possibilities that lay ahead. Melody, though, was in no mood for chit chat. "Come on, come on," she said with a clap.

"Alto's here, Soprano's here, Bass singers you can stand over there," she said as she ushered The Maker's into semi circle rows facing the burrows.

Melody paused and creased her brow as she looked down the street. She hoped that Ario wouldn't be much longer, but she knew she had to focus on the preparation in order to be ready for when he did arrive.

"You best start practicing," she called out to the crowd. The Makers obliged and started to warm up with vocal scales. Soon a cacophony of random notes and vocal runs bounced off the cliff and across the city.

Melody pulled Clef from the front row. "Hey, help me move these," she said as she gestured towards a pile of burrow ladders on the ground.

"Thure thing," said Clef. He pushed out his chest a little, quite chuffed to be of assistance and deemed more important than anyone else to take on such a responsibility. He had always had a feeling that Ario was headed for bigger and better things. He knew the first day he'd met him and he told Melody all about it as they busied themselves encircling the now formed choir with stacks upon stacks of wooden ladders.

A rabble of Winter officers could be heard approaching from a nearby street, but the trolls hastily set off to ensure they wouldn't cause any problems. The Makers hushed for a moment as their ears stood alert. A growing rumble underfoot shifted the earth violently once more. As the cliff shook, they shielded their heads with their arms to protect themselves from the showering rubble that dislodged from the cliff. Melody's face once again wrinkled with worry as she peered down the street.

"Come on Ario, hurry up," she said softly.

With each stride that pounded the cobbled street, Crone's anger jarred his bones and innards as his mind raged like a storm. He knew he could stop them. He knew all was not lost, not yet. The Maker and his troll companion were now in sight. He raised his staff as he continued to thunder down the road and started shooting.

The troll grunted as he looked over his shoulder and saw a barrage of ice blasts fly past them way too close. He wove left and right, desperately trying to avoid being struck as Crone drew ever closer. They turned a corner and a glimmer of hope fluttered in Ario's heart. The burrows were in sight. The choir stood ready. It was all within grasp, but yet still so far.

Melody's face broke into a broad smile when she saw Ario appear at the end of the street, but, in a flash, her stomach lurched with fear as Crone barreled around the corner behind them. She hurriedly began to pour the oil from the lamps over the wooden ladders. "Come on Ario!" she called out, as the Makers turned and murmured uneasily.

"Light it!" Ario yelled back in response.

Melody hesitated. The fire was meant as a Winter deterrent. She didn't want Ario to be stuck outside once it started burning; however, Crone was rapidly drawing closer. She raised her only flaming lantern over the pile of ladders, but cried out in pain as Crone blasted it from her hand. The lantern smashed into icy shards on the ground.

Panicked, Ario turned again to look at Crone, then his face brightened when he saw Tallac, Aquillo, and Lassar race around the corner. "Lassar! Light the wood! Light the wood!" he called.

Lassar skidded to a stop. She saw the pile of ladders down the street, then drew a great breath, but all she could manage was a hoarse roar and a puff of steam.

Crone now had Ario and the troll in his sight. He halted his chase, narrowed his eyes, and aimed a short, sharp freeze that hit the troll's legs, tripping him over. Ario was sent flying off the troll's shoulders and Crone laughed cruelly as he targeted another short blast. As Ario hit the ground he was frozen solid. With his momentum and icy tomb, he continued to slide across the ground towards Melody.

In that eternal second, all the anger and frustration Lassar had experienced in the last few days welled inside her. She saw Ario frozen. She saw all the Makers, Tallac, Aquillo, everyone, in desperate need of her help. She had such a fierce maternal desire to protect them all that the pit of her belly surged with ferociousness. She unleashed a mighty roar. It came from a place beyond herself; a place you can only find when you are forced to call upon all the heavens of the Earth for deep unbounded reserves. Lassar's whole body was electrified. She placed her mark as a glorious fireball traveled from her nose at great speed, singeing Crone's fur coat as it shot past. It hit the ladders, which immediately exploded into a circle of giant leaping flames.

Moments later, Ario's frozen body burst through the burning ladders in an explosive cloud of glowing embers and ash, instantly thawing him out. He skidded to a stop at the feet of the Maker crowd, who broke into a rapturous applause. Ario sat wet on the ground in a puddle of water. He looked up, slightly dazed and confused, at the cheering Makers.

Melody rushed to help him up, "Are you alright?"

Ario looked at the choir surrounded by the blazing fire. "I'm great," he said. Indeed, he had never felt any better.

Melody grabbed his hand and helped him up. Ario stood tall and proud looking at the rows of Makers. "It's time for Spring," he announced.

Crone could be heard barking with rage beyond the wall of flames—all his disappointment and all his anger spat out from him as he fired his staff at the fire. The ice sizzled and steamed, but the fire held strong.

From the end of the street, Aquillo raised his rake and turned to Tallac and Lassar. "Ready for another round?" he asked.

Tallac used his axe to lower Aquillo's rake, "We've done all we can. It's up to the Makers now," he said. They turned and looked back down the street at Crone pacing wildly around the blazing fire.

Ario took a deep breath and gave an upward flourish of his hands that Aquillo would have greatly admired. He called out to the Makers, "*C* everybody."

Each Maker took a breath and on Ario's downward motion, they gently let out a *C* note. With a tender, soulful beauty, all the individual voices filled the air and danced as one pure harmony. Ario smiled as he thought of the Magnum Opus' wise words, "Only together is life complete." He closed his eyes and felt the notes rushing to fly out of him, his arms rose up and down in ecstatic intensity as he began to conduct the Spring Symphony.

*Spring has begun.*
*The new season has come.*

The voices of the Makers flowed with delicate power. Like a wave of flowers and sunshine, their voices rose up the cliff face then bounced and showered the essence of spring all over the land. The tune broke tenderly across the forest as it reached the far seas and pattered softly like rain upon the icy mountain ridges. Every living being from insect and rodent to beast, and from the winter weeds to the grand old forest trees sensed the song and bowed in its honor. This ageless ritual long forgotten, was still remembered, buried deep within the fiber of all life.

Then, as if to celebrate the end of the cold, cruel Winter reign, the Earth shook once more. The volcano could be heard as it boomed over the land and molten rock exploded across the cloudless morning sky like a spectacular fireworks display. The Makers stood strong and undeterred and sang on. A final tide of lava rolled from the hollows of the earth and down its treacherous slope, then there was no more. The volcano lay itself to rest as the cycles of the seasons were restored.

The bass', the altos, the sopranos, and contraltos all continued their chorus in perfect unison as if woven in a timeless strain both buoyant and beautiful.

*All is one.*
*Leaf, snowflake, flower, sun.*
*Spring has begun.*

Again and again they chanted in superb harmony as every living thing heeded the call. The sun grew warmer and the snow began to melt away. Blades of grass that had lay dormant for centuries could wait no longer and unfurled vividly green. The flowers too were impatient and burst forth, dazzling with colors as bright and splendid as the symphony. Tree tops, which had remained barren for countless years, now sprouted leaves of luscious green. On those same branches, birds of every shimmering hue began to appear and warble as they joined the song of the choir.

The trolls huddled together closely as they softly howled along to the Maker's song. For the first time, they felt a peacefulness they had never known before.

The Winter citizens looked to the sky, confused at the sublime beauty that filled the air. Never in their lifetime had they been treated to such a delight of the senses. Some wanted to shield their ears, scared of what would happen if they were seen to enjoy such forbidden pleasure. But they couldn't, they had no desire to miss even a single moment of this miracle.

It would be safe to say that each and every heart, citizen and officer alike, melted and thawed as it was touched by the music of the Makers. As the magic of the symphony caressed the kingdom, all the living creatures of Winter slowly began to disappear to beyond the realm, to lay in wait for Winter's return. Each Winter person felt themselves slip away and every single one wondered in their last thought, *if music was a thing of such reverential beauty, why had they been denied for so long?*

The circle of fire protecting the Makers finally burned to ashes and dust. As Ario conducted, he looked to see Lord Crone pointing his staff at them, but it was rendered useless for he held no power in this new season. Crone's life's work stood in melted puddles all around him and he was overcome with the most wretched feeling of anger and loss.

"When Winter returns, we'll seek out the Makers and destroy you all!" he shrieked, as vengeful as ever.

The harmonies continued to ebb and flow over the land as Ario cast him a withering glare. "That's not going to happen, Crone," he bellowed back with a voice full of strength and poise. He knew he answered to no one but himself.

For the first time, Ario felt no anger or terror in the face of Crone—it had all gone. Instead, he felt nothing but pity. He understood that he was a man tortured by his own ignorance. Crone believed, like generations of his family before him, that he was better than others because of the home he was born into and the skin he happened to wear. He chose his own personal gain over the dignity and liberation of others. He had been given every opportunity to right his and his family's wrongs, but he would not or could not.

As Ario saw Crone in his true light, he felt a tune begin to tickle and tease and demand to be brought forth. He turned back to the Makers. "Follow me," he called to them.

He felt compelled to sing the notes of a song that rose from his throat and spilled from his lips. He was fine, he was not scared to sing in front of his fellow Makers anymore. He didn't give a hoot what the rest of the world would think. As always, his notes were not exact, or pure, or even pleasant, but the other Makers knew what he meant. They embraced and followed his lead, as their voices carried the tune across the sky. It was perhaps the most beautiful melody that had ever graced the kingdom.

As the tune soared, the air crackled before the choir, followed by a thunderous clap and a burst of light. The Makers let out a collective gasp as the King of Spring stepped from its center. His long, pale green fingers held a gnarled and twisted wooden staff wrapped in vines and sprouting with flowers. He was resplendently cloaked in a flowing hand woven tapestry of pastel swirls. On his head, he wore a silver crown that was twisted and knotted like a tree. It was almost lost amongst his wild white hair and great beard that was braided with tiny flower buds. The Makers stood rigid, not daring to speak, not sure if the King meant them any harm. Their treatment at the hand of Winter had taught them to mistrust those in power. But there was a warmth in his glowing emerald eyes, that made them feel safe as he smiled and kindly nodded in greeting.

Ario was in awe. While he was now familiar with the incredible power of music, he was still unprepared for this event. Once again, he was overcome by the urge to express a new tune. He didn't understand where it came from, but it was as if he had always known the notes. Ario sang the new harmony and like a flock of birds in flight, the other Makers stayed in sync. As the tune crescendoed, another crack split the air and a burst of light brought forth the Summer Queen. She was an older woman with rich brown skin and short glittering silver locks. On her head, was a tiara with a sun ray design, the likes of which was so gold that it had surely been crafted from the sun itself. In her hand, she held a long, gleaming golden staff, and at its head sat a gold sun whose yellow core glowed as bright as a star. Her crisp light linen gown was splashed with bright colors that glimmered and glistened, like sunlight bouncing off crystal. She gracefully stood beside the Spring King and she too smiled kindly at the Makers.

Ario marveled at her majestic beauty, and then a new tune sprung from his lips. The choir sung along and, this time, the Prince of Fall stepped from the light. His brown eyes twinkled against his pale white skin. A wreath of metallic golden maple leaves wrapped around his crown as his chestnut and gray corkscrew hair spiraled high. The Prince wore a tawny colored robe covered in rustic silk leaves that draped over his chunky brown boots. He grasped a deep mahogany staff, tall and smooth and carved with images of maple leaves.

Ario stared at the magnificent visitors, unsure of what to say. Each Elder returned his gaze with overwhelming fondness for the brave Magnum Opus before them. They then looked over the sea of Makers until they saw the very person they were seeking.

Crone stood away from the circle, heart racing as anger charred his soul. He had witnessed the calling of the Elders and knew what was coming, but stood obstinately as they approached him.

"We have been watching from beyond the realm," the Spring King boomed.

"Your actions are unconscionable," the Summer Queen said as her large charcoal eyes stormed with fury.

"You must answer for your crimes," bellowed the Prince of Fall as he waved his staff at Crone.

"I answer to nobody!" Lord Crone roared in defiance.

Without hesitation, the Elders raised their staffs and pointed them at Crone. His eyes flickered with fear, but he stood strong and still, resistant and proud to the end.

The Spring, Summer, and Fall Elders fired their staffs, shooting intense beams of green, red, and yellow. As they struck Crone, he dropped his staff and screamed in horror and rage. The Lord of Winter then vanished forever in a cloud of hazy light and dust—the cold, cruel reign of Winter was now truly over.

# Finale

# CHAPTER 18
## *The Celebration*

here was not a word. No one looked at each other and no one whispered. He was gone—Crone was gone. This was a moment that each Maker born into the servitude of Winter perhaps never thought would come.

The old Maker Hymn basked in the overwhelming solemnness of this moment. He smiled with tears streaming down his face, his dream of freedom had finally come true. His peers had always said... follow the rules, do what you're told. This had kept him alive to see this day, but it didn't really feel like much of a life. He now had a new dream. He would spend the remainder of his days far beyond the wall, exploring the new world and making nothing but peace and quiet.

Hymn started to sing the Spring Symphony once more. His solitary tenor voice, rich in timbre but slightly trembling under the weight of emotion, sailed across the morning. Each Maker joined him one by one. They reached out to each other and locked arms, finding solace and celebration in singing as one. They all remembered the long line of Makers that had passed before, who knew nothing but blood, sweat, tears, and the endless cold. They wept with sad hearts that felt like they would burst with joy. Every single Maker understood the legacy that was now theirs; they understood how worthy and how very important they were.

They all looked at Ario with great reverence and respect as he stepped up to lead the choir once more. He was the one that had showed them the way. They knew they had been quick to judge and ridicule him, but he rose against it all. He had fought for them and he had risked his life for them. Their song was filled with gratitude, knowing they would now live a life that generations of Makers had never dared to imagine.

Ario stood proudly as he motioned his arms up and down. Fresh pollen was carried on the warm breeze and tickled his nose; he smiled. He felt the waves of voices wash over him and he didn't think he could ever be happier. With every new note, nature bloomed and blossomed even more. The sun shone brighter, giving the earth much needed warmth after the many centuries of cold Winter days.

Out of the corner of his eye, he saw Tallac, Aquillo, and Lassar waiting for him at the side of the choir. He smiled at the rows of Makers. "Keep going," he said, leaving the choir to continue singing their beautiful spring harmonies.

Ario walked to the front row of the choir and took Melody by the hand. Their smiles beamed wide as they skipped to meet their friends. Aquillo bundled them all in a hug as Lassar gently nuzzled and licked everyone. Tallac stood there awkwardly, he had become accustomed to all the unabashed affection from his friends, but a second hug from Aquillo was crossing the line. When Aquillo began to dance a Fall jig to the Spring song, he definitely thought the celebrations had now gotten out of hand. Melody and Ario laughed and clapped while Lassar, now feeling rejuvenated by the warmer climate, puffed dainty fireballs above Aquillo's head.

The team was so lost in their jubilance, they hadn't noticed that the Elders had joined them. Tallac gave a few guttural coughs and the friends paused their frivolities as they became aware of the company. The group was instantly self-conscious and stood to attention, unsure of how to behave before such greatness. The Elders smiled warmly.

The Summer Queen knelt in front of Melody. "We stand humbled in the presence of the Makers," she said with a smile. Tears welled in Melody's eyes.

The Spring King knelt down before Ario. "Our debt to you will be timeless," he said. Ario smiled.

"I have only one request," Ario stated. The Elders nodded for him to continue. "Tallac should be the new Lord of Winter. He is kindhearted and respects the way of things as they should be. He will have a hard task of transforming his people, but he is the only one that can do it."

Tallac's eyes widened with surprise as he looked to his small friend and gave a deep nod of gratitude.

The Prince of Fall, who had retrieved the Winter Lord's staff, bowed deeply to Ario, and then turned to Tallac and presented him with the staff. "May the cold winds of winter never chill your heart. Step forward wise and noble Lord Tallac and lead Winter's new destiny."

The Maker choir had stopped the Spring Symphony to witness this momentous occasion. They joined Ario and friends in a rapturous applause as the Prince handed Tallac the Winter staff. Tallac looked at the staff, a tool of fear and oppression for uncountable years. He remembered his time in isolation with nothing but snow beasts and rodents as company. He never knew that his life could turn into something so wonderful and hopeful. He understood the gravitas of this responsibility and was overcome with raw emotion.

Tallac turned to Ario, "Thank you for helping me return to my people," he said.

Ario stepped into his arms and hugged him. "Thank you for opening your heart to us," Ario exclaimed warmly.

For the first time since he could dare to remember, Tallac could feel his face smile. He had no control over it, he was happy. Happy was foreign, happy was strange. But, my oh my, happy was good. Aquillo's eyes lit up—this was unprecedented. He opened his mouth to speak, but Melody gave him a quick elbow to the ribs. "Not now," she whispered. He nodded reluctantly.

The Summer Queen smiled as she gracefully rose to her feet. She took a few steps away from everyone and lifted her staff, then slammed it onto the ground. A ball of light burst out of thin air. She looked over the crowd, smiled, and waved goodbye. Such was the brilliance of that smile that it felt like it was more luminous than the ball of light she stepped into. There was a crack in the air, then the ball vanished. The Makers *oohed* with delight.

The Prince of Fall now stepped back and pounded his staff into the ground as another glorious sphere of light flashed into view. He beckoned Aquillo to join him. Aquillo's heart skipped and danced. It wouldn't be long before Fall would cool the land to a splendid honeycrisp and he would see his loved ones again.

With his standard dramatic flourish of the hands, Aquillo bowed low to Ario and Melody, "Farewell my lady and gentleman, time for me to go too."

Ario and Melody giggled and returned the bow as Lassar gave Aquillo a big juicy lick across the face. Aquillo embraced Ario and Melody, "I'm going to miss you guys," he said.

Melody placed her head on his chest, "We'll miss you too Aquillo."

Aquillo turned to Tallac and held out his hand, "Maybe I'll see you next season, you know, during the overlap."

"Unlikely, I'll be very busy with my new responsibilities," Tallac frowned.

"Don't worry, I'll ensure we have a reunion." Ario laughed.

Tallac growled under his breath, but gave a resigned nod of agreement and shook Aquillo's hand.

Chortling loudly, Aquillo joined the Prince of Fall and furiously waved goodbye as their sunny portal closed and vanished.

"I don't like long goodbyes," Tallac said and embraced Ario and Melody.

If there was one thing that Tallac had learned from his new friends, it was that a hug says everything that words can't say. Melody wiped away tears as Tallac took a step back. He was unsure how his new staff actually worked, but he struck it hard against the earth. Tallac was pleasantly surprised when a radiant orb instantly appeared before him. With a slight nod, he stepped into his ball of light then disappeared.

Ario led Melody by the hand and they rejoined the choir. With a final soaring harmony, the Makers' song rose above the land. Spring was now in season and the Makers cheered with joy. The newly arrived fauna scampered through rich, vibrant fields of green where the remaining flora opened their buds to the fresh day. The sun shone full of hope and promise for the era to come.

Lastly, Spring folk began to appear all over the kingdom, returning from their long hibernation. They were confused as to why their city lay in ruins, unaware of the brutal climate that had ruled for far too long. The Spring King knew he had a lot of work to do to restore his kingdom and he needed to make his way to the Spring Castle at once. He gave Lassar a gentle pat as he jumped on her back. "Let's go home, my trusty friend," he bellowed.

All the Makers cheered as Lassar reared on her hind legs, let out a roar, and shot a stream of flames from her nose. She flapped her strong, sturdy wings and leaped into the air.

Melody and Ario stood hand in hand and watched until Lassar and her King disappeared into the bright blue sky. Ario looked around as emotions of every kind bubbled and boiled. Winter City was now deserted with only the Makers left. Like the Spring King, Ario also knew there was much work to do. He had to lead the Makers back to their village and they had to rebuild. Together, they would restore the Maker Village to a magnificent bustling center. There, they would live as they were meant to, in utter freedom to create and make whatever their hearts desired and ensure the seasons rolled in their natural and harmonious way.

He shivered with excitement. What a glorious day that would be, but, for now, they needed to celebrate; they needed to revel in their liberation. They needed to rejoice that as one, they had changed their world.

Ario glanced at Melody and he knew he was the luckiest being alive. She had loved him and believed in him when no one else did. Side-by-side, they had achieved the impossible. He took her hands and spun her around. Together, they threw their heads back and looked to the sky and spun and laughed and spun and laughed, and then spun and laughed some more.

That night, and for many days afterwards, a celebration like no other rang across Winter City. The King of Spring had Lassar deliver the Makers a feast. She carried baskets brimming with bountiful vegetables and fruit that had blossomed and bloomed so gloriously from the symphony. They also enjoyed many flagons of defrosted wine that had aged surprisingly well in the Spring castle cellars. They wasted no time in building new instruments, and music and song rang out across the city as the Makers celebrated. Everyone agreed that they hoped never to eat another sneezleberry pie again.

# CHAPTER 19
## *The Workshop*

rio sat quietly at the edge of the town square watching the festivities in full swing. A large bonfire roared in the center and every Maker reveled in their new found liberty. He felt uneasy, unable to relax. Melody approached and he rose to his feet. She nodded encouragingly and he kissed her warmly, then stole away into the night.

Waiting for Ario just inside the Winter City walls was Lassar, who yelped excitedly as Ario jumped onto her back. "To the Maker Village, my friend," he whispered in her ear.

She bounded into the air and beat her strong wings as they headed north across the vast forest into the mild, still night.

Ario stepped into the workshop and walked straight to the workbench. There, was precious Renaissance. Beautiful and perfect in every stitch, fold, and turn of the tool, but still lifeless. Ario chose his instrument from the wall: a lyre that spiraled in the perfect proportions of a golden ratio. He then reached out and turned the hourglass and, once again, the sparkling sands began to fall. He took a deep breath and looked fondly at Renaissance.

The future was literally in his hands.

Ario played the Making song. With each pluck of the strings, he remembered all the wonder and beauty that he had known in his short, sweet life. He thought of Melody and how she had made him, then made him again. He thought of his friends Tallac, Aquillo, and Lassar who had fought valiantly by his side for a better world. He thought of the fragrance of flowers that now wafted across the land. He thought of all the Makers that would follow, and know nothing but songs of freedom. All of this fueled and fired his tune.

Of course, he was a little off-key. His fingers could never seem to do what his soul and his heart wanted them to. But he played with such passion, such gratitude, and with such reverence that the grand cycle of life could only bow in honor and reverence to him, and, in turn, fulfill his truest desire.

Renaissance's eyes flickered then slowly drew open, like a spectacular sunrise that promised a new day, a new age, and a new way.

Ario swept her up in his arms and held her so tightly. He had finally done what he needed to do, tears of gratefulness trickled down his cheek. As the embrace continued, she became a little squirmy and impatient and was about to launch into a thousand questions. Ario let go and smiled as he handed her the Making book.

A quizzical Renaissance wasn't sure why this Maker was so sad yet so happy and why he was giving her this fantastically old book. But before she could utter a single word, the last grain of sand dropped in the hourglass and Ario dissolved in a shower of sparkle and light. The workshop tools returned to their fixtures while the materials magically refreshed.

Like every Maker that had ever come before her, Renaissance was left standing alone and confused. "Oh my tizzy and dizzy stars," she whispered to herself, then wondered, *Wait, how to do I know what stars are?*

Before she could continue with that train of thought, the hourglass turned and the sparkling sand fell. At that exact moment, music exploded brilliantly from the tubular horns on the wall. Renaissance was steered by that deep ancestral urge as she opened the book to the first page and read.

*You are a Maker, you must create,*
*make haste for time should never waste.*

She smiled and wholeheartedly began.

And so it was in that little workshop, in a world, and in a time that most have forgot. The cycle of the Makers turned once again. The seasons rolled in perfect unison across the land as harmony and peace ruled the hearts of every Maker and every man... and so it was forever more.

# Da Capo

Made in the USA
Charleston, SC
04 January 2017